BETWEEN BLOODE AND STONE

BETWEEN THE SHADOWS

MARIE HARTE

BETWEEN BLOODE AND STONE
ISBN-13: 978-1642920642
Copyright © Feb 2022, Nov 2021 by Marie Harte
No Box Books
Cover by Moonpress Design | moonpress.co

For exclusive excerpts, news, and contests, sign up for **Marie's newsletter**.
https://www.subscribepage.com/betweentheshadows

BETWEEN THE SHADOWS

Between Bloode and Stone
Between Bloode and Craft
Between Bloode and Water
Between Bloode and Wolf
Between Bloode and Death
Between Bloode and Gods

BETWEEN BLOODE AND STONE

A NOTE FROM MORMO

There are many things in this world that don't fit into humanity's concept of what's real. Much of the magir—that's the paranormal community for you mortal types—has been kept secret. But there are some of us who've seen beyond realms, and we are right to fear what's coming.

Granted, I find vampires annoying. First of all, they're pretentious, referring to themselves as those "Of the Bloode." Bloode, as you might expect, is very important to them. It's not just that red liquid in their bodies. In a vampire, "bloode" is that essence infused with blood and magic; it's what makes them what they are.

The petty bastards are powerful, and they don't like to follow rules. Cursed by the gods not long after their creation, they are forced to keep low numbers. Vampires get along only with those in their own clan. A clan is like an extended family. Think in population numbers of ten to sixty members. I know, sounds like a small number. It is. It has to be.

Those clans belong to tribes, and a tribe can hold anywhere from a thousand to ten thousand Of the Bloode. The vampires have ten tribes, and each tribe has a different name. (See how they make everything so complicated?)

The strigoi tribe make powerful vampires. They can shapeshift into ravens and have the power of seduction over mortals. The *nachzehrer*, however, shapeshift into wolves, and they're known to be able to call on a fierce, unstoppable strength at will. And so it is with all the tribes, powerful yet held in check by the need to kill those who aren't of their clan, those who aren't kin. Hell, even within the same tribe, the individual clans clash constantly.

They're raging balls of chaos, and no one would really care if they all disappeared.

Well, except for my mistress. The goddess Hecate is lovely beyond words. Unfortunately, she's got a soft spot for hard cases. And death. She insists the vampires might be the cure to the Darkness that comes to wipe out worlds.

Her plan isn't the best. Hecate has commanded *me* to take charge of their species, starting with a brand new clan of vampires, using six of the most annoying, contentious, miserable bastards I've ever had the misfortune to meet.

I know it'll take more than dark magic to make these jack-asses get along, let alone leave me alive and breathing at the end of it all. (Don't think I haven't seen them eyeing my neck like it's bottling the finest of bloode wines.)

But I am Hecate's humble servant, and I will serve. So here we are. But it's so, *so* hard not to give into the urge to obliterate them on a daily basis.

Especially Varujan of the Crimson Veil. Because— Oh, just read on.

PROLOGUE

Mercer Island, Washington
Month of the Super Blue Blood Moon

The pain, though excruciating, felt familiar. Shadows bathed the room. The sound of battle and the scent of bloode, sweat, and excitement spiced the air. Varujan rolled away before the blade took off his whole hand. Three of his fingers lay scattered across the hated blue mat, the bright spatter of blood a welcome sight against the never-ending tedium of exhaustion and annoyance—or what that their jailer called their daily training. More like time spent in a torturous gymnasium for the damned.

"By the Black Crow, are you dancing or fighting?" Gwyn roared. "Pin him down, lads. Stop playing with your prey. He's not dinner!" But no one paid Gwyn the slightest bit of attention, the plotting bastards competing to end Varu once and for all.

Gwyn Ap Nudd, a fae hero and renowned leader of the Wild Hunt, had a pedigree the gods must envy. He was eternally young, sound of mind and body, and beautiful. His green eyes were sharp, his hearing excellent, his ability to track unparalleled.

And he *hated* being ignored.

But what could he expect with students who despised being told what to do? Compliance? Vampires didn't follow rules. Even Gwyn knew that.

Nachzehrer, revenant, *vrykolakas*. Known by their many tribal names across the world, vampires had two major things in common: they detested anyone not a vampire, and they loathed those outside their own clans. Cursed long ago to check their growing power, vampires could only coexist in small groups.

Yet despite their many conflicts, those Of the Bloode possessed similar traits. All vampires, no matter where they came from, were male in gender. They could go unnoticed by humans unless they wished otherwise, and they couldn't survive sunlight. Most of them had dark hair and dark eyes that turned red when in extreme duress or excited.

Like now. All the vampires "training" with Varu stared with red eyes, their fangs visible, their nails steel-hard claws. The scent of bloode filled the room, and hunger pulsed in the air.

Gwyn thought that keeping vampires underfed and on edge would encourage an adherence to discipline during hard times. But he only made them more ferocious and uncontrollable.

The fae aimed his majestic bow around the darkened gymnasium, targeting all of them so fast he looked a blur. But he didn't fire, which wasn't like him. "Let the training spell work through you," he barked. "You should view each other as a team, not the enemy."

In the past six months, the spell had yet to work even once.

The vampire closest to Varu made a rude gesture to Gwyn with his middle finger. Two across from the fae laughed outright, while the remaining pair watched Varu, waiting for another opportunity to slice him to pieces. That or take on Gwyn again. Only the fae's keen ability to use that bow with his blessed arrows had kept him alive these past months.

Varu studied the blond bastard giving orders no one cared to follow. Heroic, annoying, and...tasty. Varu licked his lips, famished. He could really go for some fae right about now.

That inattention cost him. Varu cursed when claws dug into his shoulder, ripping into his muscle and forcing him to cut away, losing too much bloode and tissue, his regeneration hampered by his many wounds. He put on a burst of speed he could ill afford and nearly caught Gwyn. Unfortunately, in Varu's current state, he was no match for the fae hero, who retaliated in force.

No one could shoot like Gwyn Ap Nudd. Varu dodged four of the arrows shot in the span of a second. Regrettably, he couldn't avoid the fifth and sixth arrows that followed, piercing his femoral arteries. More blood sprayed, and his fellow teammates converged on him with the bloodlust that made their species both feared and crazed.

They cut into him, not to devour, but to kill. Vampires didn't eat their own kind unless absolutely necessary. But their damage would take him too long to heal. They refused to stop.

"Maim, not murder, you monsters!" Gwyn shouted. "Remember, discipline, order. You...*ach!*" The first month he'd been with them, Gwyn had been the soul of patience and courtesy. Boy, had that gone the way of the wind—fast. "*That. Is. It.* I'm done with the lot of you!"

Gwyn glared at all of them then turned his displeasure on a creature that appeared out of nowhere, and one Varu really could have done without. Mormo—a brutally strong, white-haired bastard, neither old nor young, vampire yet not, his energy a mix of death and magic and something unpleasantly powerful.

"I did my best to help," Gwyn said bitterly. "But I honestly have no idea what your mistress was thinking." The fae shook his head. "Vampires never work well together."

Varu could have told them that from the start. In fact, he had. Several times. As had the others. But the great and powerful Mormo had ignored them all, too focused on supposed bloodedebts incurred by their clans, demanding recompense in a laughable idea of forced servitude.

And now, as Varu felt his life's essence leave him, he could finally make that payment in full. *For you, Father. I hope you're fucking satisfied with me now.*

Unfortunately, the others didn't care that Gwyn had quit, or that Varu was on the verge of true death. They continued to come after him, caught in the euphoria of the kill. Varu twisted away from them, but his movements became sluggish as he slipped on his own bloode. The revenant tore through his biceps. The nachzehrer severed his Achilles tendon. The big vryko dug claws through Varu's intercostal muscles and broke through rib bones, reaching for his heart. Varu locked eyes with the savage, doing his best to stop the monster from ripping out the organ, but a surge of power distracted him.

Everyone froze and as one turned to Mormo.

Mormo's eyes blazed red as he took in the chaos around them, studying the mess of bloode and guts dirtying his precious training facility. He looked up at the sole window in the place. It had been covered in a black sheet of metal to prevent sunlight from entering during daylight. Because day or night, they had been forced to forego rest to become a "cohesive unit."

"What? You need me to say pretty please?" Mormo grimaced as he stepped over Varu's severed fingers and pointed skyward. "Just do it, Gwyn. Today would be nice."

"Fine. You asked for it." Gwyn aimed high and let his arrow fly, piercing the metal like it was nothing. At the same time, all Varu's opponents darted for the walls, shielding themselves away from the sunlight that speared into Varu and smothered him with excruciating pain.

Agony filled every cell of his body as he slowly turned to dust. His sight left him, but he could unfortunately hear Mormo sigh and say, "It's become painfully clear to me that we're now *all* bound to suffer. Dickheads." Mormo murmured something else under his breath, then said aloud, "Come closer, you who are Of the Bloode. Much, much closer…"

Varu's attackers shrieked as Mormo released his magic. Varu felt it coat him as well, severing old ties and creating new ones, and he swore, long and loud. *And after I'd just resigned myself to a true death after all…*

Four months later, Seattle

T he dim bar stank of piss and grease, the food a step above the overpriced booze and dirty clientele. A popular hangout for college kids and desperate older men wanting to get laid, the bar didn't carry anything Varu would consider delectable—in spirits *or* women.

He glared at his new kin, so tired of dealing with fellow vampires he wanted to vomit. Alas, he hadn't ingested actual food in over three hundred years. He had no urge to try it again in this century.

Apart from Varu, Duncan probably came closest to being civilized. The revenant practiced seduction well enough. Always a cock buried in some female or other. Just what they needed on this particular mission.

Mormo wanted them to find a young woman in downtown Seattle. Considering the four-million-plus people in the city, Varu thought the asshole insane for even thinking they might suss her out with the help of a little spell. But then, Varu had forgotten who they were *really* working for.

Hecate, goddess of ancient magic, boundaries, and death. Not a bad goddess if one had to worship, he supposed. But those Of the Bloode didn't venerate deities. They took pleasure in the hunt, the kill, and in victories earned through skill and ferocity. Prayers were for the weak who needed something other than themselves to believe in.

Besides, in the four months they'd been damned to live with Mormo in a human city, they had yet to witness Hecate in any way, shape, or form. No, a vampire needed only his own fangs and claws to get a job done.

He said to Duncan, "Plan A."

"Right." Duncan nodded. The large male had lived in England for just over two hundred years before his rebirth as Varu's kin. Varu mentally cringed at the clan name Mormo had given them. The Night Bloode. How...pedestrian. But better than his first suggestion of the Seattle Bloode—which already belonged to the local upir clan. *Seattle* and *vampirism* went together as well as witches and fire. Not a great combination.

Still, Duncan didn't seem to care what anyone called him. He would get the job done with minimal fuss. No matter what clan he belonged to, no matter whose kin, Duncan was a tremendously fast fighter, smart, and a master of seduction.

The revenant caught Varu's glance and, with a wide grin, headed for the bar, shrugging away his ability to go unnoticed. Once he'd reached the attractive bartender in a shirt that looked painted on, Duncan started flirting with the witchy redhead for all he was worth. If she had any information on their quarry, Duncan would get it.

Leaving him to his task, Varu left the bar and spotted the dark SUV waiting for him in the alley. He'd told the others to leave him and Duncan behind. But had they listened? No.

He sighed. Since their recent rebirth into a new clan, they'd become used to one another's company, no longer feeling an urge to kill since they'd been bound as kin. But the need to dominate was part of what made a vampire a vampire. Hierarchy within a clan was normal. With Mormo being the obvious patriarch, the next level fell to the most powerful—namely, Varu.

Except the others continued to test him. Varu had learned enough about them to know they probably felt they had that right. But what they didn't know about him might just be their downfall.

Duncan typically followed Varu without complaint. An occasion to screw a pretty human, despite her being a witch, was nothing over which to argue. Fortunately, the somewhat problematic pair he often fought with had work away from the city tonight, so two less problems to have to handle. Which left Varu the other two idiots currently in the SUV.

He opened the passenger door and got in, not surprised to see Orion behind the wheel. The vryko, a vampire from the Greek island of Santorini, was tall, muscular, and stubborn. And like those of his tribe, he was skilled in powers of hypnosis rather than seduction. In a matter of sheer strength, Orion would likely best him.

Wisely, Varu never let that be the only point of contest between them.

With a glare, Orion peeled out of the alley.

"Head home," Varu ordered. Home, what a joke. But now bound to Mormo and his goddess, what choice did they have?

Orion didn't say anything.

Varu sighed. "Just get it off that huge chest."

"Why use Duncan?" Orion growled, sounding more like a wolf than the raven he could shapeshift into.

"Because he's funny and acts like he likes women."

"I like women."

"I like women too," came a voice heavily accented in German. "Why do you always choose the weaker ones for this kind of job?" Kraft complained from the backseat. Like Orion, he had a large frame and dense strength, his hair shaggy though, not as short and coarse as Orion's. A German nachzehrer, he could assume the form of a wolf at will and had a wonderful rage that added to his power. Too bad he also had a huge dose of dickhead in that DNA. "And why does Orion get to drive all the time?"

Varu silently counted to ten. "He's behind the wheel. Does it matter?"

"Did you know your accent appears when you're annoyed?" Orion said, wearing a smirk. "What part of Romania do you hail from? Or was it called Dacia? You know, back before Christ was born."

"Fuck off." Sometimes he forgot his exact years, but Varu knew he had only just passed his first millennium.

"Orion always gets to drive," Kraft continued to complain. "I'm tired of having to do what you tell me. Who made you boss, Varujan?"

Instead of diving into the back to strangle the irritating vampire, Varu said nothing, watching the raindrops splash against the windows as they drove through Seattle's wet streets back to the mansion. For all of Kraft's bitching, Orion drove well enough, weaving through traffic before they stopped at a red light.

The rain ceased. The moon pierced the gloom of night, full and ripe overhead as the clouds drifted apart. As a beam struck him, Varu felt a craving for blood, and he wondered if Mormo would throw a fit if they took a breakfast break. At just past midnight on a cold September night, those frequenting the bar and club scene had started to thin. Few meals wandered alone, most in pairs or packs. Easy pickings, if only Mormo would take that stick out of his ass and allow them uncontrolled feedings.

Screw him. I'm feeding on whatever I want. Having made the decision, Varu felt a little better.

Kraft continued to mutter, "I mean, what would it hurt if I drove? It's not the autobahn, but I can deal."

For four months they'd been—loosely—following Mormo's stupid orders. He told them who to track, who to kill, and who to capture when they weren't training or praying for a true death to alleviate the boredom. Varu had recently succumbed to watching television. He'd just finished bingeing *Breaking Bad*, *Sons of Anarchy*, and *The Punisher*. He was desperate for something new to watch. Or new to kill. And at the rate Kraft was getting on his nerves…

"America. Blech," Kraft grumbled. "I'm dying for rich blood. Someone who's eaten a decent *wurst* or Sauerbraten. A hefeweizen would really go down well, come to think of it." He paused then said, "Now I'm thirsty."

Varu tuned him out. Life should be about more than tracking down rogue witches and warlocks. Bagging errant vampires and escaped beasts from the underworld started to wear on a guy. Hunger wasn't helping. Nor was his irritation that Mormo refused to give any reasons behind the capture of their latest target.

Staring at the moon, Varu longed for something he couldn't quite name. "Anyone hungry for lycan?"

Orion shrugged. "I could go for fae."

Kraft stopped bitching enough to say, "Give you ten bucks to say that to Gwyn's face."

"Twenty, and you're on. But you have to convince Mormo to invite him back."

"Done."

Orion reached behind him to shake Kraft's hand.

Orion, like several of the others, didn't mind Mormo. Varu couldn't stand the arrogant prick. The secrets and the condescension, so different from what Varu had been used to for hundreds of years, rankled.

"Gwyn will gut you," he warned.

"He'll try." Orion flashed a fang, his good humor restored.

"He's going to stick you hard, many times. Turn you into a porcupine." Kraft chuckled. "He's damn fast with that bow."

"You do realize he's been King of the Hunt for hundreds of years, right?" *Orion, think, you idiot.* "He wasn't too happy with us not listening to him. He quit, remember? If he sees you again, he'll shoot first *then* ask questions."

Orion shrugged. "So what? I'm stronger than all of you put together. I can crush one tiny fae."

Varu and Kraft exchanged a glance, and Kraft said, "Sure, Orion. Whatever helps you sleep during the day."

The light turned green, and Orion started to turn. He slammed on the brakes as something—no, some*one*—landed on the windshield. The glass cracked as that someone pushed off with his feet and shot across the street into a nearby alley, running all-out.

His hunger driving him, Varu darted out of the vehicle as gunshots tore into the SUV. Knowing Orion and Kraft could handle themselves, he followed the creature who'd hit their vehicle, only to see the hooded figure disappear into an abandoned storefront. The door remained open, a cracked bay window hiding the interior.

With a speed no human could match, Varu tracked his prey inside and waited, seeing clearly in the darkness. The attack came from the deepest shadows. It was fast and furious but no match for Varu. He manhandled his prey and easily grabbed him by the throat off his feet, yet his prey's hood remained in place, concealing his features. Curious that his attacker was somewhat smaller than he'd expected, Varu studied the male, at least a good head smaller than Varu and slighter of form.

A teenager or young man, perhaps? No, make that, a young *woman.* He noticed the slight swell of breasts at the same time he drew in her scent. It burst on his tongue and caused instant elation. So very strange. He frowned, but as the sweet, sultry taste of her wound around him, his fangs grew, hunger bursting through him from head to toe. He let go of her neck and gripped her by the shoulders, continuing to keep her off her feet a few inches from the ground.

He needed to see the face that went along with that scent. Like the finest perfume… except she didn't exactly smell like prey.

The longer he held her, the less he felt like draining her. His body woke up, his fangs not the only thing growing large.

Orion yelled something outside. Distantly, as if dreaming, Varu glanced through the bay window to see Orion punch two men hard enough that they flew into a brick wall and slumped to the ground in the alley. Then he engaged with what looked like a lycan.

Hmm. Breakfast…

Kraft snarled at something that snarled back. Then he started hitting and biting and moved out of sight. More noise outside, then a cough distracted him. Varu looked back at the female, peering at the unnatural darkness under her hood. He thought he could make out her eyes. A silver glow appeared and brightened.

Then she was petting him, and he sighed with pleasure.

"That's right. Good vampire. Just a little more. Down, boy."

He lowered his arms, setting her on her feet. And then he was no longer holding her, his arms by his sides. He blinked, feeling silly. He'd missed what she'd said. But…

A lovely laugh that made him smile in return broke the silence between them.

"Oh, I'll be the toast of the town when I return with upir gold."

Upir gold? He should know that term.

A small but gracefully shaped hand with trimmed red nails trailed his forearm to his shoulder. She reached up to touch his hair, rubbing the black strands between her fingers.

"So soft. Who would have thought?" Her voice sounded like the tinkle of wind chimes, magical and soothing. So sweet.

She leaned closer, and he scented that delectable perfume again. The one that made him hungry for something other than food.

Her finger caressed his throat.

He froze.

The touch of a stranger against the most vulnerable part of him shocked Varu out of his stupor. Wait. Had she said *upir gold?* Considered a delicacy in many parts of the divine world, and a bountiful harvest to those who dealt in power and sacrifice, a vampire's bloode and brains—upir gold—could fetch a pretty penny.

He snatched her hood back, exposing a female with long black hair threaded with white streaks. Her eyes were lavender, the sclera a small presence of white, the irises glowing, her pupils, a darker purple, overly large. Her face was inhumanly beautiful. The pearlescent shine to her skin, a lovely shade of light gray— no, a pale cream color, he thought as the moonlight streaming through the window changed—emphasized her plump, blood-red lips and rosy cheeks lush with life. He could hear her heart racing, the evidence of her vitality intoxicating.

Yet for all that, she wore nothing out of the ordinary, just jeans and a hoodie and sneakers. So plain and uninteresting.

Overwhelmed by a confusing sense of lust and danger, he started to lean forward, unable to help himself.

The dagger she thrust at his throat had him springing back several feet with a snarl, flashing his fangs. How the hell had she surprised him once again?

Instead of being properly intimidated, she narrowed her eyes and *threw the dagger at him.*

He hadn't expected her to throw with such speed and accuracy. The damn thing nearly severed his head from his neck and bounced off the wall behind him.

Done playing the fool, Varu retaliated immediately, launching himself and tackling her to the ground. He pinned her down while avoiding her stare, since she'd earlier beguiled him into letting her go.

"Get off me, blood-sucker." Several more swears and insults to his lineage followed, her voice husky with anger, no longer so airy and musical.

He grinned at the epithets, not at all offended. Instead, he found himself intrigued. It had been so long since he'd had anything to smile about.

The female continued to struggle with a strength not common to humans. Definitely not a mortal, then. Interesting that she lacked the power of a stronger magir, like a shapeshifter or lycan.

She planted her hands flat on the ground, trying to push him off her. To his astonishment, she started to gain leverage.

What *was* she?

He leaned closer to sniff her neck, and she screamed.

The sound shattered his eardrums, and the force of it threw him through the already cracked bay window into the alleyway.

But immediately up and moving, he ignored the ringing in his ears and wiped away bloode obscuring his vision from a jagged head wound, even now healing. He raced after her, hearing her pounding footsteps on the other side of the building. Except he got there too late.

Exploding into the road behind the storefront, with Orion and Kraft right behind him, he watched a fast-moving van snap her up. As it carried her away, she stuck out her head, stared back at him, and flipped him off. Then the van turned out of sight.

Varu cracked his neck, annoyed, intrigued, and bless it all, amused.

Orion scowled. "What the hell was that?"

"Varu, you have bloode on your face." Kraft frowned and handed him the dagger the woman had thrown. "Here. I found this inside the building. It wants you."

Varu clasped the dagger, shocked at the sudden hum of connection. "We need to find her."

"We need to get out of here," Orion corrected. "Mormo was pretty clear about not calling any attention to ourselves. I left five bodies in the alley." He paused. "Kraft left two."

Kraft scowled. "Hey, I killed those two before I had to fight battle beasts. Not my fault I couldn't shake them to help you with those pesky humans."

"Dick." Orion huffed. "Like I needed any help."

Kraft ignored him. "I'm still hungry." He paused. "And I want to drive home."

"You drive like a ninety-year old."

"I am a ninety-year old!"

Orion scoffed. "You hit like one too."

"Oh yeah?"

While they bickered, Varu studied the dagger. Touching the edge burned, so he knew it to be silver. The leather hilt, however, had been pressed with runes. And beneath it, something beckoned the bloode inside him. So peculiar. He sniffed the weapon and scented the odd female all over it. Longing pulsed, a repeated plea to touch, to claim. But from the dagger, or was that in response to the murderous female?

Irritated, Varu concentrated on the weapon. He rubbed the leather, felt the power underneath it, and pulled back the leather binding to see a red stone the size of a dime.

Kraft cut off what he'd been saying to Orion and blinked. "I told you it wanted you. But now I can feel it pounding in my chest. What is it?"

Orion gaped. "Fuck me. I feel it too, and it's not happy. What *is* that?"

"That's a very good question." Varu's mouth dried, knowing without knowing how he knew. He held in his hand a thing that couldn't possibly exist outside legends and myth. "If you believe that Bloode Stones are real, then you'd know they have been hidden for thousands of years, created when our ancestor first bled upon the earth."

Kraft's eyes widened. "I thought they formed from his tears hitting the earth. Rumor has it the Bloode Stones can bring vampires together. A legendary bridge between the tribes."

Orion frowned. "That's not possible. Our kind is limited by bonds of kin. Hell, even those of us of the same tribe want to kill each other. I actually like my uncle, but he moved to another clan, and now I want to rip his throat out whenever I see him."

"All of us here with Mormo are outside each other's tribes, and we haven't killed each other." Kraft stated the obvious.

"Yet," Varu answered. "But that's due to whatever spells the death goddess and Dickhead Senior cast."

"Fucking Mormo." Orion snorted. "Not to be confused with Gwyn, Dickhead Junior."

Kraft chuckled, though his gaze remained on the dagger.

Varu rubbed this thumb over the stone and hissed as it made contact with the power deep inside him. The stone seemed to purr as if alive, then it started *singing*.

He hastily covered it back up with the leather binding, muting, but not cancelling, that song of kinship.

"It can't be a Bloode Stone," Kraft argued, though he didn't sound so convincing. "The six stones have been missing since the Kin Wars."

Orion huffed. "Exactly. Besides, even it if was, only one Worthy of the Bloode could contain it."

Varu nodded. Orion had the right of it. Only a vampire could touch a Bloode Stone. And only one Worthy could wield it. Varu knew he was far from deserving of any title so grand. Plus, a woman had thrown that dagger, yet there were no female vampires. No, the stone couldn't possibly be one of the legendary gems.

He clutched the dagger tightly. "So, the question is, who is she? How did she get this dagger?"

"And how did she kick your ass?" Kraft asked with an innocent expression Varu didn't buy for a second. "Because she did, and I think everyone will want to know more about that."

"He has a point." Orion remained stone-faced, but Varu saw the laughter in his eyes.

He glared at the pair. "We can talk about it once we get back. Oh, and *I'm* driving us home."

An unhappy Kraft and Orion joined him in the SUV, and after kicking out the windshield, they headed back to the house.

But Varu's thoughts remained on the dagger, wondering why his meeting with the strange female felt less like an accident and more like something that had been planned.

F araine de Cloche Jherag, known for the past ten years in the human world as Fara Redstone, settled back in the van as it sped her to safety. Best to get far from the maddening vampire muddying the already dirty waters in this American place.

Seattle. Meh.

The locals called it The Emerald City. Though she was partial to precious gems, she didn't see much green or shiny about.

They took I-90E out of the city toward the town of Issaquah. At the south end of Lake Sammamish and surrounded by the Issaquah Alps—Cougar Mountain on the west, Squak Mountain to the south, and Tiger Mountain to the southeast—the town was near enough to Seattle to be an easy commute yet kept her safely away from the vampires, who tended to stick closer to their dense food supply in the city.

They drove in silence, the crew one she'd hired for the job. She didn't know them. They didn't know her.

She planned on keeping it that way.

Fara had them take her to Lake Sammamish State Park, on the other side of the interstate from the mountains, not wanting them to know where she'd been staying. With any luck, Onvyr would be waiting for her in one piece.

They reached the gated entrance to the park, which had been locked down at dusk—her favorite time of the day.

She said to the driver, a man who didn't talk, "Drop me here."

He pulled the van aside. She glanced at the lycans sitting behind her. Initially a group of twelve—five lycans, a fae, two battle beasts, and four humans, one of which was a witch—they had been paid well to distract the creatures with Varujan of the Crimson Veil. Yet only six of them, including Fara, remained.

The witch wiped her eyes, having lost two of her partners.

Fara could sympathize. She hadn't wanted anything to do with the vampires either. But here she was, ten years later, still playing fetch for that bastard, Atanase. A master vampire, a strigoi from Romania, Atanase was one of the most powerful vampires she'd ever encountered.

Not that she'd met many, but still. Everyone knew about Atanase. Even in her part of the world.

"We should go back and take them all out," the fae next to her spat.

What a moron. The popular saying, *To Dance with the Bloode is to court Death,* had come from a poem written by the sole survivor of the Black Day Massacre. It was a tale every fae worth their salt knew, in which a village of three hundred elves lost all but one young warrior to a small but deadly clan of five ancient vampires. Yes, *five.* But no, this fae, a nasty half-sprite, wanted revenge on creatures the gods wanted no part of.

Fara didn't like him. He'd been nosy and snotty and a real downer to deal with.

So she nodded. "You really should. You're fae. You could *totally* take on all the vamps at the same time and show them who's boss."

The lycans in the back snarled their approval.

Yep. Time for her to go.

The sprite put a hand on the slide door, his pointed ears quivering with excitement. The thought of facing death excited certain fae. Despite Fara's fear at being caught by so many, she admittedly felt more alive around danger. Elves were known to be an especially curious lot. But sprites were the worst, living for chicanery, never so happy as they were when making someone else miserable.

She moved toward the door to leave when the fae yanked her back.

For fuck sake, now what? A thought struck her. Had he perhaps seen through her glamour? Because that would be bad. Very, very *bad.*

"Your payment, woman?" he sneered.

Ah, that. She reached into her pocket and pulled out a diamond.

The gem winked with a cold fury all its own. Absolutely colorless, flawless, ideal cut, and seven carats. Not excessively large by any means, but it was valued at a little under half a million U.S. dollars. If this team were smart, they'd take the money and run fast and far away from anything that sucked blood.

The fae took it and waved a hand over it as he muttered under his breath. The stone glowed for a few seconds before it resumed its regular state. He nodded. "Payment in full, as agreed."

"Outstanding." The lycan closest to her grabbed the stone out of the fae's hand. "This will buy us more spells and better weapons."

"Death to the upir," the fae agreed.

"I thought he was a strigoi," the other lycan said.

"Who cares?" The witch snorted. "Strigoi, upir, vryko. One true-dead vampire is as good as another."

"She has a point." The fae shrugged. "Let's go see if we can catch them."

Fara shook her head. "Not with me. I'm out."

"Wish us happy hunting." The fae finally opened the door.

"Good Luck." Dear Gaia, were these idiots serious? Fara exited the van and watched it turn tail, the wheels spinning as it left.

Finally.

She let out a breath, checked around for company and, seeing none, did a broader scope. Kneeling, she put a hand flat on the ground over a large rock buried in thick black soil. The moon sighed overhead, and the clouds whispered their secrets as the wind swept them away.

Fara closed her eyes and focused. Her senses expanded as the rocks in the ground began to talk to her. She picked up wildlife deeper in the park, along the trails. A few reckless humans wandered on the closed grounds, laughing as they walked on a paved trail. Two rogue dryads nestled in the boughs of their oaks, the trees playful and young on this side of the world and happy to share information.

She let herself sink deeper, tracing, until she found Onvyr. Messing around as usual.

With a sigh, she straightened and followed a public path she'd expressly told her brother to avoid. If Atanase figured out what she'd done, he would do worse than kill her. So much worse.

Hustling before one of the dryads took note, she found her older brother busy arguing with a squirrel.

Fara rubbed her eyes, a headache forming.

"I said it's mine. I'm hungry."

The squirrel chittered back, waving a peanut at Onvyr. The furry little guy seemed to have an extensive vocabulary.

She cringed at her brother's glare. That last insult in particular looked like it hurt.

Her brother flushed, the tips of his ears darkened from pale cream to black. His coloring, having adjusted to the late hour, had changed. His dark hair was now white and his light skin dark, but his eyes remained the same. Like hers, the large lavender pupil and iris merged as though one solid color, the whites of his orbs barely visible, especially with their night vision adjusting.

Fara was more a blending of their parents, neither light nor dark, but a rare dusk elf. Onvyr had lucked out. He looked like their mother, a light elf, during the day and their father, a dark elf, at night. He could often pass as either as long as no one witnessed his change.

Like Fara, should his heritage be discovered, he'd be in a world of trouble. But he'd been blessed by the best of both lineages with a purity of spirit and the same physical strength and surefooted grace possessed by all elven warriors. Even better, Onvyr didn't hate everything not fae. He had a sense of humor and an ability to laugh at himself.

And he loved her, so she had that going for her.

"Onvyr, you're screwing up my camouflage. If you-know-who gets even an inkling that you escaped, or worse, that I helped you escape, he'll slaughter our family, burn down our woods, blow up our mines, drain every living creature we've ever met, and if we're lucky, then he'll just kill us. Of course, knowing him, he'll torture us for an eternity instead."

"I know. I'm sorry." He bowed his head, and she still had to look up to see him. He stood a good head and a half taller than her, like a true elven champion. Though Onvyr couldn't commune with stone, as she could, he had other talents. Speaking with animals, though annoying, had its advantages.

"Look, tell your fuzzy buddy to keep an eye out for—"

"Upir, just two of them up ahead," he said at the same time the ground underfoot screamed a warning.

Onvyr rushed toward the threat.

Just two? He apparently hadn't read "Black Day Massacre" either. But even if he hadn't, vampires had a well-earned reputation. Back at home, one vampire alone had slaughtered dozens in a nearby trading town, his killing spree not limited to anyone, not even his own kind.

Though typically vampires kept to magir wars, decimating lycan packs and unruly mages who refused to give tithe when demanded, the ones out here mingled with humans. From what she'd gathered, the upir clan in Seattle was fairly young, but she had no doubt they'd prove powerful. Especially when dealing with upstarts who dared interfere with "just two" of their clan.

Elven upstarts—Onvyr wasn't wearing a glamour. *Shit.*

She continued to swear under her breath as she caught up to her brother, but she was too late. Onvyr used the blade she'd forged for him over a hundred years ago, the wicked edge of an ogre bone she'd fused with dragon's breath, a flame-colored metal with silver-like properties found on fae lands.

Nothing had ever broken the blade nor nicked its edges. The upir's neck didn't withstand it either. He must have been young to bleed so much, the liquid flowing from his neck a bright, arterial red.

She could only stare, unsure of what she was seeing. Tangling with a vampire typically meant death, and not for the vampire. Onvyr had killed the upir as easily as battling his own shadow.

But while Onvyr destroyed one upir, the smarter of the two let his kin be killed and struck at Onvyr's back.

Onvyr took a hit but managed to dodge the next strike aimed at severing his spine. He flowed like water, flexible enough to dip under the upir's arm and come up on his other side, retaliating with a stab that missed.

The upir and her brother danced with blade and claw, fangs out, each trying to destroy the other while the danger pressed. For all Fara knew, the upir had already put out a call for help. And while Onvyr was impressing the heck out of her with his display of battlefield agility, even her brother couldn't handle a group of upir at once. She didn't think.

But watching him move, she suddenly had her doubts. Unfortunately, his burgeoning skills might prove even more of a problem, because if others found out a solitary creature had been killing vampires, the hunt would be on to find and eliminate the threat. More problems she and Onvyr couldn't afford.

No, they had to get away. *Now.*

She darted in to distract the upir and quickly jumped back, intending to avoid injury while giving Onvyr time to handle the vamp. She received a jab of claws for her efforts. "Ow, you bastard."

The vamp flashed her a toothy grin. He'd moved so fast she couldn't keep track. Much like Varujan had in that rundown building. He'd been toying with her, she knew. He could easily have killed her.

Which was why she'd made sure to cast that protection spell that thankfully had lasted a lot longer than her enchantment. That had to have been the only reason he'd refrained from killing her once the enthrallment wore off.

This upir showed no such restraint. Faster than she could move, he was on her.

He would have cut her throat if her brother hadn't intercepted with his blade, laughing as he struck back.

Muttering at him in their native language to stop playing around, she had to do what she hadn't wanted. Expending so much magic would leave a trail, but it couldn't be helped.

Though only temporary, the spell should work. She hoped.

Fara called upon the earth to take back the upir. The vampire fighting her brother stopped moving, his feet petrifying, rooting into the ground. He shrieked, loudly, as his blood suddenly oozed out of every orifice of his body, including his miniscule pores, returning to the earth. Giving back what Gaia had once given freely in the upir's creation.

"That's disgusting." Onvyr grimaced at the sight of the upir literally melting into the ground like a pile of goo—blood, bones, and all—until the ground swallowed him up.

"It won't last long," she rasped. "He's already starting to reconnect with his parts."

A few squirrels tossed peanuts at Onvyr, who smiled widely and bowed, thanking his audience. "My friends. I am so happy to have entertained you." A nearby owl hooted while a few crows flapped and cawed.

Fara didn't have the energy to dissolve the other upir. True dead, he would likely not re-corporate, but one could never be sure with a vampire. The evil bastards had all kinds of hidden talents.

"Come *on*," Fara urged her brother. "Their patriarch will soon learn he's lost two of his kin. He'll send more of them if he hasn't already. We have to go."

"You don't need to be so uptight about it. That was an excellent battle. Short, but fun." Onvyr sighed and to the squirrels said, "Do you see what I have to put up with?"

Communing with Gaia outside fae lands sapped her strength, so Fara wasn't able to maintain her glamour if she wanted to run with any speed from the scene of their crime. And it would be a *huge* hairy deal when the Seattle patriarch learned something had killed his kin. No one fucked with one Of the Bloode without dire consequences.

If it weren't bad enough that she'd gotten on Atanase's radar a decade ago, now her idiot brother might as well have painted targets on them. If word got out they'd killed a vampire, the hunt would be on throughout the magir community.

Dragging her brother with her, she let her senses lead them. They ran with the legendary speed of their kind, over rock and earth, across a street, past moving vehicles, and finally closer to the mountain that beckoned. The makings of a cave lay in the distance, deep under the ground. Once inside the earth, with any luck, she and Onvyr should be safe enough to hide out.

But luck had never been very fond of Fara.

Her energy started to flag at the same time the stone beneath her whispered of a wave of upir approaching. Directly on their scent. "Onvyr. They're here."

"On we go, lovey." Onvyr smiled, showing his small fangs, and picked her up. To her shock, her brother ran faster than any elf should be able to move. And that was *with* her added weight.

She clung to his broad back as he flew over the ground, deeper into the Cougar Mountain forest. "Onvyr, how?"

He shrugged, not even breathing hard as he answered, "Gaia doesn't talk to me the way she talks to you, but she likes me, so she sometimes gives me the energy I need when I want to do this."

"This?"

"Run fast."

She frowned. "Then why didn't you do this when you-know-who first captured you?" She pointed. "That way. There's a cavern farther out that's calling to me."

He turned but didn't answer.

"Onvyr?"

"I had no use to run so fast before." Atanase's name remained unspoken. "And after, I wasn't me for a long time."

She had no idea what exactly the vampire had done to her brother. But she'd seen the aftereffects: poor Onvyr bloody, mangled, and unhinged. And then Atanase had shown *her* what he was capable of. Hers had been a few memorable nights of torture that felt like forever. She could only imagine what that bastard had done to her brother for *years.*

Now Onvyr wasn't quite right or rational all the time. He

could fly into inexplicable rages, no doubt triggered by his stay with the strigoi. He needed her to survive. And he needed to be free of the bloode-debt placed on her shoulders. If she failed, so did he.

Fara had to make this plan work. She *had* to.

Varujan was the key; she could feel it. She just needed time to work the sly bastard.

The upir were gaining.

But so was Onvyr.

With a great leap, he sent them airborne to hurdle a large cropping of boulders and young saplings. Impressive, and just what they needed.

With the last bit of energy in her, Fara called forth the stones in the ground, awakening in them the same magic that swam in her blood. She slid herself and her brother down through vegetation, earth, and stone as if gliding through water. Above her, the earth reformed, hiding them.

Down, down, and deeper still they flowed. Until they reached the spot she wanted. A space within which she could work.

She mentally pushed, and the rocks shifted and turned porous, opening up into a space large enough that her brother could stand without stooping. The air wouldn't last them very long. With any luck, they'd have enough to regroup, giving her time to plan.

She settled on the ground, feeling the prick of welcome from the jutting rock beneath her, and sighed with pleasure.

"Rest, sister. I'll watch over you."

"Thank you, Onvyr."

"Thank *you*, Faraine." She felt the press of his lips upon her temple and fell asleep.

CHAPTER
THREE

Her dreams didn't make much sense. Fara felt herself constantly jostled as the excited creature holding her moved into a house filled with magic. Dark, powerful, and enticing, it—no, *he*—moved with sure strides through a delightful building made with quartz, marble, granite, cement, and a host of other materials normally found in fae and divine lands.

He caressed her again, as he'd been doing along the drive back, his thumb constantly stroking her multifaceted surface. She could feel but not see or hear, and that wouldn't do.

Fara realigned herself.

Fara/Varujan blinked, and she realized they shared his senses, enabling her to absorb much more than she normally did.

Ah, much better.

He frowned. "What was that?"

"What?" came a low growl next to him.

"What is wrong now?" a heavily accented male barked from behind them.

Fara faded, becoming Varujan, and the dream turned into an experience, his bloode boiling with rage, confusion, and an odd, foreign warmth that worried him.

He stalked through a dark corridor, lit not by artificial light yet it appeared entirely visible in muted shadow. Varu mentally estimated the time at close to three in the morning, and he hungered. Damn Mormo had insisted they return immediately, ruining the breakfast break Varu had intended with two lovely women on their way home from a party. The bastard had zapped him from afar, sending a shock through his system when he'd tried to disobey.

Orion and Kraft, however, had partaken eagerly without any ill effect.

"I think our great 'leader' is hangry, Kraft." Orion smirked. "The poor, angry, little strigoi. I can hear his stomach rumbling."

Kraft snickered. "*Ja.* That's it. I wonder why he didn't have anything to eat earlier. I mean, he is all powerful. Especially behind the wheel."

I knew *my driving us home would annoy these idiots.* The only good thing to come from their night out—petty revenge. Varu caressed the dagger in his hand, saw Orion raise a brow at him, and snarling, tucked the dagger into a pocket in his jacket.

He found the others, minus Mormo, lounging around in the living room. The dark furniture, a sectional and several chairs made of leather and expensive fabrics, were soft and cushiony and provided ample seating. A large screen television took up one wall. Inset, wooden bookcases sat along the far wall, holding all manner of ancient texts and artifacts.

Cream colored walls with a hint of gold held the occasional work of art, many by magir artists and a few divine-inspired portraits. No matter where he walked through the mansion, Varu felt watched and imagined the artwork to be much more than visually stimulating. Hecate and her plethora of spies...

The floor underneath felt like marble but had a give, which would make it anything but stone. Marble was a natural stone millions of years old. The nonfoliated metamorphic rock resulted from the alteration of the composition of limestone. He paid particular attention to it, going so far as to crouch down and run his long-fingered hand over it. Odd, but he found his hands graceful and pretty, the nail beds clean, the nails themselves hard and sharp.

But the stone, ah yes, it was alive, like most of the home. Imbued with a divine magic, the mansion would stand as a fortress against any threat. Curious.

"Is there a reason you're on your knees, running your hands lovingly over the floor?" an obnoxious male asked.

He looked up to see Rolf, the only blond vampire among them, grinning down at him. The Scandinavian draugr, an oddity among blood-drinkers, had more magic than the rest of them combined. A trickster and wolf shapeshifter, he didn't fit the vampire mold. Varu had yet to determine if that made Rolf a good or bad addition to their clan.

Highly intelligent and known to play pranks despite their deadly consequences, Rolf had been spending much of his time lately with Khent, who had also come to loom over Varu.

"Hmm. Varu does seem different." Khent stroked his chin, the reaper prone to long silences while his brain came to mystifying and often correct conclusions. Once one of the arrogant Sons of Osiris, Khent had belonged to a clan that had spent ages shaping Egyptian history. It was rumored his father had often appeared to people in the guise of Set. Considering Khent liked to think himself as omniscient as a god, Varu wouldn't put it past the reaper or his father to impersonate a deity.

"Go away, Khent."

Khent's stoic expression remained. "Perhaps he's realized he should bow in my presence after all."

Rolf laughed. Orion and Kraft joined them.

They stood close, looking down at him, and the pressure of so much power sparked Varu's need to defend them. No, *him*. To defend *himself.* So many predators so close, even those he knew to be kin, triggered his aggression.

But before he could launch himself at any of them—and damn, but Rolf opened his arms invitingly, his dark eyes sparkling with mirth—Mormo appeared in the middle of the room.

"What's going on in here? Oh, Varu. How nice of you to return. I missed you so." Mormo batted his eyelashes and smiled, showing fangs.

The others laughed, but Varu was tired, hungry, and annoyed beyond measure.

He shot up and over his companions, directly aiming for Mormo. In a burst of speed he hadn't realized he could achieve, he managed to slice into Mormo's neck as he shot past. A first.

Blood coated his nails, the scent sweet with promise. He licked his fangs while watching Mormo's wound close. The ageless creature radiated power. And now, anger.

Orion gaped. "Holy crap. Did you see that?"

"Since when is Varu that fast?" Kraft asked.

Khent watched, his eyes narrowed. "Impressive."

"Well? What does he taste like?" Rolf asked.

Exhilarated at finally striking the arrogant magician, Varu stared into Mormo's red eyes and sucked his long nails clean.

Too much, came a random thought.

A rush of power shocked him to his knees, and he did his best to calm his heart that threatened to explode while his body accepted the magic, locked in a brief moment of ecstasy.

Mormo crossed his arms over his chest. "If you were that hungry, all you had to do was say so."

Kraft nodded. "Yes. We had breakfast earlier, didn't we?"

"We did." Orion agreed, still smirking.

Once Varu could catch his breath, he stood and stared. Everyone glowed a different color. Strange colors also imbued several objects in the room. He blinked, but the glows remained.

Mormo's shone the brightest, a deep red surrounded by black and a thin line of gold. "Well aren't you the talented strigoi?" He snapped his fingers, and a ball of blue light appeared. "Do you see this?"

Khent frowned. "See what?"

"Yes." Varu nodded and felt an echo of agreement, wonder, and curiosity light up inside him. "What is that?"

Mormo's eyes narrowed, and the colors Varu had been seeing disappeared, as did his sudden burst of energy. "So... Where's Duncan?"

"Still with the witch, I guess." Varu shrugged. *So, not going to discuss the ball of seething energy that was in your hand. Just another secret. Typical Mormo.*

"I have an issue with the revenant," Rolf said. "I'm twice as good looking as Duncan. Why send him after the witch?"

"Because he listens," Varu answered. "You never do."

"I listen. I just do what makes the most sense."

"That's what I'm always telling him," Orion said. "But Varu keeps issuing orders."

Mormo rubbed a hand over his face and muttered, "Dealing with you six is like wrangling sea nymphs, I swear." In a louder voice, he said, "Duncan should be reporting back soon. We need to find that female."

"Why?" Varu asked.

"I'll tell you later."

"Tell me now."

Khent cleared his throat. "I think you mean, tell *us* now, Varu."

"Whatever." Varu ignored Khent's glare. "We've been working nonstop for months, training to do Hecate's bidding. Why?" *What the hell are we really doing here?*

"That's a very good question." Rolf backflipped and somer-saulted his way to sitting on the back of the sectional sofa. "Not that I mind hanging out with my new bros, but I'd really like to know what we're working towards."

"'Bros'?" Khent grimaced. "I'm a Son of Osiris. Not a 'bro.'"

"You *were* a Son of Osiris." Rolf winked. "We're all Night Bloode now."

"Eh, bros works for me." Orion shrugged and joined Rolf on the couch. Kraft followed.

"Don't sit on the back like that. You'll crush the cushions," Mormo nagged. But no one moved. He sighed. "I hate vampires."

"Back at ya," Varu snarled. "Now talk."

"Or what?"

Rolf leaned forward. "Oh, *this* should be good."

Varu felt a spark of something under his skin and glanced at the others. The band of kinship they shared usually remained loose enough to allow independence but still kept them together. But now, they felt as one, a family of death-bringers. Powerful and hungry—and under Varu's direction.

He smiled and licked his lips, considering Mormo—their patriarch—prey.

Mormo gazed from the rest of them to Varu. "I had no idea that was possible."

"What?" Varu asked. That quickly, the power faded, and the vampires relaxed once more.

Mormo studied him with an intensity that wrapped around Varu's bones and held him with a dark magic he recognized. Hecate's Kiss. The white-haired bastard grinned. "Well, well. Who do we have here?"

"Mormo, just answer me—us." Varu sighed. "Why does Hecate really want us here?"

Mormo had yet to blink. "Why, to find *her,* of course." He peered closer, his fangs growing. "Where have you been hiding, girl?"

Varu closed his eyes, not sure why when normally he'd keep

his eyes on the threat. Something in him shifted. The warmth in his body centered in his brain, then his heart, and moved down his arms to his hands. He sank to one knee and placed his left hand on the floor. But before he could place the right hand down, Mormo snapped his fingers, and he froze.

"Oh no. You're not getting away that easily. Get up." He said something under his breath, and Varu levitated while his hand remained fixed in place.

Everyone stared as Varu continued to rise, now upside down. He would have continued toward the ceiling had his hand not been firmly glued to the floor.

"Yank him up," Mormo ordered the others, who hurried to do his bidding.

But it was too late. Varu's hand flared hot. The warmth that filled him suddenly shot into the ground. And he blacked out.

Varu blinked and looked up at five pairs of eyes. Most looked shocked. Rolf's were amused, Mormo's concerned. Huh. Concern? That was a new one. Typically Mormo only looked at Varu with disdain, annoyance, or frustration.

"Why am I on the floor?" He stood with Orion's help. He felt a little dizzy, but that soon settled. The vague notion that something was missing bothered him. He quickly felt in his jacket and brushed the hilt of the dagger, so the Bloode Stone remained. Why then did he feel… incomplete?

The others backed away, giving him space. All except for Mormo, who once again violated Varu's need for autonomy. He grabbed Varu's face with clawed hands, his hold impossible to escape.

"Stop moving," Mormo ordered. He stared, looking for what, Varu had no idea.

But this close, Varu could see the energy swirling deep within Mormo's blazing red eyes. Hints of gold and silver dotted his pupils. A waft of feminine power emanated like a wash of moonlight over his face, welcoming and mysterious at the same time.

"What did I miss?" Duncan asked as he strolled into the room like Bond on a mission. Spotting Varu and Mormo, the Brit froze. "Holy shit. Are Mormo and Varu going to snog?"

"Huh?" Orion asked.

"Make out," Duncan explained, his dark eyes wide. "I told you guys I felt a weird energy between those two."

Vampires did whatever they wanted with whomever they wanted. But no way would Varu ever welcome Mormo with anything but teeth at the magician's throat.

"Shut it, asshole," Varu snapped, wishing he could step away from Mormo.

He really didn't appreciate all the laughter.

Varu waited through the indignity of Mormo's scrutiny until the creature finally let him go. And it *rankled* that Varu had to wait for Mormo to *allow* him to step back.

I really have to kill this one.

He must have been too expressive with his anger because Mormo said, "Many have tried and failed, Varujan," and paused, his gaze vague before he focused on Varu once more. "Did you feel anything earlier? Anything... odd?"

Varu shrugged. "Maybe."

"It's the dagger," Kraft offered.

"Dagger? Is that the magic I'm feeling from his jacket?"

Orion nodded. "We were on our way home after dropping Duncan off. I was driving."

"Only because you always hog the keys," Kraft muttered.

Rolf grinned, watching others entertain him.

"Someone hit the windshield," Orion continued. "We need a new one."

Mormo sighed. "Again?"

Varu nodded. "I chased the one who hit us—a female—into an abandoned building. Orion and Kraft fought gunfire and a few lycans and battle beasts."

"And humans, but they folded with ease once we broke their

guns. No injuries for us," Kraft said. "Although Varu got beaten up by the girl."

Everyone stared at Varu.

He bit back a growl. "I wasn't beaten up. She escaped." He paused. "I thought she was human, but she was something more. She enthralled me to let down my guard." Because no way would he have let anyone attacking him to escape alive.

"A witch or mage?" Khent asked.

"I didn't get that impression. In any case, the spell wore off. Then she threw this at me." He withdrew the dagger from his jacket and handed it to Mormo. "Peel back the leather binding."

The others crowded Mormo, drawn by the jewel.

They stared in awe.

Mormo nodded, unsmiling, his satisfaction impossible to miss. "Yes. This is good."

"What is it?" Khent asked. "I feel it in my bones. It's powerful."

"The dagger or the stone?" Rolf asked. "Because both have been crafted with power." He leaned closer to sniff the dagger. "Fae power that speaks to my homeland."

"Fae power?" Varu studied the blade. "No. She was…" He thought back to his initial impression. A female with pale gray skin and lavender eyes too large for a human's that glowed. She'd been exceptionally beautiful, with a shine to her skin, a vitality he'd never seen in a human. He'd thought that the work of her spell. But what if the initial features he'd seen had been real?

His heart raced, and he wanted to grab the dagger back and inhale, as if to trap her scent inside him.

Mormo's watchful eyes didn't make him feel any better.

"What?"

"You saw her." Mormo paused, his direct gaze disconcerting. "And she was here."

"Here?"

"Inside you."

"Oh, sounds kinky." Rolf laughed. "My boy Varu was ridden by a sexy hijacker. One who left through the floor."

Varu *hated* the fact a stranger had hidden inside his mind. Magic? Possession? He hadn't felt her, exactly, except he had. And she'd been so warm and enjoyable, making him powerful and content—an emotion with which he had little familiarity. He wanted to feel it—*her*—again.

Except he loathed the idea of wanting anything beyond his control. Especially not now with his odd arrangement with his new Night Bloode kin. That was all he needed, another problematic player in this game with Mormo that he intended to win.

"I suppose it's time you all knew. Follow me." Mormo moved into the overlarge kitchen, placed the dagger on the center island, and leaned back against the counter while the rest of them sat around the island. Glasses of blood appeared before each of them while Mormo snacked on a meat and cheese plate.

Too tired to resist, Varu sipped from his crystal glass while the others downed theirs in one long, satisfying pull. Fresh fae blood. He wondered where Mormo had gotten it but didn't care, his hunger no longer assuaged by his earlier taste of the magician.

Which made him realize something shockingly important.

"We, all of us, could have taken you earlier." He studied their patriarch. The others grew still. "For the first time since you forced us under the kin bond, you weren't a part of it. Why is that?"

Mormo cocked his head. "I don't know. That's interesting, isn't it? That right after you got a boost from the presence inside you, you grew powerful enough to overwhelm me. In doing so, you pulled your brethren with you. Functioning as one clan against its own patriarch." He glanced at the dagger. "The Bloode Stone speaks to you."

"I feel it too," Kraft said.

"You all do, yes." Mormo's gaze remained on Varu. "But only one of you is drawn to it in the way Varu is. And only Varu can use it the way it was meant to be used."

Orion frowned. "I don't understand."

"Vampires were separated from each other thousands of years past in order to contain your species' great power. If left unchecked, you would have annihilated all the other sentient beings in your world before marching on the other realms."

"We are so badass," Orion said with a grin, flashing his fangs.

"And so stupid," Khent added.

"This is also true," Kraft agreed and laughed when Orion flipped him off.

Khent took over. "Our species is warlike, bent on domination. If they hadn't separated us back then, we would have killed everyone else then turned on each other. Our nature is to destroy. That's an inescapable truth."

Varu asked, curious, "So you agree that we should never accrue the power inherent in our bloode?" He'd thought about it a long time ago, back when his father had mentioned the possibility of tracking down the stones. But, like Khent, Varu had realized that giving vampires dominion over the world would be a huge mistake.

"I do. We are not meant to wield so much authority in this world." Khent narrowed his gaze on the dagger. "These stones, if this is indeed a Bloode Stone, have been buried for millennia. They are worth a fortune. Untold power to any who possess them. So how exactly did you get this?"

"That's what bothers me so much about the dagger." Varu frowned. "The female threw it at me. There's no way this thing is real." Unless she was missing some brain cells. Who let a price-less object like the stone go?

"It's a Bloode Stone." Mormo surprised them all by sharing.

"The girl did handle it. Which tells us she's no mere mortal, and especially someone we need on our side."

"You think she's got more of them?" Varu cringed at the idea of anyone like his father ever getting his hands on such power. "She couldn't have known what she had. She threw it away."

"She threw it at you," Orion corrected.

"As if I'd let her hit me." Varu huffed and turned back to Mormo. "Is this what you wanted, magician? To gather them all?"

Mormo kept watching him, and it was creeping Varu the hell out. Instead of answering, the white-haired jerk asked Duncan, "What did you learn tonight?"

"The witch has heard rumors about a big player working to find something that will change the way vampires work. Nothing specific, but the info was vague enough to add substance to your Bloode Stone theory."

"And the woman you were sent to find?"

"The witch didn't know anything about her, but she did learn something interesting before I left." Duncan wiped his mouth free of his meal. "Someone hit the local upir clan tonight and killed one of them."

The others exchanged glances. Anything that killed one of their kind bore monitoring.

"Details?" Varu asked.

"Rumor has it one of the attackers was a dark elf. The other a human woman."

"Human or human-seeming?" Varu said. Thoughts of the fearless woman stirred his rage. With icy composure, he stated, "We need to find her." *So I can drain her and get back to my complicated life. I don't need distractions right now.*

"Agreed." Mormo nodded.

Everyone gaped.

"Wait." Rolf held up a hand. "You're...*agreeing*...with

Varu?" Rolf put a hand over his heart. "I don't... I can't take the shock."

"Seriously. Are you even Mormo?" Kraft asked, peering at the powerful male. "You look like him, but the real Mormo hates Varu."

Mormo sniffed. "I don't hate Varu."

Varu arched a brow.

"I find you incredibly annoying, sure. I think you're impulsive, too aggressive, and listen for shit. You don't follow orders unless made to."

"He's got you there," Orion murmured.

"And you don't appreciate my goddess."

"I'd appreciate her more if she'd let me kill you." Varu studied Mormo's neck, which had healed seconds after being cut. "No, actually, I'd keep you alive and feed off you for eternity."

The others leaned closer. To his credit, Mormo actually looked uncomfortable.

"How did he taste?" Duncan asked. "My guess, acidic. Sour."

"Nah. He's sweet, I'll bet." Orion looked Mormo over. "Power has a sweet taste to it, and we all know Mormo's got a direct line to Hecate."

Khent nodded. "You make a good point, Orion."

"He probably tastes vanilla," Kraft guessed. "Because Mormo's nice but boring."

"I'm not boring." Mormo glared.

"And he's not nice." Rolf licked his fangs. "Probably tastes like chicken."

The others laughed, and for once, Varu found Rolf amusing.

"Very funny." Mormo once again looked too superior to have a sense of humor. "Say what you want about me, but Varu is correct."

"Again, agreeing with me. Maybe you really aren't Mormo."

Mormo glared at him, and Varu's heart stopped. Contrary to

popular myth, vampires *did* have a heartbeat and did breathe, though they didn't need oxygen to live. The heart, however, was a necessity due to circulating bloode, which held their magic.

"Are you quite finished?"

Varu gasped and nodded.

Mormo blinked, and Varu's heart started again.

"No, he's Mormo." Varu clutched his chest, willing the pain to fade.

"As I was saying, the female who threw the dagger. We need her here, now. Drop everything you're doing. I want this woman found. Varu has her image. Here." Mormo made a pulling motion with his hand, and the image of the female appeared in the air in front of them, a magical hologram of her likeness.

"Track her down. Do not, I repeat, do *not* kill her. We need to find her before the local upir do. They'll kill her. And we need her to tell us everything she knows about the Bloode Stone." Mormo grimaced. "In fact, you could say your very lives depend on this female being found and brought here before me. I want her unharmed, alive, in one piece." He turned to Khent. "Khent, I mean it. You are not to kill her and raise her from the dead as one of your servants. I'll know."

Khent sighed. "Fine. But killing her first would make everything easier."

Varu had to hold onto his temper, the thought of anyone but him handling—*no, killing*—the female making him see red.

"Where do we start?" Kraft asked. "She tore from the scene earlier. She could be anywhere."

"Backtrack from the upir attack."

Duncan asked, "Why can't you just do a locator spell like the one you used to get us to the witch?"

"It doesn't work that way."

Odd how whenever Mormo didn't or couldn't do something, he used *It doesn't work that way* as a blanket excuse.

"Duncan, get them the details," Mormo ordered.

"Fine." Duncan grinned. "I'd like another shot at the witch, anyway. You want to talk sweet? What I wouldn't give to keep that woman chained to my side." He wiggled his brows. "She was a looker, all right. And lively." He licked his lips and winked as he dug out his cell phone and made a call, walking a short distance away.

"Pair up," Mormo insisted.

Varu argued, "I'll find her faster on my own."

"Take Khent."

"I—"

"The first pair to find her gets the weekend off." Mormo vanished.

"I hate when he does that." Varu turned to Khent and glared. "Don't slow me down."

Khent looked down his nose at Varu. "Orion, trade me. I'll go with Kraft. You take Varu."

Orion snorted. "Hell no. Come on, Kraft." He paused. "You can drive on the way home."

Kraft studied him. "Done."

Duncan put his cell phone away and returned. "Upir attack happened at Lake Sammamish State Park. By the playground almost two hours ago."

Orion and Kraft left.

Rolf and Duncan eyed each other. "No tricks," Duncan insisted.

Rolf's smile widened, and he tucked his shoulder-length blond hair behind one ear. "Now, you know I can't agree to that."

"Fine, but none at my expense."

"Deal." Rolf held out his hand, and they shook before jogging to the garage.

Varu growled, annoyed at being the last to leave.

Khent sighed. "First I had to partner Rolf, now you. It's like Mormo hates me for some reason."

"Join the club." Varu hurried the slow reaper with him before realizing they could use Khent's talents to their advantage. "You still have those dead crows?"

"Of course."

"How about you do some reconnaissance? Scout out the area, see if they can track anything dead or undead."

Khent frowned in concentration. His expression eased. "They're moving. Which car do you want to take?"

"Something fast."

Khent brightened. "I suggest the Mercedes." In the garage, he swiped the keys from the rack. The Land Rover and Explorer were gone. The Mercedes it would be. He got into the driver's side, and they sped out into the night, wasting no time.

I'm coming, fae female. And when I find you, we'll talk about you being inside me. And see what it will take to turn the tables. Varu grinned, anticipation fueling his good mood. "Hurry up, Khent. We need to find her before the others do."

Mormo had said to bring her back unharmed.

He hadn't said anything about not taking a taste before delivering her.

Mormo strode down the stairwell into the heart of his mistress's domain in the earthly plane. He'd been her servant for thousands of years and treasured every single day. After the death of his mother, the first Mormo, Hecate had suckled him from her breast, feeding him the power and divine magic that allowed him to be both alive and dead and everything in between.

Like her, he needed blood to survive. Probably why the vampiric nature suited him so well.

Still, he was at least civilized. Not like the six dickheads he had to deal with on a daily basis.

"I do believe you're carrying a grudge." Her voice echoed, a lilting blend of musicality and smoky seduction. Hecate brought night, magic, and witchcraft with her wherever she went. And her home had been structured down to its bones in power and sacrifice.

"Mistress, I must ask again, why? We could do what we need without involving the six of *them*." Despite his complaint, he was coming to like Varu more than he'd thought he would. Brazen, disrespectful, yet normally in control of himself, the vampire was so like his great-great grandfather. It still boggled Mormo's mind to realize the two were related.

"My dear, you know why. You have too much to do as it is. Let our bloode clan do the busywork." She appeared beside him, a threefold goddess in one form, her faces blending constantly, like wax melting one beautiful face into the next. She frowned, and her favorite face settled in place. It was heart-shaped, her skin a shimmering bronze framed by straight, black hair that reached her back. Her eyes sparkled, jet black and set under delicately shaped brows.

A necklace holding a key draped around her neck settled between her breasts. Clad in a red sweater and jeans, she remained barefoot, though he noticed red paint on her toes and a darker crimson on her lips.

"A new color?"

She smiled. "Faraine is wearing it, and I realized I liked it."

"Faraine?"

"She's coming soon. Don't worry." Hecate put her hands on his arm as they descended to her workspace, accessible only in her presence. The basement functioned as the waystation of her creation, so she could keep track of those wishing to cross into other realms. Instead of the dense forest she used when in the divine and fae planes, here the basement resembled a speakeasy with dozens of doors constantly opening and closing, the large bar operated by Hecate's beloved undead.

She accepted a drink from an undead witch in a flapper's dress and sighed after sipping. "Divine, Catherine. And I do mean that."

The witch, who looked as lively as any living human in Seattle, laughed and returned to the bar to wait on one of Loki's annoying brats.

"Now, Mormo, tell me what's wrong. You're worried. This isn't like you."

Mormo hadn't wanted to burden her, but the existence of the stone could mean nothing but trouble. "You were right. The end approaches." He paused. "I find I don't want humanity to die."

"Of course not." She looked mortally offended. "My worshippers are human. Their lives are but a bridge between states. Life, death, creation, destruction. And magic. So much magic the frail humans possess, if only they could access it. All the races are special, but with the end of the humans, we will soon follow. All life comes from them."

Mormo still didn't understand why humans, of all the species, should be so special. But he trusted his goddess in all things. "Yes, Mistress. It's as you've said. But I can't help but wonder if we could be helping humanity more than we currently are."

"What do you think our vampires are doing?"

"*Our* vampires?" He raised a brow. "Mistress, no one owns a vampire. You only think they're yours until they slit your throat and drink you dry."

"I know. They're such lovely creatures." She had stars in her eyes.

He groaned. "They're nothing but trouble. Who knows how long your spell will hold? Even against your powerful magic, they are mostly immune. Tonight Varu pulled the others from me. They were as one, and I was nothing but prey."

"Oh, that's interesting."

She wasn't hearing him. "Witchcraft and death spells will hold for only so long, until—"

"—their bloode eats my magic. I'm aware." She continued to smile. "They don't worship the gods, so our power has no effect on them. But don't you see? That makes them all the more necessary. We must defend against what's coming."

He hated thinking about it.

"In the ten thousand years since our last battle, our enemy has grown strong. The Bloode Stones are but the first in several tasks we must complete if we're to save this world, the prophesied first to die. For if any of us shall fall, we *all* shall fall."

He swallowed. "That's what I'm afraid of."

"And let's face it, the toughest hurdle we have right now is getting the vampires in line. It's a simple enough thing to manage for someone as smart as you."

"Mistress, you might as well have me herding cats."

"There's the spirit!" She leaned over to pet a battle cat that appeared out of nowhere, stunned at its new environment.

The gray and black-striped thing was much larger than a Siberian tiger and about as friendly as one, though it allowed Hecate to pet it with pleasure. She finished, and the cat stopped purring. It snarled at Mormo, then turned tail and stalked toward the bar, where the witch had set out a huge bowl of milk.

He tried again. "Beloved Mistress, I really think you're misunderstanding the situation."

"Oh, I understand just fine." She turned to him, and her faces began to blend again. "Gather Ambrogio's tears. Blood the dusk elf, and bring me the bones of the abomination with her. Only with true sacrifice will we survive this first challenge." She gripped his wrist and dug red-painted claws into him, drawing forth a well of blood from which she drank.

When she let him go, he continued to bleed, so much he worried he might actually perish. This time for good. Hecate loved him, he knew, but sometimes she forgot that part of him would always remain the tiniest bit mortal.

Hecate watched the blood seep into the floor, greedily ingested into the heart of her home. "Ah, there we go."

He wavered on his feet, unsteady until she drew him close for a kiss.

Power unfurled, energizing him for the next hundred years.

"Ah, my sweet. I love you, dearest."

He knelt, unabashed at the tears streaming down his face. "And I you, Mistress. I worship everything about you."

"Thank you. I needed that." She left him with a smile on her face.

He stood, rejuvenated, until he realized she'd also left him with a still hungry battle cat that didn't appreciate life in a divine bar, far from his fae home.

"By the Goddess," he muttered and did his best to convince the damn feline not to hold a grudge.

F ara woke feeling more tired than she'd been before she'd
gone to sleep. A fuzzy remnant from her dream remained,
the sense of reveling in thick power, a dizzying rush of glory,
death, and hunger weakening her to the point of passing out
again.

Onvyr shook her. "We need to go. I sense them coming."

"Wh-what?"

"Faraine, wake up." Onvyr slapped her gently, but still.

"*Ow.*" She couldn't see a blasted thing, but she'd felt that slap
for sure. "That was unnecessary."

"I can't see, I'm hungry, and a mole swung by to let me know
the upir are coming."

"How many, do you think?"

"More than one, I know that. But the mole said there's something else that brings death besides the upir clan, and it's scared."

"Just great." How had her nap taken things from bad to
worse? Fara reached out and used her brother to stand. Once on
her feet, she grounded herself in the rock underfoot and drank its
energy into her cells, allowing Gaia's gifts to take root inside her.

It wasn't much, but it should be enough to allow her to get to safety to recharge, once again assuming her glamour.

Onvyr tightened his hand over hers. "Oh, that's nice. Can I have some?"

"Sure." She asked for more for her brother, and the stones all around them answered.

The cave lit up, power shining from the rocks lining their hiding place, gradually subsiding from a blinding glare to a dim glow. Her brother looked well enough, the fury in his eyes dulled to his normal night-eyed stare. Except now that she looked at him, she noticed his pupils, still lavender in color, had *elongated*. He had the eyes of a feline. Or a dragon.

"What the heck? Onvyr, your eyes are weird."

"Is that a compliment?" He stood with his head cocked, listening to what, she couldn't hear. "They're coming in fast. Are we staying or going?"

"How long was I asleep? Shouldn't they have come and gone already?"

"I don't know. A few hours maybe, but not enough for the sun to come up. Maybe the vampire you buried has risen and called in his friends." He glanced at his skin, which remained dark.

"I really wish you hadn't killed that upir."

"I'm sorry." He looked embarrassed.

"It's okay. But please, no more. We can maybe pretend you got lucky by killing a young one. But if you kill any others, we'll have not only you-know-who but the Bloode Empire on our tail." Not to mention every magir faction wanting to put an end to creatures more powerful than vampires.

She still didn't understand it. Though powerful, her father had only ever bested a vampire with the help of fellow warriors. But Onvyr had killed a young vamp by himself. She had a feeling he'd been on his way to taking out the more mature upir with him before she'd cautioned him to stop.

"I'm not sure if we should stay or go." She sighed. "If we stay, we can wait them out and regain some strength. But we can't sit here forever. And if they do track us and try to wait us out, we'll end up facing a bigger threat than if we leave now and find a new place to hide."

"So we run." He nodded. "Let's go."

"Fine. First, your glamour." She waited while he sighed and forced himself to look human. He retained his height and brawn but now possessed coloring and features similar to hers. "Good job."

"It feels like I'm all stretched out."

"Because you never practice holding it. How many times have I told you to get used to keeping your glamour in place?"

"Who needs to look human in fae lands?" he muttered. "Fine, you're right." He looked past her shoulder. "Oh, shut up."

She frowned. "Who are you talking to?"

"The mole."

"I don't see him."

"He just ducked back under. Come on. Send us topside so we can run." He turned his back. "Hop on."

"I don't need you to carry me."

"Are you sure?"

"Yes. We need to move fast. I have a feeling we might need to split up. If you or I get captured, we can rescue the other later. But if they get us both, that's not going to end well."

"Good point."

Fara focused, asking for Gaia's help, and they rose up through the earth as easily as they'd sunk into it.

She heard several beings in the distance running toward them. With her elf sight, she looked some distance away to see the moon spotlighting the red eyes and ivory fangs of unhappy bloodsuckers threading the forest and coming fast.

Right. Time to go.

"Hurry, Faraine." Onvyr raced off, and it took everything she had to keep up with him.

It felt as if they made progress, the noise behind them growing fainter.

She started to slow down, losing sight of her brother ahead.

Then she felt it. The quiet but creeping sense of being stalked. She put on a burst of speed, adrenaline fueling her once more.

But though Gaia had replenished much of what she'd lost, she still needed rest and time to fully recover. She started to slow again. In the distance, she heard Onvyr roar.

How had they gotten ahead of her brother? "Onvyr!" She ran faster, her lungs burning.

Overhead, she noticed a few birds flying with her. Odd to see crows flying at night.

A tall vampire appeared in front of her, and she nearly ran into his arms, stopped only by the tree root that tripped her.

She tumbled and righted herself quickly.

"Easy, female," the vampire said, his voice deep, soothing. He was incredibly handsome, his expression almost kind, which scared her even more. "Come with us and no harm will befall you."

Onvyr continued to growl far ahead.

She backed up and at the last moment dove to her right over a fallen tree, shot to her feet once more, and started running. The dark laugh behind her sent chills down her spine.

Dodging trees, shrubs, and rock, alternating her path, and flat out running as fast as she could seemed to give her no advantage. The handsome vampire ran a few feet next to her and waved. To her right, Varujan appeared, grinning so wide his fangs glistened in the snatches of moonlight that bathed his face.

Oh, crap. This isn't how I'd planned to use the vampire. Being his dinner is not going to help me with Atanase.

Scared but determined, she continued and would have escaped

—she wanted to think—if the handsome vampire to her left hadn't appeared right in front of her.

On a gasp, she turned and banged into Varujan.

He closed his arms around her and lifted her up, bring her face to face.

"Hello, there." He radiated smug satisfaction.

She squirmed, and he tightened his hold around her, his arms like steel bands. Before she could even try to enspell him with her very last witch stone, he tilted her head to the side and bit deep.

The swift dart of pain quickly turned to pleasure. He pulled with his lips, sucking her blood, and sighed.

Fara lost herself to his dark embrace, praying this wasn't the end though not sure she minded if it was.

VARUJAN HAD NEVER KNOWN any taste so sublime—a word he'd never used to describe blood. Blood was food—a necessity. Tasty, bitter, sweet. Sure, all those. But the female in his arms felt like life at its purest.

"Why do I get the impression you do not mean to share? Come, crows. Back home with you both," he dimly heard Khent say.

An instinctive growl left him, and Varu hugged his prey —*mine, only mine*—tighter. The blood he'd swallowed gratified his hunger on another level entirely. He licked her wound shut, sealing it, then tucked her closer to his body.

A glance at the others who'd approached showed Rolf holding a large man over his shoulder, a blade tucked into his jeans. "Found this one in the woods. Fought like a demon. Impressive. Figured we might as well take him back with us too."

Duncan nodded. "If he's not with her, we can enjoy a late lunch."

"Great minds think alike." Rolf grinned.

Khent cleared his throat. "If you're done sampling the merchandise, can we please get back? I have more important things to do."

"Like what?" Orion asked as he jogged toward them, Kraft on his heels. "Oh, don't worry. We took care of the half dozen upir back there. Thanks for waiting," he said to Rolf with no small amount of sarcasm.

The draugr ignored him. "Well, Khent? What *are* you in a rush to get back to at the mansion? Inquiring minds want to know."

Khent frowned. "Not that it's any of your business, but there's a new murder mystery streaming on YouTube. It's a vampire mystery series with some of my favorite actors."

"Oh?" Duncan stepped closer. "Just please tell me it's a new guy playing Lestat. Loved the books, but I did not understand the movie casting. At all."

Khent shuddered. "No, nothing that horrific."

Orion rolled his eyes. But Kraft agreed. "They should have chosen someone taller."

Varu couldn't care less about any of it, gratified to finally have his prey in his arms. He cradled the female, feeling her heart beat in time with his, slowing until they started together, creating a new rhythm that calmed.

Orion watched him, his expression odd. Then he murmured something to Kraft, and they flanked Varu back to the car, watching every little thing he did, which had him growling nonstop.

The pair finally left to get the SUV. Khent drove the Mercedes, his smirk in the rearview annoying. Sometimes Varu wished all vampire myths were true, but vampires could and did project reflections. "Are you sure you don't want to leave her in the backseat and sit up front with the adults?"

"Show me an adult and I might."

Khent raised a brow. "You can let her go. I doubt she'll be conscious after you put her under."

"I'm not taking any chances." He had no intention of describing his need to hold onto the female. Khent would think him under a compulsion, and he wasn't. He didn't think.

Unconscious, she couldn't be using any kind of spell to force his protection. He was aware of her on every level. He continued to savor her taste. Inhaling her captivating scent, memorizing the fragile line of her throat, the shape of her eyes, her lips... He studied her form, bemused at the desire building as he watched her lovely breasts rise and fall.

His body responded for the first time in over a century, ready and willing to join with another. Male to female. Ready to mate. As much as he didn't trust the need, part of him reveled in it. The idea of filling her with his seed became more than idle thought but a possibility, something he dwelled on as he spent the rest of the car ride with his hand protectively over her belly, already anticipating the pleasure of her warmth.

Varu had always been an intelligent strigoi. No sense in wasting an opportunity for some pleasure in his life. He'd have her then kill her, letting none of the female go to waste. Perhaps that would get any mating nonsense out of his mind.

They pulled into the garage, and he was startled to see that he'd been unaware of most of the ride back. He glanced up to see Khent's gaze in the rearview mirror.

He bared his teeth in warning, but Khent only rolled his eyes and left the vehicle.

Before Varu could get out, the car door opened and Mormo and Duncan stared down at him.

"What?" he snarled.

Mormo huffed. "Still *such* an ass."

Duncan chuckled and took the woman from Varu's arms. Varu did his best to pretend he didn't care that he no longer held onto his prey. He'd been the one to capture her, the one to imprison her for the journey back. And everything in him rebelled at his empty arms.

Orion and Kraft joined them. He followed the group into the house, watching closely as Duncan settled her into a spare room with a large bed. Rolf put the unconscious man on a nearby chair, propping him up so they could study the pair.

Varu looked from the woman to the man. "They look alike. Siblings perhaps?"

"Or family of some kind." Mormo nodded.

"They smell alike," Rolf said. "They look human, but they're not."

"Interesting." Khent leaned closer, making Varu uncomfortable. He wanted badly to push Khent away. "To continue the glamour while unconscious takes no small amount of power."

When Khent leaned even closer, Varu forced himself not to yank the reaper back. He didn't like Khent so near, but he disliked his odd reaction to the female even more.

Khent glanced back at him and smirked. "I'm merely studying our prey."

Finally losing his temper, Varu snapped, "*My* prey. I captured her."

"With *my* birds sighting in and *my* help herding her toward you."

"Please. I had her the minute we stepped on that mountain." Not a lie. Varu had sensed the woman's presence easily, feeling her as he'd earlier felt the Bloode Stone. He frowned down at her. "I think she's connected to the stone. She feels the same."

Mormo watched him. "Interesting."

Orion snorted. "You keep saying that, Mormo. But you never tell us exactly what 'interesting' means."

Kraft blinked. "*Interesting* is an English word used to describe something that catches your attention. You should read more, Orion."

"Shut up, dickhead. I was trying to say that Mormo keeps too many secrets."

"Yet you sounded confused about the meaning of a simple word. You make little sense."

"Yeah? You're an asshole. You know what that means?"

"That you are glad we're kin and best of friends?" Kraft added something in German, and Orion answered him in Greek.

Rolf started laughing.

Khent kept smirking.

And Varu did his best not to rip Duncan's arms off when he moved in from the other side of the bed to touch the woman's forehead.

"She feels warm." He looked up at Varu. "But I don't sense the stone when I touch her."

Orion stopped arguing long enough to say, "I don't smell or sense it either, and I felt it earlier when we fought in that alley. Kraft? You held the dagger. Do you sense it now?"

"No." Kraft shook his head. "It's as Mormo said. The stone calls to you, Varu. And perhaps this thief does as well."

"Thief?" Duncan asked.

Kraft nodded to the woman. "She handled a Bloode Stone, yet she is no vampire. How then did she get it?"

"And can she get more?" Mormo murmured. "That's another *interesting* question." He smirked at Orion, who glowered. "I have work to do. Rolf, Varu, stay for a moment. The rest of you, go clean up and see to the vehicles."

Orion gave a loud sigh. "Fine. Always with the menial labor."

"Oh, menial. Now that's a good word for you. Unskilled, lowly, those are words you should understand." Kraft gave him a fake smile then darted away when Orion started after him, sniping again.

Khent and Duncan followed, shaking their heads.

Once the door closed behind them, Mormo crouched next to the female.

Varu watched Mormo carefully, gratified to see Rolf watching Mormo just as keenly.

Which was why the attack from the previously unconscious man took him by surprise. And why Rolf nearly lost his head when it should have been impossible to overtake one vampire, let alone two.

Fara groaned and put a hand to her head, not aware of much except a dull ache at her neck and a throbbing in her chest. Her heart seemed to be pumping especially fast.

She heard grunts and thuds, a lot of swearing. The sounds of a fight.

"Die, vampire scum." Onvyr swore in *mrykálfar*. More thuds and grunts, then… laughter?

She blinked her eyes open and stared up into the concerned red gaze of a beautiful man with long, white hair. He had sharp cheekbones and arched brows, a thin nose and firm jaw. He was in no way human, yet he didn't strike her as a vampire. More like elven with a dash of something else? Demon, maybe?

He smiled at her. "Hello there."

She couldn't help smiling back. "Hi."

"Do you think you could ask your friend to relax?"

She followed his gaze to see her brother's arm locked around a large blond man's neck while Varujan launched himself at the pair. All three fell to the ground, a tangle of limbs and blows while the blond man laughed, apparently unconcerned about being choked to death.

Scared Varujan might kill her brother if she didn't intervene, she sat up and wavered, feeling dizzy. The white-haired man braced her. "Thanks."

"My pleasure."

Varujan snarled at her helper, oddly enough, before dragging Onvyr away.

Trust her brother to continue to make trouble for them. "Onvyr, enough! Release that man. Onvyr. Look at me!"

Her brother glanced at her, but his eyes seemed blank. She didn't think he was seeing her, no doubt overwhelmed with memories of vampires and torture, forever locked in the world of pain Atanase had created for him.

"Oh, Onvyr." She whispered a prayer in mrykálfar, a soothing poem her mother had once given them, courtesy of her love of Gaia. The earth always sang back. Even in this magically enforced place with evil creatures, Gaia's love murmured a bless-ing, singing up from the earth, through the floors and walls.

To her relief, her brother heard and relaxed, sagging in Varu-jan's hold until he passed out cold.

Varujan dropped him and leaned down, his long-fingered hands, tipped with dagger-sharp nails, outstretched.

"Don't hurt him," she ordered, which had him glaring at her. "He's unconscious."

"And breathing. For now." Varujan glared at her as if *she'd* been the one to attack. His palpable rage had her inching back, wanting more distance between them.

The blond next to him grinned, showcasing fangs. Shocked, she studied him, not sure what he was. Vampires tended to have dark hair. She couldn't imagine a vampire being vain enough to use hair dye. Then again, she had yet to meet a vampire with a sense of humor that didn't involve bloodletting, and the blond doofus had been laughing throughout the fight.

The white-haired man sat next to her on the bed, startling her into looking at him once more. He nodded. "Faraine."

"How do you know my name? Who are you? Why am I here?"

"I'm Mormo. You've already met Varujan."

"Yeah, you were *inside* him. Remember?" the blond said with a wicked grin. "I'm Rolf. How about you come inside me for a bit? I'm draugr, and we're much more fun than the strigoi."

"Shut up, Rolf." Varujan straightened and stepped away from her brother. Finally. Unfortunately, he took several steps closer to *her*, which had her heart racing even faster. "What are you?"

"I'm nobody. A human." Her go-to when questioned.

"Try again." Varujan crossed his arms over his chest. He was tall but not musclebound. His short hair teased his neck, which gleamed white against a black leather jacket. Though he wore human clothing, she would never peg him as a mortal. Power clung to him like a second skin. She felt edgy around him, conscious of his danger as much as the fact that the stone liked him, which made *her* want to like him.

No way in hell.

She tried again. "I'm hu—"

"You put a spell on me earlier." He eyed her.

She looked at him with her practiced no-guile expression. "I'm a powerful witch."

"Liar." Varujan scoffed. "You're not human—not a witch, druid, or warlock." He studied her, and she prayed her glamour held. "I know what I saw in the shadows. You're fae, aren't you?"

"I have no idea what you're talking about." Damn it. He'd seen her true features before the spell took effect? How had that happened?

Rolf joined Varu to study her. He took a sniff, and she felt familiar magic. He'd said he was draugr, and that might explain his tie to fae magic, as his tribe were reputed to have distant relations to the fae.

He gave her what he no doubt thought was a kind smile but looked only slightly less than wicked. "You smell like home, little sister."

Varujan didn't blink as he watched her. "Makes sense."

"Home?" Fara asked, trying to steer the conversation away from her identity. "Isn't Seattle your home?"

Rolf crouched to look directly into her eyes. "Loki take it, but I think I can almost see you."

She scooted away until her back hit the headboard of the bed. "You keep away. And let my brother go," she warned Varujan when he lifted Onvyr over his shoulder. "He was just defending himself. You attacked us in the woods." She swallowed hard, not liking how easily Varujan handled Onvyr's heavy weight.

"If you want your brother to live, tell us what we want to know."

"You haven't asked me anything yet." *Threaten my brother, will you?* "Dumbass."

Rolf burst out laughing.

"It's like she already knows you," Mormo said with a wide grin.

In a blink, Varujan tossed her brother on the bed and yanked her to him, bringing her so close she could feel his breath on her face. "*What* did you just call me?"

Her mouth dried. His eyes had turned a bright red, and he didn't look amused. *At all.*

"Um, I said, that's dumb. You should ask."

"That's what I thought you said." He dropped her to the bed, took a step back, and watched with a haughty look of superiority.

I really hate vampires.

"Well?" Rolf asked.

"I'm the bearer of the dagger." She'd come up with the lie

some time ago, in the off chance she was ever captured by an enemy. "I was cursed a long time ago. I can't remember who or what gave me the dagger, but I was entrusted to deliver it to whomever the stone chose. And it chose you." That was no lie. The Bloode Stone wanted Varujan, not the person she'd been ordered to deliver it to.

"We're to believe it chose Varujan of the Night Bloode, formerly of the Crimson Veil?" Mormo asked, his gaze keen.

"Y-yes."

"Are there others?"

"No." At Mormo's frown, she added, "Not exactly."

All three males leaned forward, and Varujan asked, "What does that mean?"

"I, um…" How to explain that the stones she'd been ordered to deliver hadn't been nearly as powerful as the one Atanase deemed his own—the same one she'd decided to give to his son?

Mormo stared. "You've had others. Where are they?"

"Others?" She had thought about what exactly she might say if questioned about the other five stones, but she'd expected to get caught by vampires, who had no truthsense. Mormo, apparently, could tell when she lied.

Varujan took a step closer, looming over her. "Let me ask the questions, Mormo. I'll get you all the answers you need."

She could almost smell the menace radiating from him, a decadent perfume of malice and darkness that made him one of the most feared of his tribe. *And I thought he would be easy enough to manage? What the heck was I thinking?*

"I'll talk," she said in a rush, her back plastered to the wall, as far away from the vampires and Mormo as she could be. "None of this is my fault. I didn't ask to be involved in vampire business."

"So you do know what you were carrying," Mormo said.

She nodded. "I have an affinity for power gems. Whoever cursed me knew this. I can't remember, exactly…" Not necessarily a lie. Being tortured by Atanase had warped her memory some, so that the basis of her bloode-oath lay enshrouded, making her unable to sever it without fulfilling her duty or with Atanase's help. Talk about cursed. "The gist of it is I was ordered to find gems like the one in the dagger. The one I gave Varujan."

"*Gave* me? You threw a dagger at my neck," Varujan growled.

"That you clearly avoided. With your speed, you were never in any danger." Unfortunately, her explanation didn't seem to appease him. "Look, I've answered your questions. I—"

Mormo interrupted, "But how did you find the stones? How many have you given away and to whom?"

She didn't know how much to reveal and needed time to plan. "My head hurts."

Varujan didn't look as if he believed her, but Mormo seemed to soften.

Rolf sat next to her on the bed, freaking her out. Something about the blond vampire struck her as odder than the others she'd seen. "How did you handle the Bloode Stone in the first place? You're not a vampire, are you?"

"No, I'm not." She swallowed, not liking his proximity. "I told you I have an affinity for power gems. They talk to me. The curse enabled me to pick up a trace of Varujan's Bloode Stone. I found it buried deep in the Fann Mountains of Tajikistan."

Mormo frowned. "In Central Asia?"

Fara shrugged. "I have no idea why it was there. The curse focused my ability to sense it, and when I found it, it let me hold it for a moment."

Mormo blinked. "You touched it?"

"Yes. But briefly. There's too much death essence in the stone. It hurt to hold it." She shivered, not pretending at all. As much as she loved stones and gems of all shapes and sizes, the sentience within this last Bloode Stone had *not* been easy to manage. Only by using the dagger, a piece properly crafted by Atanase himself, had she been able to transport it. The smaller stones had been easy to move. The larger Bloode Stone? Not so much.

"Fascinating." Rolf cocked his head. "She seems like she's telling the truth."

"She's lying." Varujan, obviously not her biggest fan, scowled down at her.

Mormo shook his head. "She's being honest enough about that. Not everything, no, but she really did handle the stone." His gaze felt heavy, searching. "Where did you get the dagger?"

"I don't know."

"That's a lie," Mormo said softly.

"I can't say his name." She remembered all too well her time with the master vampire. A swift glance at Varujan showed how much the two males looked alike. Yet the inherent cruelty shining in Atanase's eyes lay buried behind Varujan's flat stare.

I have to get out of here before he kills me. Or worse. But what to do about the Bloode Stone?

"The truth." Mormo sighed. "Well, we'll get more out of you soon enough, I suppose. You're staying with us for the foreseeable future. As is your brother." He nodded to Rolf, who grabbed her brother from the bed and left the room with him.

Her heart raced. "Bring him back."

"You'll see him again soon." Mormo stood next to Varujan, not looking so friendly and open any more. "You're our guest."

"Prisoner," Varujan corrected.

"Semantics, but okay." Mormo smiled. She didn't see any fangs this time. "You will stay here and recover. You are free to move about the house, but you're not free to leave. I can't speak for your safety if you decide to wander too freely. Perhaps Varu will watch over you?" He looked at Varujan, who glared down at her, and laughed. "Or not. Rest, Faraine. We'll talk later."

He walked out, leaving her alone with Varujan of the Crimson Veil.

Oh boy.

She glanced at his graceful hands, the claws at his fingertips slowly receding.

How easily he could gouge out her eyes or pluck her heart from her chest. Just as Atanase had before putting her back together, one painful organ at a time. And poor Onvyr had been the master vampire's plaything—and hostage—for years. She shivered and met Varujan's gaze once more.

He said, "The group you happened to be running with the other night attacked me and my kin. Why?"

"Not running *with,* running *from.*" She sighed, doing her utter best to sell this fiction. "They were after me for the dagger. But I made a break and landed on your vehicle. For that I'm sorry. I was trying to escape when you came after me. I was only defending myself."

"And giving me the finger while a van drove you away with those same friends?"

Shoot. "They were different friends. And I flipped you off because I was riding high on my escape. Sorry." She totally wasn't.

Varujan didn't blink. "Say what you want, but you tried to take my head off. *Upir gold* sound familiar?"

"Again, I was just being nasty to you because I was scared. You tried to kill me!"

"Only after you crashed into our SUV and magicked me into letting you go." He scowled. "I still want to know how you did that."

I'll bet you do. That witch spell hadn't been cheap. "It was the stone."

"You're saying the stone controlled me?" His dark eyes narrowed. "Is that why you were with me, in my mind, a few hours ago? Because I held the stone?"

"Yes. I think. The stone feels almost alive. It's like nothing

I've ever seen or felt before. Some powerful magic enabled me to carry the dagger. I know the story of Ambrogio's blood or tears, whichever way you choose to believe the legend. The point is only those Of the Bloode can hold a Bloode Stone. I know that. But I held it all the same. Not long, but long enough to know it wants other vampires. Not…humans."

He smirked. "Not fae, you mean?"

She said nothing.

"Rolf is taking your brother to the basement."

"Don't hurt him."

"Tell me the truth."

"I did, as much as I can."

"Hmm."

Hmm? What did that mean? Did he believe her or not? She blinked, feeling more than tired, exhausted to the very core.

Varujan stepped back. "Think hard, Faraine. Because vampires aren't known for being nice. Tell us what we need to know and your stay might not be unpleasant. Or at least, not fatal."

"You hurt my brother and I'll hurt you."

He gave her a slow grin that should have scared her senseless. Instead, it stirred an odd heat inside her.

"I mean it. I want Onvyr cared for."

"Your wants are not important." He nodded to another door. "There's an attached bath and some clothes in the wardrobe. Make use of them. If you're smart, you'll use your time here to share what you know." He paused. "But if you think to trifle with vampires, you can't be all that intelligent after all."

"I told you I was cursed."

He ignored that. "Feel free to wander about the house. I'm sure once the others discover how lovely you taste, you'll be the most popular person in the place."

He stared at her neck and licked his lips.

Her heart threatened to pound out of her chest. "You bit me."

"And I'll bite you again." He smiled. The expression chilled her to the bone. "Soon, I'm thinking. Rest now. I'll see you soon... *human.*" He sneered, turned, and left, slamming the door after him.

Fara hurried to lock the door behind him—as if a locked door would repel vampires and whatever Mormo was—then fell back on the bed and stared unseeingly at the ceiling. "I am *so* screwed." And of course, never, ever, in a good way.

CHAPTER EIGHT

Varu stalked down the hallway to his bedroom. Oddly, the interior dimensions of the house didn't always match up to physical reality. Hecate had done something screwy with the inside, making it much larger than what it looked like from the street. And the basement always smelled off, as if myriad creatures from other worlds lingered, often clinging to Mormo when he'd come back from a visit below. Yet Varu had never seen anything but the dark room they used for entertainment, filled with a large television, speakers, a pool table, and a bar.

Hecate still didn't have his worship, but she did have his grudging respect. At least she knew how to fulfill her servants' needs. Used to powerful beings, Varu had been around many who couldn't care less about anyone's comfort but their own.

Yes, he knew all about the strange and powerful. So for some female to think she might fool him twice? Once he could understand. He hadn't known what to expect when fighting her in that abandoned shop. But now? She wanted him to think she was human? Ha.

He snorted, not altogether unhappy to learn Faraine was a terrible liar. He didn't have Mormo's truthsense, but even he'd been able to tell that she'd been lying about most of what she'd said earlier.

Except the part about being unable to mention who had put the curse on her.

Someone had been hunting down Bloode Stones and using Faraine to do it. Why her? Why Bloode Stones? The connection to vampires made little sense unless the person behind it all was Of the Bloode. No one wanted vampires to be any more powerful than they already were. A clan of fifty or so could decimate a city fifty times its size. Imagine what clans, working together, could do. Or tribes of thousands working with other tribes of thousands. With little time, vampires would rule the world.

The only creatures behind such grand scale annihilation had to be vampires or gods. Which made Hecate his number one suspect. What did the witch goddess want with him and the others? Why send them after so many rogue magir already? Why after Faraine?

Hecate wanted the Bloode Stones, obviously. What, though, was her end game?

And why did it bother Varu so much that Faraine was now a part of it all?

Duncan followed, uninvited, into his room. "So, what's the deal with the hottie?"

Varu rolled his eyes. As much as he adhered to the diction of the present age, Duncan always felt young to him. And at over two hundred years of age, the revenant had more than a century over Kraft, the youngest.

"The 'hottie' is a bald-faced liar with an agenda. We need to keep an eye on her."

Duncan nodded, leaned against the wall, and watched as Varu paced the floor. Irritated, Varu had a tough time relaxing or sitting still.

"What?" he snapped.

"What did she taste like?"

Varu blanked, feeling again that surge of life, of perfect union as he'd sipped and held Faraine the Liar.

Duncan whistled. "That good, eh? No wonder you're agitated."

"I'm not agitated."

Behind him, Kraft appeared and apparently overheard, because he said, "Oh, you're agitated."

"We should spar." Duncan grinned. "Three on three."

"More like one on one," Kraft said. "Mormo gave the rest of us orders. Rolf is guarding the brother. Varu, you're to see if you can get any information out of him."

"Then who's guarding the female?" He wanted to use her name, but the last time he had, he'd felt funny. As if by saying *Faraine,* he'd tied himself to her in some way. Had to be the after-effects of that damn stone.

"No one's guarding her," Kraft said. "Mormo put a ward over the house, so she can't leave. And we've all been warned not to kill or maim her." He sighed. "It's been way too long since I hunted down real prey."

"You just had a meal."

"That day-old blood? Meh." Kraft rubbed his gut, the nachzehrer in a state of constant hunger, no doubt to feed that huge body. He yawned. "I'm still hungry, but I'm also tired. A few of us are turning in."

He left, and Duncan watched him go. "Lazy." He glanced back at Varu. "So, what do you say? Want to spar with me?"

"After I talk to the brother. Meet me in the gym in half an hour."

"Will do." Duncan turned to leave. "And the female? I'm thinking I might take a sip myself, see what the fuss is about."

It took everything inside Varu to not react, especially because Duncan was watching him closely while pretending not to.

Showing any weakness was not to be tolerated. Varu knew better than that. "Have at it."

Duncan grinned, showing fang, and left.

Varu waited a beat before shaking out his hands and waiting for the bite of his sharp nails to heal. He'd clenched his fists so hard he'd drawn blood. Damn that female.

He muttered under his breath as he joined Rolf in the basement, eager to tear into her brother for answers.

He found Faraine's brother awake and aware, standing with his back to a wall while Rolf crouched, on the balls of his feet, on the back of the sectional sofa. As if the weird draugr knew of no other way to perch. *Great, and now I'm sounding like Mormo, nagging about the proper way to sit on a couch.*

"Do I know you?" Faraine's brother asked Rolf.

"I don't think so. But who knows? The world is a very big place." Rolf chuckled.

Varu approached the pair and stopped next to Rolf, his attention fixed to the supposed human. "What are you?"

"Uh, I'm a guy. My name's O—" He coughed. "John."

"O John?" Varu raised a brow, met Rolf's amused gaze, and stared back at the man. "Try again."

O John clamped his mouth shut and looked up with an obstinate gaze. Like brother like sister.

Before Varu could press the point—with his nails and fangs—Rolf said, "Let me try. Hey, O John. If you want your sister to live, answer some questions."

If anything, the male's expression grew even more mulish.

Rolf sighed. "Fine. Varu, go bring me one of her arms."

Varu half-turned, as if he meant to follow Rolf's orders.

Before the lying male could launch himself after Varu, Rolf jumped forward and put a hand on his chest, freezing him in place. Varu didn't think Rolf used any magic or compulsion, but the male stopped moving all the same.

Rolf stared at him for several heartbeats before pulling back. "Your name. No lies."

"Onvyr."

Rolf nodded. "A fae name."

Onvyr growled.

Varu didn't want to be but couldn't help feeling impressed. Onvyr stood as tall as Rolf and had a breadth of shoulder and musculature hard to ignore. His earlier strength showed him to be a formidable threat. Nothing Varu couldn't handle, of course, but he admired a predatory nature, and this fae had it for sure.

"Let's see it," Varu ordered.

"See what?" Onvyr asked.

"Take off the glamour."

Onvyr looked around him.

Rolf sighed. "No one but the two of us are down here. And we already know you're not human." After a pause, he added, "Or we can bring your sister down and nicely ask her to take hers off." He bared his fangs.

"Fine." Onvyr shrugged it off, and the glamour slid off his skin and vanished in a haze of shadow. He still wore the same clothing, but instead of a tall blond man, he had pitch-black skin, pointed ears, long white hair, and lavender eyes. A true dark elf. Varu had been correct in assuming the male to be a threat. Dark elf warriors had on occasion been known to kill weaker vampires.

Onvyr sighed. "Happy now?"

"I'd be happier if I could tear your throat out," Rolf said with a smile. "But I think maybe we should wait and see what information you have for us first."

"I know nothing of use." Onvyr shrugged, and his powerful biceps contracted. "I was held captive to make my sister search out and deliver your Bloode Stones."

"Then how are you here?"

"She broke me out. We escaped and came here. She said we

had to." He looked at Varu, his eyes narrowed. "The stone wanted him." Onvyr sneered. "A nasty piece of strigoi."

Instead of launching himself at the offensive fae, Varu considered Onvyr's anger. "You've met my kind before, I take it?"

"Oh, yes. And you deserve nothing more than a true, painful death." Onvyr's smile suggested he'd be happy to make that happen right here, right now. He flashed a small fang and cracked his knuckles. "But then, your cowardly tribe never fights fairly, do they? If I take a swing at you, you'll make sure to involve the rest of your clan. No honor, no strength in self, you dark bastard."

Varu smiled through his teeth. "*I'm* a dark bastard? Take a look in the mirror, asshole."

Onvyr snorted. "At least I cast a reflection."

All vampires, except the very ancient and powerful, cast reflections.

"Met many vampires, have you?" Varu asked.

"Enough."

Enough that cast no reflection? Varu pondered that, curious as to who the fae had encountered. He himself knew of only a handful of strigoi that old. "And did your vampire friends hold you captive? Torture you for fun, maybe?"

Though torture and fun were redundant for most vampires, Varu had never seen the need to prolong another's suffering. Fighting and battle, on the other hand, had merit. Pain for pain's sake appealed to the older generations, like his father's.

Onvyr didn't answer, but his expression grew more focused.

Varu could smell his aggression. Rolf must have sensed it too, because he took a step back and opened his arms. "No, my turn. Let's play, shall we?"

Onvyr growled and shot forward, picking up Rolf and body slamming him to the floor in the blink of an eye.

Before Varu could move forward, Rolf snarled at him to stay out of it and countered.

Varu sighed and moved back out of the way to watch. He knew what it felt like to want to take Rolf's head off, and the dark elf had earned that right with that first body blow. Nice moves. Violence checked, his aggression never overtaking his strategic counterattacks. Onvyr met Rolf punch for punch for a while, and Varu could tell that even Rolf was astounded that the dark elf could keep up.

But Onvyr must have been tired, because Rolf managed a slash to the male's face and another to his gut, cutting through his clothing.

The sweet scent of fae blood had Varu's mouth watering.

Rolf's as well, for Rolf darted in to lick across Onvyr's cheek.

Onvyr roared his displeasure and amped his attack.

Until Rolf brought out his real power to fight an opponent of equal measure. A true compliment.

In seconds, Onvyr lay bleeding and glaring from the floor. He flipped off Rolf, which had the draugr laughing.

"Good fight, fae." Rolf was never happier than after a battle. "Well met. And now, my prize?" He licked his lips.

"Fuck off."

"Try again," Rolf said, still smiling though his tone had grown steely.

Onvyr sat up, clutching his side. "You're an asshole, but that was some kind of attack combo." He stood, looking a little shaky, but as he focused on Rolf, he started to relax. "Do you have to drink from me?"

"I really do," Rolf apologized with a half shrug. "But you can choose where I drink from if that makes it easier."

Onvyr looked torn. He looked from Rolf to Varu, considering, then sighed. "Fine," Onvyr conceded. "You can take it from my wrist."

"No problem."

Varu watched as Rolf turned all solicitous and helped Onvyr

to sit on the couch. Before Rolf could bite into the dark elf's arm, Onvyr stopped him. "No. I'll do it." He glared up at Varu, who had nothing to do with any blood taking, and bit into his wrist.

A gush of blood welled, and Onvyr held his wrist out to Rolf, who nodded and leaned over to drink, his blond hair shielding him. Such a well-mannered vampire.

Perturbed at the sense of intimacy, Varu growled, "Rolf, we're not here to make friends. Get the information or I will. He only needs a working brain and mouth to function. The rest is excess."

Onvyr looked alarmed at that. Finally. Varu didn't like the idea of not being feared by a lesser species.

Rolf ignored him, continuing to feed, only pulling away to show Onvyr's skin newly healing thanks to a dose of vampire saliva. The blond draugr then licked his finger and dragged it across Onvyr's face and again over his side, accelerating his healing. "Ah, that was delicious. Your blood packs a punch." Rolf blinked a few times and turned to Varu. "Wow. Did his sister give you the tinglies?"

At that, Onvyr's entire demeanor shifted from friendly to deadly and he darted to his feet.

Eagerly anticipating the battle, Varu wasn't prepared for Onvyr to look beyond him with wide eyes and stop.

The fae frowned. "What? I'm not stupid. I could take him."

A snarl and low grunt answered him. Neither came from a humanoid throat.

Varu turned to see a giant battle cat stalking past him. "What the hell?"

Rolf gaped. "Where did he come from?"

"She. And she's not impressed with you," Onvyr told Rolf. "But she says the strigoi will be a major problem."

Rolf didn't look too pleased, but Varu nodded. "She shows a marked intelligence."

"Hey." Rolf watched the giant feline pad past him with a sniff. "I'm dangerous. I'm a killer."

Onvyr cocked his head as the big cat's ears and tail twitched, and she rumbled something in her throat. "He did nearly kill me. But he was holding back. No, really."

Rolf joined Varu, watching Onvyr chat with the feline. "He's talking to the beast."

"I know." Varu wondered if Faraine could do the same. "But is he just crazy, or is he really communicating with it?"

"With *her,*" Onvyr said. "And yes, I am. She's aggravated with some guy named Mormo. And she wants more milk. Where's the dead witch?"

Varu stared, still unsure of Onvyr's sanity. But one thing he had learned from watching the dark elf. Onvyr knew more than he'd shared. He'd likely been tortured by a strigoi with power, which left only a handful of suspects. And most importantly, he was the bargaining chip which kept Faraine in line.

"We keep him watched and safe," he said to Rolf in a low voice. "And through him we find out what the hell fae and strigoi have to do with Bloode Stones and with us."

"Yeah." Rolf sighed. "Sure." He yawned. "I'm tired. Daylight just broke and—"

They both watched as Onvyr's coloring shifted, his skin and hair color inverting, so that he now appeared very pale with black hair and black brows.

"Neat trick," Rolf murmured before yawning again.

Varu shook his head. "Go sleep it off if you need to." He could go weeks without rest, but the others seemed to need to nap all the time. Pathetic.

"Thanks."

Disgusted with his feeble kin, he waited with Onvyr and the big cat, enchanted by the beast that let him pet her. Like all vampires, Varu was drawn to predators, and he especially liked felines. He'd never seen a cat this big in the human world. It was easily the size of an Amur tiger. And it liked Onvyr, which likely meant the male might have some worth after all.

Between the cat and Onvyr, they served as a necessary distraction. Varu was still doing his damnedest not to think about Duncan biting Faraine, or imagining tearing his kin apart limb by limb.

And losing the battle horribly.

F ara showered, dressed in a pair of loose sweatpants and a tee-shirt she found in the armoire, putting on her dirty bra because no way in hell did she want anyone to get the idea she might be a meal *and* entertainment, and finally gave in to her curiosity.

She left her room wearing her glamour and tiptoed down the hallway, heading away from a cluster of rooms in one direction and instead toward a brighter area that opened up into a living room. As she moved, she'd swear she felt someone watching her. Cameras maybe? Humans loved their technology, and even though the vampires weren't mortal, they seemed to live in a mortal dwelling.

Yet... She crouched and stroked the floor, enamored with the divine life breathing through the marble-amalgam. So powerful, familiar yet foreign at the same time. Not Gaia's breath, but someone else's. Someone with the power over connections, in particular with death. Which actually made sense considering Fara was in a house filled with vampires.

"Did you drop something?"

She jumped to her feet in a shriek, holding her chest. "*By the Veil.* You scared me."

A woman stood there, gaping at her. She appeared human, with sandy-brown hair pulled back into a ponytail. The woman had average height and looks, until she smiled. Then the beauty in that grin overshadowed everything else about her.

"Sorry about that. I'm so glad to see another woman around here." The woman blew out a breath and held out her hand. "Hi. I'm Bella. I help out with the house. You know, the cooking and cleaning and all those pesky minor details—without which everything would cease to exist." She chuckled.

Fara considered Bella a moment before taking her hand and shaking it. No extra burst of strength or odd temperature, Bella's hand felt normal. Human. "I like your red nails." They looked the exact same shade as Fara's.

"Thanks. I needed a new color and felt compelled to try this one. I think it's vampire-red. Go figure." Bella grinned.

Relieved at finding someone not trying to kill her or feed from her, Fara smiled as she dropped her hand. "What's it like working for vampires?"

"You don't want to know. For a race that doesn't actually eat much, they make a huge mess in the kitchen. Most of my work involves buying clothes or laundering them. How they tear through so much is a mystery to me, frankly. Then there are the wacky requests all day long. Especially for videos and streaming channels—they're all addicted to movies."

"Huh."

"It's kind of like a frat house for killers," Bella said with more cheer than the phrase should allow. Fara didn't know what a frat house was, but Bella didn't seem bothered by it. "The nice thing about working here is that the place is usually pretty quiet during the day. Soon as the sun sets, though, they're up and moving." Bella yawned. "I'm getting ready to turn in, actually. Had a late night. But Mr. Mormo wanted to make sure you had something to eat."

"Oh, I'm fine." Her stomach chose that moment to rumble, and she flushed. "I was just going to head to the kitchen and check it out. I don't want to keep you." Because the sooner Fara found a way out of this place, the sooner she and her brother could steer clear of so many death-bringers.

She needed to figure out how to handle Varujan. Her plan to control him—*remotely*—would no longer work. A bummer, because she couldn't use the spell she'd been planning on to help her manipulate the strigoi. She didn't want anyone knowing how powerful, or weak, she might be. Bad enough Atanase knew, and he'd made her brother pay dearly for every mistake she'd already made.

"Well, before I turn in, let me show you around this floor, at least. The outside doesn't mirror what's in here." Bella winked.

Fara had no idea what she was talking about, but she nodded and followed Bella around.

"The main living area has a great big TV with all the channels you could ever want. Then we keep going through to the open dining room. Great views, huh?" Bella paused as Fara stared out past a yard to a body of water.

Fara swallowed. "Where are we, exactly?"

"Oh, that's right. You were asleep when you came in." Bella patted her on the shoulder, and Fara swore she felt a small shock. "Static electricity. Zaps me every time. Sorry." Bella sighed. "Isn't it beautiful out there? The sun just rising over the water? Gorgeous. That's Lake Washington. Mr. Mormo nabbed this place for a steal. It's got to be worth close to ten million now. But then, property on Mercer Island ain't cheap." Bella grinned. "Okay, so onward."

Bella showed her the grand kitchen with top-of-the-line appliances and high-end stone work. Two refrigerators filled with food

Fara couldn't imagine a vampire eating and more snacks in the pantry.

"Um, not to be too nosy, but I thought vampires don't eat?"

Bella shrugged. "That's what I thought too. Some of them do, a little bit. And Mr. Mormo does." She leaned closer to whisper, "He's not a vampire, but none of us are sure what he is. I've heard Varujan and Khent call him a magician, but I just stick with Mr. Mormo or sir. But I can tell you he's not human."

"But you are?"

"Maybe."

Fara must have looked skeptical.

Bella groaned. "Okay, yes, I'm human. But I feel boring around all these hunky supernatural types. I like to think I might have some witch blood in me. Or maybe ancient fae."

No, not any fae that Fara could tell. "How did Mormo find you?"

"Oh, that's a story that's going to take some wine, for sure." Bella winked. "But I'm starting to lose my late night buzz. Let me show you the areas to avoid." They walked toward the entrance to a long corridor bathed in shadow, and Bella stopped. "The guys have rooms down this hallway. I try to steer clear. Although I wouldn't mind Duncan or Khent taking a bite of me sometime. Khent's so intense." She shivered. "Duncan's nice and *sooo* handsome. They all are, but he seems less bite-y and murder-y than the others."

Bella was a strange one all right.

"Anyhow, you might want to stay on your side of the house. Next to yours is a room prepared for your brother. Farther down your wing, there's a library, weight room, and believe it or not, a spa room with stairs down to the pool house." Bella's eyes sparkled. "Yeah, an indoor pool. This place has *everything*."

"The patio out back looks lovely. Do you think I could have my meal out there?"

"Sure. I'd join you if I wasn't so tired." Bella yawned, proving her point. "I'm sorry. It was a long night. Plus, I had to make yet another appointment to have a windshield replaced." She frowned. "I mean, are they eating them or what? That's five windshields in the past two months."

Bella walked Fara back to the kitchen. "Oh, before I go. There are a few sets of stairs to avoid. Mr. Mormo occupies pretty much the whole second floor, so I'd advise you to stay on the main level. And the basement is where the guys hang out if they're not sleeping. Pool table, another big TV, and down and around another hallway is a gymnasium for training. It gets confusing downstairs, so maybe don't go there unless you need one of them for something important. That's it! I'm down your hallway, so I'm going to sack out. I'll see you again in a few hours, I hope." Bella patted Fara on the shoulder, and this time there was no static shock. "Great to meet you, Fara."

"Yes, likewise." Fara smiled and watched Bella walk away.

As soon as the woman left her sight, Fara hustled to the glass doors by the dining area. She tentatively reached for the handle, surprised it opened for her without setting off an alarm. She took a few steps outside and breathed in the fresh air. She liked the cold stamp of autumn, the scent of Lake Washington bathing her in the breeze.

The house had been built on an incline, with the main floor looking down over the backyard. Past the patio a floor down, she could see a large expanse of lush green grass leading to a wooden deck in the shape of an L. Next to the dock, a boat hung suspended in a covered slip. Out facing the water, parallel to the house, several deck chairs faced Lake Washington and several boats puttering past.

On either side of the vast yard, tall wooden fences separated the property from its neighbors.

Looking behind her at the house itself, she realized what Bella had meant about the inside not matching the outside. The house didn't appear to have the depth or width for the many floors and space she'd seen when inside. Heck, out here, there was no second floor. Just the main level and one below.

What had Bella said the others called Mormo? A magician? Not a human one. Not with those eyes and fangs, and of course, that huge reservoir of magic swirling inside him. She'd felt his power, just as she'd felt the energy surging in the others.

Yet another reason to find a way out of the present danger. She could work on controlling Varu later, after she and her brother went free.

Fara decided to try to get as close to the water as she could, basking in the sun. She walked toward the edge of the deck near a set of stairs. And ran into an invisible wall. *Shoot.*

She swore under her breath and rubbed her nose, smarting at the sting there. She tried again, but the barrier blocked her. It remained invisible but firm, so not a way to escape from the back, despite the clean air wafting over her.

Turning to head back inside, she froze when she saw a new vampire staring at her from the doorway. The sun should have killed him, yet it didn't touch him. She could see a veil of shadow overlying his frame. Not good. She'd been counting on at least the patio for protection.

Tall, broad shouldered, and handsome like the others, this one looked a lot more charming. He had dimples he showed off as he smiled at her from a face that looked tan, as if he spent time under the sun. Dressed in jeans, a button-down Polo, and loafers, with a stylish cut to his short brown hair, he looked human enough if otherwordly handsome.

Then he smiled, flashing a set of fangs. "Hello, Fara."

She didn't trust that smile, though she felt herself respond to the inherent charm he was flashing around. "H-hello."

He waited in the open doorway, his hands in his pockets. "I'm Duncan. Welcome to the house."

"It's very nice." *And I'm not welcome. I'm a prisoner.*

His smile grew wider. And that handsome factor notched upward by a bazillion points.

Then she realized she'd been staring into his dark eyes. A big mistake. She forced herself to blink and looked back at the water, doing her best not to fall for the oldest vampire trick in the book —mesmerism.

She ignored her racing heartbeat, squashing her fear, because encouraging a predator to play chase with terrorized prey wouldn't do her any favors. Instead, she pasted on a fake smile, turned, and calmly passed by him as she walked inside.

"How are you liking it here?" Duncan asked, his breath brushing her ear.

Way too close. She swallowed. "I like it very much, though it's colder than I'd thought it might be. I'm going to have something to eat."

A pregnant pause followed by a low chuckle had her fighting the urge to run. "Me too."

She put the large kitchen island between them, careful to meet his gaze only briefly. "I was planning to have some yogurt or eggs or something." She opened the refrigerator and stared in surprise at a now empty interior save for a cup of yogurt sitting on top of a carton of eggs on a shelf at her eye-level.

"Grab me a bottle would you?" he asked and sat at the island.

She watched in shock as a bottle of pink protein drink appeared next to the carton. Taking everything out, she put the eggs and yogurt on the counter before turning to slide the bottle toward him.

Though the sun illuminated the room, a subtle pall seemed to seal the inside from harmful rays. Duncan clearly sat in a ray of sunlight yet didn't burn or sizzle one whit. With a wink aimed her way, he twisted the top off and drank the bottle down in one long gulp while she watched his throat move.

He finished with a loud "Ah," and she hunted down a spoon.

"Third drawer on your left."

"Thanks." She scooped a delicious bite and realized how hungry she'd been. Working earth magic earlier had sapped her energy. She finished the yogurt and wondered if she should have another or turn to domesticated bird eggs for protein. Though she knew humans liked chickens, she'd always preferred *kval*, though they didn't seem to exist in the places Atanase sent her to. So she'd usually made do with native fruits and vegetables and the occasional sweet to curb her cravings for fae food.

Duncan moved past her to the refrigerator and fetched her another yogurt and a bowl of *warm*, scrambled kval eggs.

She blinked.

"We live in a magic house. Don't question it."

"I won't." She forced herself to eat the yogurt before slowly devouring the scrambled bits spiced with a delicate flavor she couldn't place but really liked. She couldn't help a sigh of pleasure. "It's been so long since I've had good eggs."

"Kval, eh? And you're human. How about that."

She froze. So stupid. She blamed her exhaustion for making such a simple mistake, especially since everyone knew how much the fae loved those birds. "Kval? I thought these were regular eggs. From a chicken bird." Wait. They didn't say chicken bird, did they?

He smirked. "It's okay. I won't tell. Enjoy your food, *human* woman."

She pretended she hadn't given a vampire more ammunition to use against her and stacked her plates in the sink, allowing herself to enjoy the breakfast. Then she wondered where they kept their ingredients for tea, something all civilized creatures everywhere seemed to enjoy.

"What do you need?" Duncan asked, standing way too close all of the sudden.

She tried to step back and felt the counter behind her. "Um, space?"

He laughed, a pleasant sound, until one noticed the sharp fangs peeking out from behind those full lips. "How about a nice cup of *chà*?"

Chà, a traditional drink of the dark fae.

She didn't want to be that easy. "I was hoping for tea. I'm not sure what that 'chou' stuff is."

"*Riggghhht.*" He drew out the word. "Well, for those of us pretending not to be fae, chà is a kind of tea the fae seem to like."

"I'm not fae. I'm human." Her lies sounded weaker each time she told them. *By the stones, I'm better than this!*

"Then how about proving it?"

"What?"

He stared at her neck and smiled. "With a taste."

BEFORE THE BRITISH bastard could sink his fangs into Varu's prey, the female's brother was there, once again wearing a human-seeming. Varu watched with narrowed eyes from the dining area. He didn't understand what the big fae said to his sister in a language clearly fae, but she obviously understood. She blushed.

The sight didn't look right, her pale skin turning pink. It should be a light gray sparkling with lavender notes, the flush of her fae blood like a cool, colorful shadow. He could almost envision it, the sight of her emblazoned in his memory.

Onvyr stood between Fara and Duncan, but he didn't seem angry. Mostly because he kept talking to the feline that refused to leave his side, this time conversing in English.

"Yes, they're apparently all like this. I know." Onvyr snorted. "At least this one waited before threatening to pounce."

The cat made a growly sound and flashed her teeth in warning at Duncan, who stared back in awe.

"Aren't you gorgeous?"

At that, the cat sniffed, preening.

Gorgeous and vain, but Varu thought the feline deserved to be.

"I can't..." Onvyr paused, glancing from her to Varu. "Yeah, he's not having it. You're right."

Varu didn't know what the battle cat had said, but it seemed to amuse Onvyr, which couldn't be good.

Varu scowled. "Okay, party's over. You two, go to your rooms. You're not exactly guests here."

Duncan looked over his shoulder at Varu. "Well, well. What a surprise. Varu's babysitting after all."

"Duncan, don't make me bite you." He paused. "I thought we were going to spar. Why are you up here molesting Mormo's fae?"

"Just the one fae. I didn't want a bite of the male."

"Onvyr," the fae growled. "I have a name."

"Whatever." Duncan smiled past the male's annoyance, not at all bothered he might have offended him. "I'm much more interested in our delectable *human* guest." He winked.

Fara scowled. "I'm not lying."

The cat grumbled, and Onvyr tried to shush her, which didn't go over well, because the tiger hissed and stomped away.

Onvyr cringed but yelled after her, "You don't know what you're talking about." He put a protective arm around Fara. "Sorry, Fara. You didn't deserve that."

"What?"

Varu noticed that they really did look alike. Did that mean Fara's glamour, once removed, would show a dark fae? A light fae? Or was she actually the light gray beauty he'd first seen?

He couldn't contain his curiosity. "Remove your glamours."

She blinked at him. "Wha—No. I have no idea what you're talking about, strigoi."

"Stubborn like a mule," he thought Duncan said under his breath. Then the revenant cleared his throat. "I was actually coming down to see you, Varu, when I noticed Fara outside."

All eyes turned to her.

She shrugged. "It's nice and sunny. I just wanted to see the view from outside."

"I thought you said it was cold?" Duncan crossed his arms over his chest, studying Fara too hard, to Varu's way of thinking.

"It was nice out before it grew cold." She smiled at him, but the expression didn't reach her eyes. "I thought you were leaving to spar."

"We are." Varu's tone brooked no argument. "Come, Duncan."

"Fine. But I want to know more about that tiger. Beautiful." He turned swiftly and took Fara's hand in his before anyone could move. Then he kissed the back of it. "Milady. I hope to share a bite later, perhaps?" He chuckled as he left her staring after him, her mouth agape.

Onvyr sighed. "I hate vampires."

"No kidding," she muttered.

Varu found himself biting back a smile, which puzzled him. The female should be vexing, not entertaining. Yet she was. He forced himself to draw on his typical icy reserve, channeling his father. "There is no escape. You're both ours. Remember that." He saw her glare and her brother's eye roll and nodded. "Exactly. But if you'd rather serve as a meal, by all means, walk down that hall, last room on the right. I'm happy to make you my post workout snack."

"Nope. We're leaving right now." Onvyr grabbed Fara by the arm and dragged her with him back toward their rooms.

Varu watched her leave, noting her smooth stride, the way she made little to no noise when she walked, like her brother.

And there, when she glared at him over her shoulder—a flash of *lavender* eyes.

He smiled, more than satisfied, and joined Duncan in the basement. His mood improved when he gave Duncan the thrashing he deserved. Then he let himself catnap on the couch in the living room upstairs, right outside his prey's quarters. Keeping an eye on their valuable prisoner.

And if he happened to make sure the others left her alone so he could question her later, so much the better.

CHAPTER
TEN

A secret castle
Under the Apuseni Mountains, Romania

"Two hundred lashes is the best you can do?" Master Vampire Atanase of the Crimson Veil shook his head, disappointed in their newly-promoted lieutenant.

The strigoi, Atanase couldn't even remember his name, shrugged. "Master, he's barely clinging to life."

They both studied the lycan hanging in the central courtyard, his heavy torso pulling his limbs as he sagged, his eyes having lost that spark of rebellion days ago.

"If I bring him past the edge, he'll start to sour."

There was a reason vampires weren't ghouls. Eating the dead had never proven palatable, to Atanase's way of thinking. And the blood, if not ingested right away from the dead, could grow intolerably bitter. Yet, only a few hours in on this particular night, after a few hundred lashes and some blood-letting, the lycan was about to escape strigoi interrogation by dying? What had the lieutenant been *doing* with their prisoner?

He met the eyes of his lead general, Iancu, who shook his head and gave the lieutenant a dismissive look.

Atanase glanced around, noting the crowd. The strigoi often gathered under the first rays of moonlight, when their night truly began. Out here, in the center of their vast castle grounds, grass quivered under the breeze that sang through the hidden cave. Sequestered as they were a good quarter mile beneath the surface world, living in the loving darkness, the strigoi knew no master but themselves.

They housed the largest clan of their tribe with over three hundred of their kind in residence. The Crimson Veil had never been overrun or warred upon in their stronghold. Not where they were at their most powerful.

Underground rivers and streams provided fresh water, and the mass of overhead rock gave them protection from the sun. Only small holes in the ceiling, and this vast one over the expansive central courtyard, allowed light to pervade, shuttled in courtesy of a series of tilted mirrors carrying the moon to them.

Like now, as the moonlight bathed them, showing the lycan at his worst, covered in bloody strips of torn flesh too slow to heal, his claws ripped out and on the ground by the young lieutenant.

A *weak* lieutenant who had yet to get a confession or information they might barter to the Blue Crow clan, who had something Atanase wanted.

Still so far from getting results, he thought, displeased.

In a flash of movement to quick to be detected by those who stood watch, Atanase leaped to his lieutenant and beheaded him with one swipe. "Ridiculous attempt to declaw the bastard. Really? He'll just grow them back. You have to hit the wolves where it hurts most." He pointed to three of his finer hunters. "You three, go kill this thing's mate and young. Bring their heads back with you."

The courtyard froze, everyone processing that: one, they'd

lost their patriarch's protégé to the master, and two, that the lycan leader they'd captured would soon lose his mate. And everyone knew how clingy lycans were with those they considered family.

The lycan surprised Atanase by giving a nearly imperceptible laugh then choked on his own blood. "No... mate... "

Atanase shrugged. "No matter. We'll just kill the rest of your pack."

That had the lycan shocked and subdued. Or at least shocked. The furry bastard looked ready to kill. *Ah, he was just faking. The lycan isn't as done in as he'd pretended to be.* Which the lieutenant would have known if he'd been doing his job correctly.

The hunters waited for Atanase's nod, and when he gave it, they disappeared.

The patriarch of the Crimson Veil roared from inside the keep and stormed out, his intent to kill radiating like a summer storm. Atanase kept a straight face, but inside, he relished the coming confrontation. Mihai in a rage was a sight to behold. And Atanase knew that his patriarch had been training the true-dead lieutenant for over a century. No doubt the mentor had bonded with his pupil, at least a little bit.

Mihai's weakness was legend. The male had a touch of empathy that no amount of killing, torture, or mesmerism could fix. Though Atanase had spent over a thousand delightful years trying.

He grinned, watching as both Mihai and Iancu, their tribe's lead general, approached.

In the hierarchy of things, masters ruled over the tribes, generals governed tribal war councils, and patriarchs led their tribes' clans. The Strigoi tribe had twenty clans, with the Crimson Veil—Atanase's clan—being the most powerful.

The Red Fever clan had its share of strength, for Iancu claimed them as kin.

But though Mihai and Iancu had fought too many times to

count, each balanced the other to such an extent Atanase couldn't say which male was stronger.

Iancu never could muster that intense rage that swelled in Mihai, like a tidal wave ready to destroy all it touched.

Like now.

Mihai's eyes turned a scarlet-red, his fury seething as he stared from his decapitated kin to Iancu, who shrugged. Tall, muscular, and dark-skinned with flowing black locks, Iancu epitomized the perfect strigoi. That lack of feeling for another made him strong, a general who never put his men in a position to lose.

The magir world trembled when Iancu mustered an army, though he'd had no need for a major battle for more than two thousand years. Boredom had set in, and so Iancu worked to create warriors who wouldn't fall to magir, humans, or gods. It was slow-going getting there, but Atanase figured his kin had nothing but time. So much time...

Mihai, however, broke the monotony with his rages and his not-so-hidden grief.

With a grin, Atanase settled on a nearby bench to watch, along with the hundred or more strigoi no longer training but watching with him.

The moonlight streamed through the open ceiling by way of several carefully placed mirrors to take advantage of the great glowing orb in the night sky. In the deeper recesses of the castle and tunneled grounds, fae torches and mage llumes provided lighting, what would look like normal daytime to the livestock they kept herded in a separate area of the stronghold.

"What did you do?" Mihai snarled at Iancu. As tall and broad shouldered as Iancu, Mihai had brown hair cropped short, his skin a pale glow with hints of lavender that at times flashed in his eyes, a hint of past fae heritage, no doubt.

Though all vampires were born male and possessed vampiric traits, on rare occasions, the biological mother might appear in some small way in her son. Like that tendency Varujan had to stare *through* his father, not giving the proper respect a grand master should be due. All thanks to his stubborn witch of a mother. And a good thing Atanase had killed her the first chance he'd gotten.

He frowned, thoughts of his long-dead mate always enough to put him a foul mood. "*I* killed him," he snapped at Mihai. "He was terrible with the lash and scared of his own shadow. Or so Iancu constantly tells me."

Hatred seemed to bleed from Mihai's pores, like a sweet smelling perfume that saturated the air around him.

Pleased to have gotten a reaction, Atanase nodded to Iancu. "Show our patriarch why he should know better than to mentor fragility."

Iancu flashed a fang and bowed. "At once, my lord."

The intensity of battle didn't last as long as Atanase might have liked, and halfway through the blood and limbs flailing all around, he grew bored.

He snapped his fingers, and a servant attended him at once. "I'm hungry."

"Yes, master."

In no time, Atanase fed on a human mother while her daughter cried and begged for him to stop. Both mother and daughter appeared older, the younger woman at least past her first menses. But her pleas had the opposite effect than what she intended.

So eager to see her tears, her rage, her connection to another that motivated her to *fight,* Atanase made her mother's feeding as painful as possible.

"Please, no," the young woman sobbed, growing more beautiful in her tears. "She raised me all on her own, worked two jobs, has never done anything for herself. She deserves more than this!" Shrieking, she tried to move past the strigoi holding her in place. "Take me. Take me instead. Please, she's all I have left. I love her."

Her zeal to save her matriarch fascinated him. Atanase reveled in battle, the very reason he and all his kind had been created, or so it had been said.

The mighty Ambrogio, a warrior of world-wide renown, had been cursed for dallying with his true love, one of Apollo's hand-maidens. Legend had it that the sun god had turned Ambrogio into the first vampire. But his love for the handmaiden had been so strong, not even a living death had sundered them.

Atanase stared at the feeble human, trying to understand her. Ambrogio had been human once. Had loved and suffered for it.

The young woman cried and continued to reach out for her mother as Atanase shook the older woman to wake up, to at least fight back a little. Instead, she lay limp in his arms, his fangs buried in her jugular.

Had Ambrogio ever been so pathetic? Begging the sun god for his love?

No. Because once made vampire, the very first strigoi, Ambrogio had been too powerful to contain. So more gods involved themselves, soon cursing Ambrogio, his mate, and all their kind. To only bear males, slowing their numbers, and to make it so that only kin—vampires in small groups—could gather without bloodshed.

A master vampire could of course control his tribe, allowing clan members to interact without fighting. But sometimes Atanase found it better to take that control away, and he watched the human woman bargain for her mother's life while Iancu and Mihai continued to whale on each other.

Sated for the moment, Atanase crushed the older woman's ribs and heard her moan, so at least she could still feel. Then he pulled back and watched for a reaction as he broke her wrists. Which, unfortunately, made her pass out again.

"Ech. Enjoy what's left." He tossed her to his nearby servant. The strigoi smiled and bowed, dragging the human by the arm back into the keep.

The younger woman grew shrill and continued to try to escape her handler, yelling and swearing at him. She fought harder and ripped her shirt, exposing a lush, womanly form.

"You can rape me, you can drink my blood, you can kill my mother," she ended on a sob. "But you'll never break me."

The strigoi holding her barked a laugh, inciting many others around the courtyard, watching the spectacle, to do the same. Even Mihai and Iancu ceased to watch her with their master.

Atanase rolled his eyes as her handler explained, "Woman, you're beneath our notice. Rape? Fuck a human?" He laughed. "A strigoi would ever sully ourselves so. Now, drinking your blood, that we might do, but only if our master deems you worthy." He looked her over and raised a brow. "I'm thinking not."

Atanase waved to his kin and powered his voice to be heard throughout the courtyard. "What say you, my brothers? Should we add her to the stock or throw her in with the first meal?"

Everyone had an opinion. Mihai and Iancu added theirs. Fortunately, Mihai's compassion seemed to have exhausted itself, because he wanted to drain the woman dry *now* and forget the first meal.

Which had Atanase chuckling.

The human yelled epithets in between tears, snot running from her nose, her eyes bloodshot as she struggled to no avail.

"By the Night." Atanase cringed. "Take this pathetic mortal away from me. Bleed her and give her bones to our friends in the marsh." A magical place, the marsh shouldn't exist as it did in the caves beyond the Strigoi stronghold. Yet the stagnant pools of water and thick miasma of power called to those who consumed flesh and bone. Ghouls. Thought of as the scum of the magir world, they actually did a great service to those who needed to dispose of corpses without all the fuss.

Atanase turned his attention to the lycan barely breathing and chained up like a fresh flank of pig. No, make that, wolf.

"Mihai, come."

The strigoi shot a lovely uppercut to Iancu's face, snapping a fang, if Atanase wasn't mistaken, and walked away, giving the general his back. A well-played insult.

And that was why Atanase favored Mihai, truth be told. His patriarch might be weak when it came to emotions, but he could turn that same weakness into a strength and incite the greatest reaction in his opponents.

Iancu roared and would have attacked, but Atanase moved between them, giving credence to the rumor that he could in fact teleport, he moved with such speed. With pleasure, he reveled in the fear on his kin's faces. *Good. They should know terror when they think of their master... unlike my stubborn son.*

"You're done." Atanase smiled at Iancu. "For now."

Iancu froze in place, his need to obey bred into his bloode. He bowed his head. "By your command."

Mihai glared at them both before pulling back his anger. He too bowed his head, though his bow was a lot more shallow. "Master." He straightened and bit out, "About the lycan, he has no family. We were trying this new approach. It was working. He'd already given us information about his pack and the dusk fae settled near their camp."

Atanase perked up at that. "And?" More of Faraine's kind would help move along his plan to secure the Bloode Stones.

"And then... " Mihai swallowed. "And then Devon thought we should slow down the torture to work more curses through him." Mihai glanced at the chains, and Atanase noticed the small runes carved into several of the links. "The sorcerer we employed was coming up with a heavier hex."

Atanase realized he'd inadvertently interfered in his own mission. "But you were too slow, and then Master had a need to tear off Devon's head, is that what you were going to say?"

"Yes, sire."

Atanase saw his patriarch ready himself to receive a blow for calling out Atanase's mistake. But it never landed. Instead, Atanase grinned, always doing something unpredictable to keep his strigoi off balance. "Next time, stop me before I start having too much fun." He kissed Mihai on the forehead, a sure sign of favor.

Others around them laughed and began talking among themselves again. The danger to the patriarch had passed, and the clan felt secure in their master's incredible power.

All was well, and Atanase had been amused. A very good beginning to his night.

Until Iancu had to open his mouth and ruin everything. "My lord, I was coming to find you before... this." He glared at Mihai, who glared back.

"Yes?"

Iancu steeled himself. "The prisoner is no longer in the hold. I fear the dusk elf has escaped."

CHAPTER
ELEVEN

F ara woke feeling refreshed. She stretched and shook off her
glamour, relieved to feel her strength returning. With a
yawn, she walked into the attached bathroom and stood under the
shower, missing the hot springs of home.

Humans put a layer of artificiality between them and nature,
and as a dusk elf with ties to Gaia, she'd felt freer when walking
through her forest and communing with the rock and earth
beneath her feet.

Yet she'd been dissatisfied too, she had to admit as she stood
under a spray of lovely warm water. She grabbed a bottle of some
kind of soap for her hair and lathered, enjoying the comforting
scent of flowers as she massaged her scalp.

A sudden rush of feeling centered her, and then a flash of red
and she was feeling shock and then deep interest.

Masculine interest.

She dropped her hands to the side and swung around but saw
no one nearby. The clear glass walls of the shower hadn't
steamed, and the large, open bathroom remained empty, no visible
place to hide. But she could have sworn she wasn't alone. She

shifted and got a face full of water, making her sputter and blink to clear her vision.

The sense of another had vanished, as if it had never been.

She shivered, no longer so comfortable with memories of home, which she shouldn't have felt in the first place.

You're in a house filled with vampires, you jabbering derendel. The elven insult hit its mark, and she flushed, wishing she was better at subterfuge and survival than she'd been showing lately.

Ten years ago, she'd felt dissatisfied with life and had wanted something more. So she'd ventured into the human world. Unfortunately, she'd ventured too near to the strigoi stronghold, having inadvertently journeyed to a place rich with biodiversity and rock, the presence of strigoi, ghouls, and human byproduct creating a unique substrate of mineral matter.

Having realized her error too late, she'd been brought to Master Atanase's attention. In order to avoid being killed, she'd tried to show him she had value apart from being a food source. She'd found a crystal that enhanced the master's ability to purify blood.

Intrigued, he'd asked her what she knew of Bloode Stones.

Unfortunately, she'd known quite a bit, had even been intrigued to discover the legendary stones, not putting credence into what they might do when found. Thus had begun her journey to find them. Except when she'd realized what she'd done by handing them over, she'd refused to bring him any more.

And then her brother had vanished.

She sighed, wishing she'd been smarter about her dealings with a creature who'd been manipulating others for thousands of years. If only she'd pretended to not be able to commune with power gems in the first place. Or hadn't ventured outside her world and been happy with her life as it was.

Her life hadn't been adventurous or spectacular, but it had been safe with family. With the few friends like her, dusk elves hiding from those who would seek to destroy her because two enemies had seen past needless enmity and fallen in love. Her family had at least understood her growing need for isolation, to lose herself in Gaia's breath and help purify the stone in her world.

Why had she left? Because she'd felt she deserved more out of life. But did she really?

She exited the shower and dried off. Staring at herself in the mirror, she looked beyond flesh to the weak character within.

So much damage she'd inadvertently caused, and all because she'd placed a higher value on her own life than those of so many others. Because of her hubris, her brother had suffered. And at the rate she was going, the entire human world might suffer as well. If Atanase got his hands on the Bloode Stone she'd thrown at Varu, worlds would end. The human plane would be the first, but not the last, to fall to vampire rule.

She shivered, scared of what she'd allowed to happen. But no more. She had a job to do, and no matter what that arrogant Varujan might think, he was going to obey her. With the help of the Bloode Stone, of course. She just had to convince the stone to like her better.

That thought in mind, she shifted back into her human-seeming, the glamour settling over her once more, her womanly features much like her fae ones except for the blunted ears and smaller eyes. And that dull skin, of course.

Speaking of skin.... She frowned, hoping her brother hadn't let the others see his true self. She knew he hated his glamour, but he also had to know the importance of keeping their secret.

She hoped.

After dressing in a fresh set of clothing, including a brand new set of underclothes that hadn't been in the armoire last night, she left her room and tiptoed toward her brother's, only to find him absent, the room a mess.

But not the site of a brawl, rather Onvyr's perpetual struggle with the concept of neatness.

She left the room and continued down the hallway, hoping to investigate the library and spa when a burst of magic swirled like a mini-tornado toward her, appearing from out of nowhere.

Sparks of electricity shocked her as it neared, and she flinched from the wave of power seeking out her own.

Before she could flee, a battering ram knocked her to the floor, leaving her breathless and doing her best to keep the heavy object from crushing her.

"Remain still, fae," Varujan ordered and barked a few curses in a foreign language. She didn't understand until he glanced down at her and switched back to English—one of the five mortal languages she knew. "Rolf lost control of a practice spell." He frowned at her, lifting a strand of hair that obscured her vision and tucking it behind an ear.

She bit her lip, hating the fact he'd accidentally managed to find a spot that made her want to melt into a pile of warm goo. Many fae disliked anyone touching their sensitive ears. Fara had always considered the tips of hers an erogenous zone.

"You really should be more careful," he murmured as he stared into her eyes, his lips curling into a smile.

Devastating.

The male looked lethal enough when he glared or flashed his fangs. But the sight of his smile enthralled her.

Oh no. She tried to blink, to look away from what had to be his obvious powers of seduction, but she could only shift her gaze to his mouth. Those firm, red lips, so close....

He licked his upper lip, and the hint of his fangs reminded her that a predator had her caged to the floor. Her heart should race in fear, not arousal.

"Oh ho, what is this?" Rolf chuckled as he approached and stopped to stare down at them. "Has the female cast a spell over you again?"

Varujan shocked her by laughing. "Apparently so." He moved back, crouched on the balls of his feet, and stared, the amusement leeching from his expression and leaving a killer there for her to see. "Come, fae. Mormo wants you."

She wanted to ignore the hand he offered her.

His sardonic smile told her he knew that. "Take my hand," he murmured, his gaze on hers. Compelling her so easily.

She took his hand and let him bring her to her feet.

Annoyed at how smug he seemed, she reached out to the stone and communicated. Not that she'd ever been able to explain to Atanase how that worked. She didn't exactly converse with the stone, though she did talk to it. It responded with feeling, having a sentience all its own.

A little help here, please?

She stared at her hand held tightly in Varujan's much larger one, his fingers strong, the nails sharp and clean but not overly dense, almost human-like.

He frowned at her and slowly pulled his hand back.

All while Rolf watched as if enjoying his favorite movie.

"Come with me," Varujan said, still frowning but likely unsure why.

The stone hadn't commanded him to obey, its power more subtle than that. In the years since Fara had been working with Bloode Stones, she'd come to understand that the smaller stones had used guile and suggestion to get others to do what they wanted. What *she* wanted, actually, until she'd handed them over to Atanase. Then the stones' power shifted to him.

Although she still wondered if she could have taken that power back. But under Atanase's watchful eye, she hadn't had the nerve to try.

With Varujan and this larger, more powerful Bloode Stone, she had the sense it would react differently than the ones she'd given to his father. She could mentally reach it with ease, so it had to be nearby.

"Are you ignoring our charming leader?" Rolf goggled.

She blushed and forced herself to look away from the seductive Varujan. "What? Um, no. I was just, I ah...."

Rolf's wide smile made her face feel even hotter. "I see."

Varujan said something she couldn't make out to Rolf, which made the draugr laugh, though she didn't think that had been Varujan's intent. Varujan snarled at him before grabbing her by the hand and yanking her with him down the hall toward a set of stairs that went up.

"Let me go."

"No," he growled, turned to face her, and glared with red eyes.

A bad sign.

He crowded her until her back hit the wall. "What are you doing to me?"

"Doing?" *What?*

"You're trying to control me, aren't you, fae?"

"N-no." That blasted, traitorous stone.

"I can feel you inside me." He put her hand over his chest as he searched her gaze. "The stone sings to me constantly in a low hum. But I think maybe that's you."

She didn't know how to process *that*. "It sings?"

He shocked her anew by shoving his face in the crook of her neck. Then he licked her.

She felt the heat all the way to her toes and would have landed on her ass if he hadn't caught her.

"Ah, so maybe it's not you after all." His red eyes gleamed and slowly turned back to black.

She should have felt good about that. Except he followed his lick with a kiss to that same spot.

To her embarrassment, Fara let out a low moan, her body suddenly hungry for the creature nuzzling her throat. The one with very sharp teeth.

VARU COULDN'T GET ENOUGH of the handful of fae female in his arms. The lust fogging his sense confused him. And Varu didn't do confusion.

Leery of falling for the ripe prey who managed to subvert his commands, he forced himself not to bite her—and By the Night was that all but impossible—and stepped back, keeping her upright with hands on her shoulders.

Her gaze met his, and he saw the dazed passion blazing in eyes that flashed lavender, her entire body shimmering in her glamour that faded for the briefest second.

Such beauty, such grace in that fine, trembling form.

He wanted to see her. Without her clothes. Covered in nothing but him.

And enough of that.

Calling on his discipline and forcing out that stupid hum that never seemed to stop, he dragged her with him up the stairs toward Mormo's office.

The unnaturally grand level of the home never failed to impress him, the scent of power and the feel of so much magic making him tingle all over. And not the good kind of tingling, the way he'd felt with Fara just moments before. This was a warning, a predator's way of reminding Varu he was not in charge around here.

That never failed to piss him off. Mormo might be a magician working for a goddess, but Varu was a Night's blessed vampire. A strigoi from the Crimson Veil. He bowed to no one.

Not even his father, which had gotten him cursed to work with Mormo and Hecate, after all.

Calming himself, he continued through the open level toward the robed creature in the back, fiddling with the Bloode Stone dagger.

"She's here," Varu said and nudged Fara toward Mormo.

She glared at him over her shoulder, apparently having regained her wits, and stalked to Mormo's side.

Varu did his best not to grin, reminding himself that the female wasn't amusing. She was a threat and an unknown. Not someone to think about breeding with.

Breeding? For fuck's sake, no.

He forced himself to ignore his growing arousal, willing it to fade while he focused instead on Mormo and that blasted gem.

"Ah, Faraine. Thank you for joining me." Mormo smiled, solicitous and annoying because of it. "Can I get you anything to eat or drink?"

"Kval eggs, perhaps?" Varu mocked. "We know what you are. Why not show us?"

"I'm human," she snapped.

"No, my dear. You aren't." Mormo sighed and put a hand on her forehead.

Fara gasped as the glamour faded. Unlike her brother, she was neither dark nor light, but that pale shade of gray Varu had seen when he'd first met her. Her hair, a long, shiny black with streaks of white, looked as soft as down. A pointed ear peeked through, and he remembered touching her ear earlier, sensing her pleasure from the caress.

Her facial features morphed from human to elven, the high cheekbones and slope of her nose regal, her dainty chin and sparkling eyes more than attractive. And, he had to admit, the sight of her tiny fangs made him wonder what they'd feel like if she bit him.

Night take him, but why did he find that thought so arousing?

"You done staring?" she asked, her voice like ice.

"You look much better as yourself." Mormo nodded. "Right, Varu?"

"Yes. Even if you are fae." He cocked his head, noticing that her body looked pretty much the same in either form. "And small."

"I'm not small."

"For a dusk elf, no." Mormo held the dagger up to her. It lacked the Bloode Stone. "Do you know where the gem is?"

She blinked. "It's not here?"

"What?" Varu stepped closer and accepted the dagger, staring at the bevel where the stone had rested. "Bring it back," he ordered her.

"I don't have it." She stared at the dagger. "When would I have taken it? I just got here last night. I was told not to come up here."

"That's true." Mormo took the dagger back from Varu. "Perhaps my mistress borrowed it."

"Your mistress?" Fara asked.

"Hecate. My goddess."

Fara gaped. "Your mistress is *a goddess?* She manifests here?"

"Supposedly." Varu narrowed his eyes. "I haven't seen her."

"You have, you just don't know her like I do."

"I'm crushed." Varu turned to Fara, not liking the awe on her face. "Oh please. She's just a deity. And she's not my deity. None of us worship her." He paused. "Do you?"

"Me? No. Hecate is a goddess of magic, witches, and death. I'm surprised you're not partial to her. Vampires do like to kill things a lot." She didn't look impressed by the fact.

A lot less respectful than she should be. "You know, little dusk elf, you should be careful of how you talk to me." He glared at her, flashing his eyes with anger.

And saw her swallow, that delectable throat begging for a bite. He licked his lips and heard her swallow again.

With a laugh, he turned to see Mormo studying the dagger with a frown.

"What's wrong?"

"So many things." Mormo sighed and slid his hair back behind one ear—not pointed like Fara's. "But for now, let's talk about Ambrogio, Selene, and Apollo. And your history in particular," he said to Varu.

"My history? Why?"

"Because your great-great grandfather left a legacy that only a few can carry out. And you're the one I'm counting on."

CHAPTER TWELVE

Varu frowned. "I'm not sure what my history has to go with anything." He glanced at Fara, who looked a little too interested. "And she has no need to learn anything more about me than I wish her to know."

Instead of cowing, like a proper female should, she snorted. "I already know he's arrogant, deadly, and bossy. Can we get on with this? I have things I need to be doing. The sooner I can give you what you need, the sooner I can leave with my brother."

Mormo took a seat in a plush chair near his mini library—stacks of shelving occupied by books and the odd potion or fetish he often used for his spells. Varu had made the mistake one day of asking the magician what he really did with his time and had been treated to a potion making class that had been both interesting and beyond his comprehension on every level. Not that he'd confessed that, of course.

Fara sat on the couch next to the chair, and Varu sat next to her, secretly amused at how she tried to hide the fact she stiffened whenever he got too close.

Mormo waved his hand toward her, and a plate of fruits and

cheese appeared on the table. "Please, eat. You need to restore your strength. The glamour must take constant energy."

"It does." She shrugged and bit into a strawberry, her small fangs tearing through the fleshy fruit. "But it's natural now. Been doing it for a while."

"How long is a while?" Varu asked as Mormo created a goblet of blood for him. Thoughtful, and not something Mormo often did. The white-haired bastard was trying to make a good impression in front of their guest for some reason.

Mormo winked at him but said nothing.

He took a sip. Lycan, fresh. With a grudging nod of thanks, Varu focused once more on Fara, wondering how she'd react to him drinking blood in front of her. Lesser beings tended to get nervous when reminded of their mortality, since he could just as easily be drinking from her right now.

She didn't seem fazed at all. "Ten years. That's how long I've been cursed."

Mormo nodded. "Ah, yes. The curse that allows you to find precious gems and Bloode Stones. And you still can't remember who cursed you or why?"

Varu felt an exchange of energy between them.

"I can't tell if you're lying," Mormo murmured, "which is interesting all by itself."

Fara continued to nibble at the food on her plate. "I'm not lying."

Varu knew right then that she was. But why? Because she wanted the stone for herself? Because she had ulterior motives? Was she in fact a threat to them? And if so, would Mormo or Hecate try to kill her?

The goddess hadn't involved herself—that he knew of—in anything they'd been doing for her since becoming kin. But Varu had the feeling he rarely knew what really went on in this place.

Like why an otherworldly battle cat kept showing up out of nowhere.

Fara froze. "Can someone please take care of that?"

Mormo started. "What...? Where did you come from?"

She grumbled at him before coming to sit near Varu and nudged his hand with her head.

Pleased to pet her, he lengthened his nails and ran them along her fur, scratching under her chin and around her ears, his gaze on Fara, who looked properly terrified.

"Th-that's a battle cat."

"Yes." Mormo sounded annoyed. "One who was supposed to have gone home yesterday."

The cat gave him a lazy snarl, as if Mormo were too beneath her to even bother.

"Yes, I know. I feel the same way," Varu said to her.

Fara's eyes widened. "You can talk to her?"

"No, but I can tell what she's thinking by the way she's ignoring Mormo. And we all feel that way.

"Very funny." Mormo didn't seem amused. He glared at the cat. "And you, get home. I'm sure Freya is wondering where you've gotten to."

The cat huffed, took a step closer to Fara's food, sniffed it, then made a face and turned away, leaving by way of a new set of stairs Varu hadn't seen before. Then again, doors and stairways came and went in the house regularly.

"I'll be right back." Mormo followed the beast out of the room.

Leaving Varu alone with Fara.

He watched her eat the rest of the food on her plate, which soon replenished itself with a bowl of some kind of porridge. "You're going to eat that slop?"

"It's oatmeal."

"It's disgusting." He grimaced.

"You drink blood. That's disgusting."

"That's normal."

She stuck a spoon in the glop and watched him as she ate it. "Mmm, this sure is good."

He grimaced, which caused her to laugh. Once again, not displaying the fear and awe he was used to. But as he watched her tiny fangs appear, her laughter didn't bother him so much.

"It really is good," she said. "Would you like to try a bite?"

"Perhaps a bite later, after you've processed the meal," he offered instead, and was gratified to see her remember to whom she was talking. "Or now, if you'd rather." He stared into her eyes, but the savvy female broke eye contact, focusing on her food. "Later then."

"Leave me alone."

"Fae, you exist at my whim. I can kill you whenever I want."

"No, you can't."

He studied her, the frail yet delicate elf full of vigor and defiance. His father would have crushed her for daring to argue with him. But Varu had always been inclined toward truth and intellect. He respected those with the fortitude to try to deny him. Of course, they all caved to his will eventually. Even the others of his Night Bloode clan gradually agreed with him and carried out his orders.

Varu didn't act like their commander out of any sense of misplaced pride. It was something inside him, a part of his makeup that made him need to control, protect, and manage others around him. Which had made him an outstanding leader in his clan and a problem for his father, who believed in the old ways of mastering all those around him. Atanase of the Crimson Veil answered to no one, and when his son dared doubt some of his questionable activities, he hadn't taken kindly to the assumed disrespect.

"Like two beta fish in a small bowl," he'd once heard Mihai describe his relationship with his father.

To which Iancu, that dickhead, had responded, "Best kill him now, Master Atanase, before he grows into those fangs."

Varu had been a hundred years old at the time. His father sixteen hundred years his senior.

Thinking of Mihai made him wonder how the patriarch was getting along in his absence. As the master's son and a tribal captain, Varu had done whatever Mihai wanted, often clashing with his father on purpose, just to put a kink in Atanase's grand plans.

And his father *always* had grand plans.

To annihilate the nearby city of Cluj-Napoca.

To make a vampire/lycan war with the European packs.

To show the draugr tribe who really ruled the Norwegian territories, nearly wiping out a score of ancients who would have retaliated in force against the strigoi.

Varu scowled, recalling his father's most asinine plan from five hundred years ago—to find all the Bloode Stones and conquer the major realms.

No, his father couldn't be that obtuse and narrowminded, could he?

"Your brother knows a master vampire," he said, watching for Fara's reaction.

He didn't get one. "My brother is not always right in the head," she said, sounding sad. "Time spent with a past enemy hurt him, deeply. He's still recovering."

"I see." That made sense, considering how odd Onvyr had been acting with them all. Friendly, then not, then friends again. He studied her. "How is it you're gray, but your brother is both light and dark elf?"

She scowled. "How do you know that?"

"He showed us last night."

"Onvyr." She huffed. "I told him not to do that."

Varu scoffed. "Female, we already knew you were both fae. He was smart enough to show us the truth."

"Smart enough or gullible enough?"

Varu shrugged. Either way, the elf had been honest. "He's fierce, your brother. Powerful." He paused. "Word has it someone killed a young upir from the Seattle clan. They want vengeance."

"It was me," she blurted. "I did it."

Her attempt to sound proud would have worked better if her voice hadn't shaken.

"Oh? How did you do that?"

"Fae magic."

"Show me."

"No, if I kill you, the others will retaliate."

"No, they won't. They hate me."

"I hate you."

He grinned. "You want to hate me, but you don't."

"I do too."

"You're a poor liar."

She glanced around, as if that could dissuade him. "Where's Mormo?"

"In the basement. Downstairs. In another dimension." Varu shrugged. "Who cares? I want you to show me your magic, fae."

"Blow me."

He blinked, startled to hear those words coming from such a sweet-looking mouth. But her horrified expression capped it. He burst into laughter, something he hadn't done in.... Well, he couldn't remember.

Mormo returned to find Varu laughing uncontrollably while Fara sat with her hand over her mouth, watching him with wary eyes.

"I think he's lost it," she told the magician.

"I don't think he ever had it to lose." Mormo sighed. "The feline is back home. Now, what are we talking about?"

FARA WATCHED VARUJAN—VARU—COMPOSE himself, shocked at how charming she found his laughter. He'd looked as surprised at his reaction as she'd been. But seeing the austere strigoi with a smile really scared her.

Because she liked it. A lot.

As had the Bloode Stone.

It was no longer embedded in the dagger, but she felt it close. The gem had to be near, maybe on one of Mormo's many tables covered with potions and magics she wanted no part of. Or perhaps the goddess, Hecate, had grabbed it and taken it only she knew where.

Fara had no idea, but she had a real problem with the gem not responding to her the way it had before. Ever since being handled by Varu, the stone seemed to gravitate toward the strigoi. And that was a problem.

If Fara wanted to use Varu to battle his father, she'd need ammunition. From all she'd gathered about Varujan of the Crimson Veil, he had always been loyal to his clan and worthy of handling the stone. Hell, he'd handled the dagger readily enough.

He scared her, and he didn't scare her. Not enough, at least. She planned on using him to win this war a master vampire had started. One she'd been unwillingly helping the evil bastard to build.

"I want to tell you a little bit about Varujan," Mormo said, breaking the sudden silence.

Fara realized she'd been staring at Varu, and he'd been staring back, a brow raised in question.

She flushed. "Yes, of course." She picked up her oatmeal and continued to eat, famished despite haven eaten a full plate already. "I'm listening."

"I know I'm an awesome specimen, but please, contain yourself," Varu said with a smirk.

She wanted so badly to flip him off, but his expression cautioned her not to try. He looked a little too willing to serve her up for lunch.

Varu turned to Mormo and sighed. "Do we really need a family history? The fae—"

"I have a name." She was pushing it, but he really got under her skin.

"—doesn't need to know more than that I can kill her in a blink. She'll do whatever we tell her to do. And like it," he added with a sneer.

"No wonder everyone hates you," she mumbled.

Mormo coughed. "Yes, well, that's beside the point. Varu is descended from Ambrogio himself. He's the great-great grandson of the first vampire. The Primus."

Fara blinked. "What? I thought vampires came from hell, an offset of demons who took to the mortal plane." That the whole Apollo-Ambrogio story was made up.

Mormo shook his head. "The youth of today. No. While vampires love that the rest of the worlds think they're hellspawn—"

"I don't." Varu frowned.

"They're actually descended from humans and gods."

"Not gods." Varu sounded as if he hated the thought. "Well, maybe. Cursed into being, maybe."

Mormo sighed. "I suppose we'll have to skip back a few thousand years before Varu's birth, to the time before the Ending."

"Ending?" Fara asked.

"Of all that was good in this world." Mormo shot him a look. "Before his kind shook up all of existence."

. . .

Varu nodded. "Continue. I do think I'll like this discussion." Because vampires *had* changed the power structure in the many worlds once ruled by gods. Men and magir had been forced to remake their territories, to concede to a force far greater than any they were used to. And the gods, those loathsome beings, could no longer compel anyone into worship.

Vampires refused to pray to anything. They did what they wanted when they wanted, deservedly. They'd been doomed to live an existence filled with nothing but infighting, never-ending wars, and terror until the masters had realized such a life would only end in misery for their kind. Only with strict laws and structure had the Bloode Empire formed tribes that could coexist, and with such rules, vampires began to breed. Slowly. Their numbers would still never rival those of other magir or come close to human numbers. But what they lacked in progeny they more than made up for in power.

"You might want to rethink that," Mormo said. "Because what you think you know about your ancestors and the truth are two different things. And yes, I know what I'm talking about. My mistress was there at your beginning. And she'll be there at your end."

He paused to look from Varu to Fara. "And that end is coming sooner than you think."

CHAPTER THIRTEEN

F ara waited, now eager to hear about vampire history. Most people had never met a vampire. If you met one, you died. Vampires didn't hate everyone, but they considered non-vampires *lesser beings*—Atanase and his general had used that term about her and her brother many times. Even magir, fellow people made of magic, held no importance to vampires. Unless they considered breeding, and then vampires became super choosy.

They were also super secretive. Despite working for Atanase for over a decade, Fara knew little about vampires other than that they lived to fight and to kill. Torture seemed to be a hobby for their kind. So she'd spent much of her time away from strigoi lands, doing her best to avoid anything with fangs.

Searching for the Bloode Stones had surprisingly taken her far from any vampires. So anything she could learn about the master and his kind would be more than welcome.

Mormo cleared his throat. "Yes, so, from the beginning. Varu, don't interrupt."

Varu groaned. "Can we get on with this?"

"It all started with a secret love. Between a human warrior named Ambrogio and a woman named Selene. History would have you believe Ambrogio was a merchant, but in that they'd be wrong. Ambrogio served as a great warrior in Mesopotamia, and for his efforts he was noticed by a cache of magir who allowed him to lengthen his lifespan. He wandered between lands and peoples, learning and developing a penchant for trade."

Varu shook his head. "Ambrogio was Roman."

"Rome wasn't founded until 753 BCE, according to scholars, so no, Ambrogio was much older. I think he reinvented himself as an adventurer from Italia in later texts." Mormo shrugged. "Anyhow, he wandered into a Greek temple devoted to Apollo, the Grecian sun god. And there he found Selene, one of Apollo's handmaidens. A priestess, actually."

"Apollo had priestesses?" Fara asked, curious.

"Yes, though humans tend to mask anything relegated to female empowerment and give agency to gods and priests, the Feminine has always been a power of creation and life."

Fara liked that way of thinking.

"Fine. Ambrogio was older than I'd thought." Varu frowned. "He and Selene had an affair. Apollo didn't like a human sullying his virginal maiden and cursed him. Selene followed. Then bam, we have vampires."

"No." Mormo glared. "Didn't I tell you not to interrupt?"

Varu opened his mouth but said nothing more, surprising Fara that he had any sense when it came to listening to anyone but himself talk. She let out a little sneer.

He glared at her, and she pretended not to see it.

"Anyway," Mormo said in three long syllables, "Ambrogio fell in instant love with Selene, who was anything but a mortal. She was Apollo's sister, and she liked to play mortal now and then because it broke up the tedium between wars. Everyone likes to think Artemis is the goddess of the moon, but Selene predates her by thousands of years."

"Wait. A goddess?" Varu looked he'd just been slapped across the face with a mermaid.

Mormo smirked. "Yes, my friend, a goddess. Selene loved a mortal, and that's why her brother lost his marbles. Not because his handmaiden didn't give him the proper respect, but because his sister wanted to bring a human into the family. Apollo lost his shit—excuse the expression," he said to Fara, "and cursed Ambrogio to a lifeless existence apart from Selene.

"But Apollo hadn't counted on her true love. She followed Ambrogio, and when he fell upon her, lost in madness, she let him drink from godly veins. He nearly drained her dry, if that can even happen to a god, and between her blood and Apollo's curse, he became a vampire. In fact, when he realized he'd nearly destroyed Selene, he wept. And those six tears that hit the ground became the Bloode Stones.

"Hundreds of years later, worried at how powerful he'd become, and how powerful his progeny might one day be, he and Selene agreed with the gods to limit their young to one per couple, that they would only ever have male children with vampiric traits, and to ensure that their kind would always keep to smaller groups."

Varu looked as if he were having trouble with what he'd learned.

Fara was shocked, for sure.

Varu shook his head. "Not sure I believe you about Selene's origins"

"Not sure I care." Mormo snorted.

"Why are you telling us this?"

Mormo turned to Fara. "You see what I have to deal with on a daily basis? He has no patience. And he's actually a sight better than the others. Don't get me started on Kraft."

"Mormo," Varu growled.

"Ambrogio is in fact your Sire. The Father. The Primus. *He* had the power that's been diluted over time. Like I told you, at first, when he and Selene started having babies, no one cared. Especially when those female children scattered and showed no signs of drinking blood or having killer instincts. The only thing they inherited from their parents were long lives. Then one of them had a child. A male child. And he became the next vampire. Each of Ambrogio and Selene's daughters gave rise to the Ten Tribes."

Which Fara knew to be the Draugr, Revenant, Nachzehrer, Vrykolakas, Strigoi, Upir, Reaper, Jiangshi, Sasabonsam, and Pishachas tribes. She frowned. "But if Varu is Ambrogio's great-great grandson, and he's strigoi, wouldn't that mean Ambrogio was originally strigoi?" And that would make the strigoi stronger than all the others, but she hadn't realized that to be the case.

"No, he was Primus. All others came after him," Varu said, a thoughtful expression on his face. "My father is strigoi, my grand-father before him."

"Now, let's not get ahead of ourselves." Mormo held up a hand. "I'm going somewhere with all this history. Bear with me. For a hundred years, Selene's girls kept popping out babies, and vampires scattered across the human continents. They came into contact with other magir, mated with some, and though it's said only male progeny come out vampire, many vampire males started to develop minor traits because yes, the mother contributes half a baby's genetics, magir or not."

"Even vampires," Fara murmured.

Varu shook his head. "No. I have nothing from my mother."

"Oh?" Mormo cocked his head. "Because I met her a long time ago, and you do have a few things in common with her."

Varu froze. "What?"

"Wait, wait, we're getting off topic."

Fara watched Varu, fascinated by the tangle of emotion that crossed his face before disappearing completely.

Mormo continued, "So Ambrogio and Selene limited their race to smaller numbers and an affinity to make war on each other. The girls scattered with their tribes, the first and last queens of their kind. Sad that they eventually died before they could whip their kin into shape. But the point is, the vampire population settled. Ambrogio's tears remained where they had fallen when he'd been cursed and cried, and those tears formed the Bloode Stones.

"He and Selene buried them, because they knew the power of the stones. And wherever the pair went, peace followed among their kind. Until one day a nosy little bastard named Adrastas—that would be your great grandfather, Varu—found those tears. He united the strigoi and made war on the pricolici, which is why there are hardly any of them around anymore. When Ambrogio returned and learned what Adrastas had done, he took the stones back."

"After killing Adrastas," Varu snapped. "Don't make Ambrogio out to be some saint."

"No, he was a killer, cursed to be one for the sin of falling in love with a goddess. Selene was crushed to lose her boy, but Adrastas had issues. They hid the stones and soon disappeared, never to be seen again. Some say Selene took Ambrogio back to Mt. Olympus with her, others say she and he left for the moon, never to return. Others say the pair eventually died, no longer truly immortal. No one knows."

"Not even Hecate?" Fara asked, enrapt in the story.

"Well, if she does, she refuses to tell me."

"Great." Varu glared at Mormo. "This is a fascinating history, But what does—"

Mormo interrupted and turned to focus on Fara. "Adrastas died, but he'd already had a son named Vasili. Vasili continued the strigoi, growing the tribe, and eventually procreated and had Atanase, who in turn lent his seed to a lovely magir who gave birth to Varujan. Of all the children Ambrogio and Selene birthed, the only direct descendant still alive is Varujan."

Varu frowned. "That doesn't make sense. My father is still alive."

"But he's not a direct descendant, and by that I mean, his parents were not both descended from your creators."

"What?" Fara was confused.

Mormo explained, "When Ambrogio and Selene's daughters scattered, the male vampires found mates that appealed to them and had a son or daughter. They normally killed any female child outright, though the occasional vampire gave his daughter away. The males they kept and raised as kin. But through some odd twist of fate, all of Varujan's forefathers, with the exception of Atanase, had vampire genetics passed from both father *and* mother. Varu, your father's mother was magir, a fae, I think. *Not* descended from Ambrogio and Selene. But you have vampiric genes from both your parents. Your father was strigoi. Your mother, pricolici, if I'm not mistaken.

"That's why the Bloode Stones call to you. Because you're the closest thing to Ambrogio and Selene as can be." Mormo turned to Fara. "But you. I'm not sure why you can handle the gem. Unless of course you have some distant connection to the vampire family tree that I can't see."

Fara blinked. "Um, no. I can trace my heritage all the way back to a daughter of Freyr and cousin of Danu."

"Hmm."

She didn't like the way Mormo was thinking. Or the way Varu watched her, with more interest than she found comfortable.

"Okay, so the history lesson goes to show I'm a direct descendant of Ambrogio," Varu said. "The stone sings to me. Great. Now what?"

Mormo studied Fara. "Now she fills in the missing pieces. I'm sorry to say I can't read her, and I'm not sure if it's the stone's interference or some fae magic I can't understand. My truth sense with this one only extends so far."

"I can't help you." Won't *help you, because I need Varu if I have any hope of freeing myself and my brother from his father.* She didn't trust Mormo's agenda with the Bloode Stone, or his connection to the witch goddess. "But maybe I can work on the Bloode Stone with Varu, see if together we can fix it or something. I don't know."

Mormo nodded.

Varu watched her with an unreadable expression. "No. She knows more than she's saying."

"Varu, she—"

"Let's bleed the brother. Then she'll talk."

Fara glared. Every time she thought she could work with the guy, Varu acted like some kind of cold-blooded killer. Which of course he was. But still. She'd seen him laugh. Felt his breath on her lips. She could feel something inside him that wasn't all death and dismemberment.

She was pretty sure.

"Touch my brother and any hope of cooperation goes out the window."

"Of course." Varu bowed his head her way. "I was only joking. Vampire humor."

She didn't trust him one bit. "Ha ha."

Mormo didn't bother trying to hide a smile. "Great. Well, with you two working with the Bloode Stone, that frees me and the others to find a few more missing things."

"You mean missing lesser beings." Varu frowned. "What have you been doing with all the people we've brought back to you, anyway?"

Fara stared from Varu to Mormo. "There are others?"

Mormo answered easily enough, "They had information we

needed, then I sent them on their way." The way he ended his sentence, in that creepy tone of voice, froze her to the spot.

"Alive?"

Mormo turned into someone she didn't recognize. He smiled, and she saw a mouth full of sharp teeth, his eyes glowing and surrounded by a line of black and gold. His long hair flew around his head though there was no breeze. "Those who will not serve will die. Remember that, Faraine de Cloche Jherag." He reached out with a clawed hand and brushed her cheek.

Fara screamed, monstrous visions coalescing to drive the fear and pain of losing all she loved into a maelstrom of death. Her beloved ancestral forest saturated with blood and covered with scattered limbs. Trees ripped from their roots, stone crushed and decimated as fires raged through the many worlds. Wars fought between magir and human, the boundary between divine and mortal skewed, lost in the chaos of unbecoming.

And there, her brother a husk while a master vampire drained him dry, accompanied by a horde of living dead consuming everything in their path.

Then she knew nothing more.

Varu caught Fara in his arms and hissed at Mormo, not sure what the hell the magician thought he was doing.

The magical field around him settled, and Mormo blinked as if coming out of a trance. He'd never been so close to dying, whether he knew it or not. Only concern for the fae in Varu's arms kept him from destroying Hecate's beloved servant.

"She's mine," he roared and pushed out with everything inside him. A fierce power lit him from the inside out, and he watched as Mormo blinked in surprise before disappearing in a flash of red light.

Gone, but not from this world, Varu didn't think. But as a soft breath brushed his chest, he didn't care.

Varu laid Fara down on the couch, still seething. How *dare* Mormo touch Varu's prey? *Mine,* that same power roared inside him. *Mine to take, to taste. To keep.*

The call of her blood had his heart slowing, beating in time with hers. She didn't move, but he could see her chest rise and fall. A fae essence layered with the subtle texture of power and something fertile. Like the bud of a flower beginning to unfurl, her power called to his, and he watched as her eyes opened and she reached out to him.

Her eyes no longer lavender, but red.

The color of blood.

Entranced, he gave her what she wanted. And kissed her.

CHAPTER
FOURTEEN

F ara had no idea why she couldn't stop trembling, likely fear leaving a tail of uncertainty in its wake.

But as she saw a light blur take shape into a familiar face, rabid hunger overwhelmed her, and she reached out. Needing....

Varu's eyes blazed as he lowered to her and gave her the kiss she wanted. Craved. Demanded.

The feel of his lips, both soft yet firm, molded with hers as he lowered himself onto her, their bodies flush, his so much larger and stronger than hers.

But the panic and fear she should have felt wasn't there, replaced by a feeling of safety and desire and pleasure. All-consuming. She nipped at his lips and sighed as a fang grazed her tongue. The taste of fae blood, sweet and earthy, filled her mouth, and she heard Varu groan as he deepened the kiss.

He notched that hard arousal between her legs, rubbing with more insistence as the kiss deepened. She'd never felt its like, the ecstasy and agony of not having enough of him, of feeling empty and needing, overpowering all sense.

Then his hand moved, and she keened as he closed it over her breast, pulling the taut nipple into a hardened bud. Fingers gripped her hair, folding her deeper into his kiss as he plunged his tongue in and out of her mouth, mimicking with his body what she desperately wanted.

He shifted again, mounting her through their clothing. She leaned up, needing him closer. He thrust again and again. Until finally, she lost all control and found her release, gradually blinking her eyes open only to see his close as he threw his head back and stilled.

She felt his heart racing, the pulse of his release as powerful as hers.

And as shocking.

She stared, wide-eyed, wondering what, By the Veil, had just happened.

Could a strigoi have given her more pleasure than she'd ever experienced in her lifetime, and with their clothes *on*? She'd had sex that wasn't sex with... *Varujan of the Crimson Veil?*

It took him a moment, but then clarity returned to his gaze as well, and he stared down at her, not with horror, but with some-thing close to it.

He leapt from her, swearing in several languages, one she recognized.

She sat up slowly, her head buzzing and her body replete, soft. Wet.

She blushed, not sure what the heck had just happened. She rubbed her eyes and still saw Varu standing there, the thick bulge between his legs less apparent.

"Yes, I came in my pants," he muttered and glared at her. "Because of you."

"I, well, I, ah...."

He dragged her to her feet and held her up on her tiptoes as he growled, "Right after you came so hard you nearly passed out."

He kissed her, the passion still taut between them, stirring her to desire once more, as if she hadn't just experienced the greatest bliss of her life.

Then he dropped her to her feet and stormed from the room.

She wanted to be more annoyed and less lethargic, but that orgasm, on top of whatever Mormo had done to her, had wiped what remained of her energy. Fara slowly left Mormo's floor for her own, heading for her bedroom.

Fortunately, she didn't run into anyone on the way.

After cleaning up—embarrassingly having to change into clean panties—she forced herself to put Varu from her mind and searched out Onvyr. She found him in the spa room, looking around at everything.

The spa room consisted of a sauna, steam room, and a few massage tables. Oils, perfumes, and lotions sat on a counter against a wall.

The room had been painted a soft beige with hints of green. Several plants scattered around the corners, counters, and tables made the room feel surprisingly like home. As did the rocks embedded in the floor.

Her brother saw her and smiled. Clad in human clothing like her, in jeans and a tee-shirt, his hair combed back, light fae features no longer hidden, he comforted just by being normal.

Well, normal for Onvyr.

"I found a bird flying around in here, and he said the weirdo two-leg running the place imported these lava rocks from Efnesvir in Nidavellir." Nidavellir—the land of the dwarves, had stone Gaia had created especially for the dwarven smiths in their gem capital—Efnesvir. The minerals making up the stone existed nowhere else.

She walked barefoot over the slew of stones set in a pattern on a path, from one wall to another.

"The bird said the weird white two-legs, I think he means

Mormo, called it a reflexology path." He frowned. "What's that, exactly?"

"It's like massage for your feet." Enchanted by the feel of magic she'd always wanted to sample but had never gotten the permission to see, as dusk elves were usually killed on site on most fae lands, Fara walked over the stone and asked it all manner of questions, absorbing the knowledge and feel for the potential it held within.

"These are some of Gaia's favorites," she said, in awe, and continued to walk back and forth over the path while her brother investigated the sauna and steam room.

He came out of the steam room with his shirt in hand, his black chest covered with moisture, his long white hair slicked back from his face. His grin looked so real, so much something of the past, that her heart swelled. Happiness bubbled inside, and she laughed as she encouraged her brother to follow her over the magical stones.

Walking behind her, he marveled at the small rock trail and challenged her to move over it with one foot, hopping, then skipping, then somersaulting. Playful Onvyr, his eyes sparkling with mirth, seemed whole again, something he hadn't been in a very long time.

Tears filled her eyes, a wonder that she should find such peace here, of all places, among death-bringers.

She turned to go back over the stones when her brother stopped suddenly. She glanced up and saw his smile vanish. The warrior in him glared at her with a killing expression.

"Onvyr?"

"Why do you smell of strigoi?"

"Ah, well, we were up with Mormo, Varu and me, and we tripped. Kind of." *Into each other's mouths.*

He growled, "I'll kill him," turned, and raced out of the room.

She followed, hearing a chirp that must have been that bird

he'd talked to but that she hadn't seen. Such an odd place, this house that gave sanctuary to vampires, Mormo, a human servant, and animals.

Hurrying after Onvyr, she saw him head down the bad corridor—the one that led past the vampires' rooms.

Taking a deep breath for courage, she let it out and hoped to not run into anyone on her way. She saw her brother rush down a stairwell at the end of the hall. Great, the basement, where most of them spent their time.

She got halfway down the hall before a large vampire with shaggy dark hair intercepted her.

"Well, *gute Nacht*, sweet fae." He smiled, showing sharp teeth. "Are you my breakfast this fine evening?"

"Yes, hello." She pushed past him, ignoring his surprise. She didn't have time to be amused or afraid, too concerned for her brother, should he find Varu.

"Why do we run?" the vampire, likely a nachzehrer from the accent, asked.

"My brother is looking for Varu."

"Ah, then I'll go with you. I look forward to any battles Varu might have." He chuckled as he walked *way* too closely behind her.

They descended into a large room, the center of a T of connecting hallways.

The vampire with her put up a hand and paused. He cocked his head. "That way."

She followed him, aware she walked behind a nachzehrer willingly, and ended up in a spacious gymnasium. In the center of which, her brother argued with the blond, Rolf, and one of the vampires who had stalked her in the woods. A tall, long-haired male with regal features and a disdainful expression.

"We owe you nothing, vile creature," the snotty one said.

Her brother shrugged then punched him in the face so fast and with so much strength, he lifted the vampire off his feet and shoved him through the air into the wall, where he landed. Hard.

Everyone stared in silence.

Rolf started clapping. "Oh, man. That was epic. I mean, something I will take to my grave. Damn it. Does anyone have a cell phone? Anyone get that on video?"

The vampire her brother had smashed stood tall, straightened his broken nose—she heard a sharp snap and cringed—and launched himself at Onvyr.

They fought with snarling savagery, but when she tried to move to intercept, the charming one, Duncan, appeared and held her back.

"Hold on, love. Let the boys get it out of their systems."

"He'll kill him." Her brother or the snotty vamp, she wasn't sure whom she meant. She only knew she didn't want her brother getting hurt.

"Well now. That's an interesting perspective," Rolf said as he joined them. "Who do we think is going to kill who?"

"Whom," a taller, broader vampire said. "Twenty on the dark elf."

"You're on, Orion. Twenty on Khent," the nachzehrer said.

"Khent to win." Duncan shook his head, his accent odd. British, maybe? "Khent's a right prick when he's riled. And that fae broke his nose." Duncan laughed. "Outstanding."

"I though we were supposed to be getting ready to patrol. Didn't Mormo say to gear up and head to Tacoma?" Varu asked as he entered the gym. He paused at sight of Fara, and his eyes turned red.

Unfortunately, so focused on Fara, he hadn't noticed her brother toss Khent aside like an unwanted pebble and attack in a rush.

But Varu had spectacular reflexes. At the last moment, he dodged the sharp nails aimed at his neck and powered up, catching Onvyr in the gut with a powerful punch, shoving him into the air.

Several feet up.

"Oh, that was quite brilliant." Duncan seemed to approve.

Not done, her brother screamed a battle cry as he arrowed down with speed. He crashed into Varu, and the two rolled and struck at each other so fast she couldn't see who was winning.

"Now that's entertainment." Orion slapped Khent on the back.

The arrogant vampire glared and shrugged Orion's hand away. Then he turned his bad attitude on Fara. "You. Why am I not surprised?"

"I didn't do anything." *Except maul your buddy, Varu, with my mouth. And body. I'm despicable. Anyone but that vampire, Fara! Remember who his father is!*

Khent shook his head. "Why do I not believe you?" He stared into her eyes, but she didn't feel him try to mesmerize her. "I think they fight because of you."

Great. Now the others were looking at her. Standing a little close, apparently, because Varu appeared and yanked her away, putting himself between the others and Fara before her brother barreled into him.

She heard an *oof* before the two were plowing into another wall, leaving a massive dent.

"See?" Rolf rubbed his hands together. "Varu's going to win, but to make it better odds, I say Onvyr lasts more than fifteen minutes."

The group of lethal idiots—gambling, really?—continued to banter about their bets as the fighting wore on. She worried her brother might get really hurt. For a few minutes. But as he continued to fight with more and more ferocity, she worried he might die. The vampires with her didn't seem so amused as they watched the battle grow intense.

"Mormo said we have to keep him alive," Rolf muttered and

rubbed his head. He looked so like her kind, she expected to see pointed ears when his hair shifted, but they were rounded instead.

Wait. "Keep who alive?"

"Yeah." Orion, huge, muscled, and intimidating, gave her an apologetic look. "Sorry, pretty fae, but Varu, as annoying as he is, has to stay in one piece. The dark fae has to go."

"Stop." She darted past him toward the two fighting, despite knowing the effort a futile one, and had a thought. Dropping to the ground, she put her hand flat and closed her eyes. Feeling the welcome touch of sentient stone, not Gaia's, but someone else who understood the earth, she asked for a favor.

"What the hell?" one of the vampires said.

She opened her eyes to see the tiled flooring cracked and broken as a funnel of rock encased both combatants, holding them away from each other.

Onvyr struggled to calm himself, but Varu stood without moving, glaring a hole through her forehead.

Ugh. She liked him better when they were kissing. At the thought, she blushed, and Varu's glare faded, replaced by a more thoughtful expression.

"Onvyr, relax," she said and pushed a pulse of fae touch through the rock, causing it to crumble.

At that, he let go of his tension and sagged. "Oh. Whoops." He glanced at Varu, saw the bloodied face healing, and grinned. "But I'm so not sorry. Next time I'll kick your fucking ass."

Khent, unfortunately, wasn't restrained. He walked up to her brother and punched him in the face.

The crack made her wince.

"I can kill you and bring you back more times than you'd like to imagine. Don't push me, elf." Khent shared that glare with her, then stormed from the gym.

Rolf whistled. "I said more than fifteen minutes, but we had an unfair interruption in play."

"No way. You owe me money." Orion cracked a fist into his palm. "And we'll add that to the two hundred I'm still waiting on."

"And my fifty," Kraft added, the two glaring at Rolf.

But at least the attention had shifted from her brother. She hurried to him and watched him wipe the blood from his mouth. Kraft appeared next to him and smiled.

"No," she said, instinctively calling on the Bloode Stone for support. "Mormo said he's off limits." Not exactly, but she'd protect her brother. And they needed to have a talk about not attacking the greater threat every other day. Man, they had to escape before her brother ended up killing himself. Suicide by vampire.

Kraft glared, shook his head, then took a step back. "Fine. But Mormo is a shitty boss. I'm just saying."

She kept a mental link to the stone, drawing on its power even as it started to burn her deep inside. She wasn't a vampire and the stone, though it liked her, knew it.

Varu gripped her upper arm and tugged her to his side. "We need to talk."

"Oh. They're talking, guys." Rolf tittered, and the others laughed with him. She thought he might have something wrong with him, mentally. He winked at her and walked away with the others. "We'll be waiting in the garage, Varujan of the Night Bloode. Yo, Khent, bro, let's partner up."

"I'm not a bro," she heard Khent complain. "You sorry bastard. Get your hands off me."

Her brother looked from her to Varu, glaring at the hand on her arm. Then he glanced up and smiled. "Oh, hey."

An owl, of all things, flew in circles before landing on her brother's shoulder.

"What's that doing in here?" Where had it come from?

Varu sighed. "Don't ask. We have all manner of creatures

around here." He tightened his hold on her arm, not hurting, but not allowing her to escape. "Including mouthy fae."

Onvyr stepped out of the pile of rock, and Fara asked it to reset, pleased when it reformed as though it had never been apart. "Hey Fara, we're going upstairs. I'll get something for you to eat in the kitchen. Bella's back." He stroked the owl tenderly on its breast and loped away, leaving her with Varu without a qualm.

From wanting to kill Varu because she smelled like him, to leaving her alone with the killer. Her brother was giving her a headache.

She swallowed. "Um, you wanted to talk?" She wished Varu would let her go, then tried to use the stone again.

When he released her, she didn't know if it was because she'd controlled him or not.

"Yes, female. Talk. Explain your actions from earlier." His eyes turned red, as they tended to when around her, apparently. "When do you plan to finish what you started?"

"I... *What?*"

V aru was glad strigoi didn't feel embarrassment. Because if they did, he'd surely be turning red in the face. He had no idea why he'd ask that question when he had no intention of touching her again. Sexually. He did still plan to feed on her of course. She tasted like nothing else.

But Varu was no freak to mix food and sex. Typically, his kind only indulged in sexual pursuits to breed or when keyed up after a hunt. Then there were those, like Duncan, who were more sexual than others. Strigoi, as a rule, mated to breed offspring. Having spent so much time at war, he hadn't had much time in the past century to indulge in pleasure. Plus, the act involved losing control, trusting his partner.

Oh, he could function well enough. He knew how to please a female, had more than his share of bedmates eager to have him. Not out of any sense of self-aggrandizement, but he knew he had the looks most of his kind did, to better lure prey. Plus, he held a great deal of power, or at least, he had when back with the Crimson Veil.

Here, unfortunately, he was at Mormo's beck and call.

So, for a male who didn't want to lose control and had no

intention of sexing up his next snack, asking for a repeat of earlier —when he'd come in his pants like an untried fledgling—that question was ludicrous.

But seeing how unnerved Fara was, he thought maybe he should pursue the matter. She seemed as anxious about repeating their intimacy as he was.

He'd do better to make her think he'd planned their rendezvous upstairs all along. *Tactics, my boy, will take you far. It's about the long game.* Words his grandfather had once told him that stuck.

"I don't know, dusk elf. Seems to me you need more of what I can give you." He looked her over, past her lovely body to her neck—a favorite grazing spot—to her full lips, and stared into her eyes. Yes, he'd bed her and forget her. But the pleasure would more than make up for her tendency to irritate him.

Obey me, female.

But instead of wrapping his will around hers, he felt as if his intent slid off her. Like finding a slick surface, he could find no purchase in her mind.

He scowled. How could a mere lesser being put him out of her mind?

"Seems to me like maybe *you* lost control, not me," she had the temerity to boast.

"Me? You came so sweetly, Faraine, that you pulled me with you. Your little death could do no less than bewitch a strigoi."

"Little death?" She frowned.

"Your orgasm." He smirked and laughed when her pale gray skin sparked with a delicate lilac. His heart raced, and something inside him gave as he stared at feminine perfection. Because yes, he without question wanted to bed her. To slide inside her, with lips and cock and mind, and take and taste until he sated himself on the beauty before him. "Ah, Fara. You will be mine."

"Dream on, buddy." She poked him in the chest, and he laughed again.

But inside he didn't feel amused. He felt confused and unnerved. Because Varu didn't do trust and mirth and sex. He planned, he strategized, and he decimated his opponents.

Faraine was clearly on the other side of the battle line with a power over him he didn't understand.

"Ah, so you think to challenge me, female?"

"Yes, *male,* I do." Her scowl faded, and she blinked in befuddlement. "I mean, no. There is no challenge. I'm not sleeping with you."

"I said nothing about sleep." He gave her the grin that had seduced more women than he could count... back in the day, when he'd been younger and into such physical pleasures.

"I. You. I just...." She stormed away from him, or tried to, but he grabbed her by the hand and spun her around.

"You will stay away from the others if you value your safety." He forced himself to shrug. "But if you don't care, by all means, keep prancing around with that pretty neck all bared and lovely."

She put hands around her throat. "Back off, strigoi."

She sounded angry. And aroused. He breathed her in, taken with the warm musk of her need.

A problem. He needed distance. Now. Varu had no need for affection. *And when the hell did affection enter this absurd picture?*

He tried to shake off his odd sensation of communion, heard the soft song of the Bloode Stone, and glared. "You're using the stone."

She couldn't hide her guilt, though she tried to. "I am not."

"Witch."

"Fae, you mean."

He swore at himself for being such an idiot and stormed away before he did something he'd regret. Like kiss her again. With his luck, he'd end up fucking her on the gym floor where he'd once lost several fingers.

FARA LET herself collapse as soon as he left. All alone, she stared at the ceiling, taking in the moonlight and the stars through a large, open skylight.

What the heck was wrong with her? Being near him, teasing, taunting, she'd wanted nothing more than to kiss him again. A monster related to the butcher who'd tortured her brother for years, who would kill her just as soon as he could. And she just had to grind against that particular strigoi.

She closed her eyes, trying to recall the peace that had come from her walk across the dwarven stones.

But peace refused to come.

She sighed and got to her feet, forced herself to think calm thoughts, and went upstairs to rejoin her brother. She had no urge to see what else lay in this basement level, swearing she could hear other people laughing and talking though no one entered the gym or the corridor leading to it.

Once back upstairs, she felt an odd shift, as if she'd gone through an ethereal passage of some kind. Yet she found nothing but moonlight streaming through the glass wall by the dining room.

"Hey, Fara. What's up?" Bella winked at her as she added a plate of food, something with a lot of meat, in front of Onvyr.

To her relief, her brother seemed to be healing as he ate, his metabolism offset by the speed-healing common to all warriors after a battle.

Fara noticed something different about Bella though. "Ah, your nails. They're pink."

Bella wiggled her fingers. "What do you think? I'm calling it vampire-love. Because it's pink, and we have a ton of vampires around the place."

"Um, nice?" Fara joined them at the kitchen island. "But is it wise to antagonize them?"

"It is when they're not here." She laughed. "Mr. Mormo sent them off on a hunting mission."

"What exactly are they hunting?"

"No clue. But he always seems to have jobs he needs them to do." She looked around. "Where's Varu?"

Fara forced herself not to feel awkward. "He joined them."

"Oh. I was supposed to help you two find a place to work. Do you want to be in a bright study or a dark library? Looking at you, I picture something earthy. Lots of plants, soil, rock. And light wood."

"Yes." Fara realized Bella didn't seem at all put off by her fae appearance. Or her brother's, for that matter. "You've seen fae before?"

"Yep. Though usually like him." She nodded at Onvyr. "Dark or light. Not so many gray. I think I saw one dusk elf before. You guys are pretty rare, huh?"

Fara nodded. Rare because her kind weren't allowed to exist.

Onvyr grinned and continued to eat. Boy, could he eat.

"Anyway, Mr. Mormo told me to tell you he's busy on another job for the mistress, but if you have any questions to ask the owl." She nodded to the large white owl with yellow eyes. Onvyr's friend.

The owl flapped its wings and flew away, disappearing around the corner of the living room.

Fara looked back to see Bella staring at her brother. Bella saw her noticing and blushed. "I can't help it. He's hot."

"I am, truly." Onvyr smirked.

Fara would need to warn him to steer clear of Mormo's staff.

After seeing how creepy the magician could be, and how power-ful, she had no urge to annoy him ever again.

Varu had scared her at first. He'd been terrifying, especially because he looked like Atanase. But since getting to know him better, especially through the stone, she didn't think him evil. Murderous, maybe. He was strigoi—it was in his nature to hunt. But the Bloode Stone softened her perception of him. Perhaps dangerously so.

She'd need to be on her guard. And good gods, to never, ever kiss him again. What had she been thinking?

The stone sang to her, a short sharp note of longing.

Oh boy. She needed something to bolster her nerves. "Hey, Bella. Do you have anything sweet to eat?"

Bella looked away from Onvyr. "Sweet? Sister, you came to the right place. Pie, cake, something cold, or—"

"All of the above."

"Gotcha."

A FEW HOURS LATER, Fara sat in a room across from the spa, studying the dagger and the Bloode Stone, which had reappeared on its own, once again embedded in the blade's hilt.

She brushed her fingers against it now and then, careful to keep her contact brief and open, welcoming. She wanted nothing but to acknowledge its magic and might, appreciative, helpful.

The stone liked her help and her praise. An arrogant stone, she thought with humor. But then, most power gems with any kind of sentience were.

When she listened close, she thought she could make out words as it sang to Varu. It really liked him. *A lot.*

She thought about all she'd learned from Mormo, about Varu's link to Ambrogio, which shocked her. And she had to wonder why this stone was so much bigger than the other five she'd found. They were the size of sunflower seeds, small shards in appearance, but just as red and feeling of a similar footprint of power.

Yet she knew Atanase would want the biggest for himself.

She had seen what a Bloode Stone could do in the wrong vampire's hands. A draugr, one Atanase had hand-picked to test out the power of the first stone she'd found for him, had been given the gem in the middle of a room full of strigoi. By rights, they should have torn him to pieces when Atanase pulled back his power over them.

But the draugr had held that stone in hand, and it had accepted him. Not like this Bloode Stone pined after Varu, but with a soft reception nonetheless.

She'd been stunned and terrified to see what she'd done— putting such power in the hands of a killer. And then bad turned to worse.

Atanase had thanked the draugr, taken back the stone, and smiled.

As if a switch had been thrown, the savage strigoi leaped on the draugr and tore him to pieces in seconds. Bits of flesh and bone scattered as strigoi who normally didn't eat their own sucked down his blood and destroyed him.

She'd stared, sickened, and flinched as Atanase wrapped a long-fingered hand around her arm, his claws sharp, deadly. "Careful, pet, or I'll let them have *you*. Now prove yourself useful. Find me the rest."

So she had. Year by year, working without fail, never stopping, searching all around the world to find those remaining Bloode Stones. And each time, after handing one over, she died a little inside, knowing Atanase grew more powerful with each acquisition. He wanted chaos, war, dominance. An end to any kind of life worth living.

She'd decided to quit altogether. He only had three stones,

after all. Her death would be a just reward for what she'd done. The torture had been unbearable but a just penance.

And then he'd captured her brother.

She sighed and stared at the stone, asking it what to do.

But the silly thing only put the thought of Varu in her mind, offering her a chance to join him once more. To enter his mind and settle into his bones as he did whatever the others had been ordered to do.

She wanted to spy, badly, but he'd feel it now. In tune with the Bloode Stone, he'd have no problem sensing her intrusion. And then he'd make her pay. With her luck, the gem would let him. And then what? Death by exsanguination?

Fara cringed. No, she'd do better to focus on how to use the stone to bend Varu to her will. Which meant figuring out how to get rid of Atanase and put Varu in power. And then of course, she had to figure out how to destroy the gem without getting herself or her brother killed. Because if Varu decided to keep the gem to rule, she'd only be trading one monster for another.

In the end, she'd still be that stupid dusk elf who'd managed to destroy civilization, one race at a time, while the vampires added the magir to their human livestock and crushed anyone who dared stand up to them. Gods and all.

CHAPTER SIXTEEN

"Why are you here? You're on my nerves," Orion grumbled as they met with the Seattle Bloode lieutenant on neutral ground. While the others had been tasked with apprehending a thief and picking up a package from one of Mormo's witch friends, Varu and Orion had to handle the upir clan.

With the waning full moon overhead, the hour a quarter to midnight, and the breeze off the Sound punishing with the cold, the meeting couldn't have been more perfect.

Varu had a need to kill. The Seattle Bloode clan would do nicely. Maybe not the lieutenant, since Mormo would bitch about what a waste that might be. But a lower tier upir, surely, if the lieutenant was stupid enough to bring any. By rights, members of different clans felt a need to fight. But Varu and Orion were stronger than most, able to contain their bloodlust. Usually.

Varu growled, "Just shut up and let me do the talking."

"That's all we need, you being diplomatic." Orion let out a dramatic sigh. "What's the deal? You were staring at the elf like you wanted to do her right there. You hot for the fae or what?"

"Keep your voice down, jackass," Varu hissed. "With what

she brought us—" *the Bloode Stone* remained unsaid, "—I'm sure she's on someone's radar. And we don't know whose."

"Sorry." Orion groaned. "I'm hungry."

Varu did his best to ignore the stone's song, which kept reminding him how good it had felt to kiss Fara. Not remembering the way her heart had been his to destroy with one punch, or her throat his to rip out with one bite. But how soft her skin had felt. How warm she'd been. How sweet. Funny how that song started to sound like actual words that made sense.

His cock started to rise, and he swore as he tried to get a hold on his sudden desire.

Was the female controlling him from a distance? He concentrated on the stone but felt nothing but its inherent power, nothing fae coming from it but a longing to hold her once more.

Damn it all.

"You okay?" Orion raised a brow. "Scared of what's coming? Or scared another of us will take the sweet offering back at the house while you're gone?"

I see one sneer or hear one comment about Fara and I'll end him. Kin or no kin.

Before Orion could utter his last words, a faction of upir arrived. A dozen strong vampires with an ax to grind arrived on the abandoned pier.

What a moron. Bringing that many upir with him was sure to end in several deaths.

"We want the elf."

Varu felt his bloode boil and forced himself—and that blasted stone—to calm down. "I am Varujan of the Night Bloode." *I hate that fucking name.* "Who are you?"

The upir frowned and opened his mouth, but a taller upir dragged him back and shoved him at his brethren. "Put him in check or I will."

Varu liked this one's style, pleased that at least one of the gathered upir wasn't such a hothead. Vampires loved to fight, true, but intelligence always won in the end. One of the few things he and his father agreed upon.

"I am Eric, Lieutenant of the Seattle Bloode. Well met, Varujan. We know of the Night Bloode, as well as the Crimson Veil, and are honored to speak with you."

Huh. Now *that* was how he should always be addressed. With respect and a tinge of fear.

He glanced at Orion, who rolled his eyes. Yeah, such a dick.

Varu turned back to the upir. "Eric. Why did you want this meeting?"

Eric looked strong but young. In his eyes, a world-weary expression had yet to develop. The upir looked excited, doing his best to appear cruel and stern but not quite landing it. "A male dark elf killed one of our own, a fledgling, not past fifty winters."

"Just say he's fifty years old, Jesus," Orion muttered.

The lieutenant's eyes narrowed, and Varu held back a surprising laugh. After that mess earlier with Fara, he hadn't thought he'd feel amusement so soon. But damned if he wasn't starting to enjoy himself. It helped that the upir wanted Onvyr and not Varu's prey.

"So a dark elf killed your upir. What of it? That's not our business."

"But it is," Eric continued, and his eyes flashed red. "We witnessed you track him and a woman and take them from our territory. Without our permission."

Orion perked up. "We totally did." He cracked his knuckles and his neck. "Like stealing prey from an upir. A cake walk."

Eric's expression darkened. The upir with him bared fangs and extended their nails to claws. "Give us the elf and the woman and you may go free."

Orion laughed. "Seriously? Come on. At least tell us we'll go home injured but alive. Not just free. That's lame."

"Orion." Varu agreed but wanted to test something.

That he and the lieutenant hadn't already gone for each other's throats was unusual, though Varu was strong enough to hold himself back, and Eric just might have hidden depths. Orion should have mowed through them all too, but instead he made jokes and sat back. Yet he hadn't realized anything was amiss. The upir clan hadn't either, and Varu doubted any of them had the fortitude to hold back their animosity on their own.

Is this you? Did you settle them down for me? he asked the Bloode Stone, which responded with a laughing *Yes* before singing about longing and sex and vampire babies.

Which freaked Varu the hell out.

Apparently, the stone didn't like his attitude. The song receded.

Orion's expression turned demonic, and he pounced on the closest upir.

Oddly, Varu still felt no sense of hate for the enemy clan. "Alive. Injured but alive," he yelled as the vryko slashed through the upir like tearing through paper. Embarrassing for the upir and more than a little scary for anyone who had never seen Orion move before.

Varu stood back, studying the skirmish, and knew he would never want Orion for an enemy. Unless he wanted a really good workout. Then sure, he'd have to kill the bastard, but he'd later be sorry to end such a skilled fighter.

With a sigh, Varu called on the stone and apologized.

It flared in his mind, and he imagined its power pouring over the combatants as Orion landed just one more punch to Eric's face.

"Not really putting much effort into this, Varu," he apologized. "That okay?"

Surprised at how amenable the normally obstinate vryko

could be, Varu saw more to commend the Bloode Stone than he'd realized. *You're a wonder.*

A red glow, and how he knew it was red he had no idea, but a warm red glow suffused him.

Orion blinked. "Your eyes are shining."

Varu sighed. "It's the stone. Sorry." *Can you dim it a little?* he asked it.

Sure. It smiled with pleasure in his brain, the answer clear. He had another thought. *Hey, can you soften up Fara for me?* He envisioned her obeying him and being pleasant like Orion.

It chuckled. *You're on your own.*

Huh. Hadn't expected that.

Varu settled things with the lieutenant, focusing on the now. "Look, we've taken care of the elf for you. But our patriarch felt badly about your loss, so he's sending your patriarch the potion he's been looking for."

Eric blinked and said, garbled, "He's been unable to find that potion for fifty years." He massaged his jaw, trying to realign his face after Orion had crushed it. "Please send our thanks."

"Yeah, Mormo's a real peach," Orion drawled. Then he laughed. "He's actually a huge asshole, but we'll tell him you said thanks."

Eric grinned. "So's ours. But I never said that." The others with him started joking, as if a rival clan from another tribe wasn't standing near them.

And Varu knew he could never, *ever*, let the Bloode Stone fall into the wrong hands. Not because a battle to rule the world wouldn't be glorious, because it would. But because he liked order and discipline. And vampires running amuck would be nothing but chaos.

They left the upir to join the others out in town.

"Mormo really is an asshole," Orion said as they hopped into the car.

In a rare good mood, Varu had no problem letting him drive. "Not arguing."

"But I probably shouldn't have said that to another clan." Orion turned to Varu instead of starting the car. The big vampire scowled. "The stone. We should have been ass-deep in blood and bones. But we joked and talked before I beat some respect into them." Orion looked him over. "Is it in your jacket?"

Varu had left his jacket at home, not in the car, accounting for Orion's confusion at seeing Varu in a simple tee-shirt, no dagger in sight. "No. It's at the house."

Orion's eyes narrowed. "You don't have to be holding or touching it?"

"I guess not." He paused. "It's still singing to me. I think.... I think it's alive."

"Fuck fuck *fuck.*" Orion growled. "Do you realize how powerful that is? How incredibly *bad* it would be if someone like Ivanoff or Atanase had it?"

"Atanase's my sire, so yeah, I do know."

Orion blinked. "Seriously? *He's* your father? But, ah, he's a killer. I mean that in a good way. And a psycho. I mean that in a bad way."

Varu sighed. "I know. Trust me."

"Right. He's your sire." Orion started the car and turned toward Kraft's last location. After a minute or two, he added, "Him being your dad explains so much."

"Shut it, vryko."

"Roger that."

ATANASE FINGERED the small Bloode Stones in the locket around his neck, the power never far from his grasp. He regretted his earlier outburst, but Iancu would heal in a few days. And likely his hand would grow back if he could get his hands—*no, just the one,* he thought with humor—on that potion the sorcerers had brewed them a few months ago.

Probably.

Unfortunately, not all strigoi were alike. Some, like Atanase and Varu, could regenerate limbs. Others needed magical help to do so. While still others had enhanced senses that never left them, even if they lost vital sensory organs.

Eh. Iancu would either heal or he wouldn't. Atanase didn't much care.

After enjoying the blood of a few virgins and one especially spicy nonvirgin, he went back to the cell where his problems had started and made plans to fix said problems permanently— namely, a fitting end to a troublesome set of dusk elves.

But sadly, he had more on his mind than reveling in torture and bloodplay. He had a witch to see. With any luck, she could scry the location of his missing prisoner.

His blood boiled just thinking about how long Onvyr had been missing, no doubt laughing about his escape from a master vampire too stupid to realize he'd been gone for *four fucking months.*

No one but Atanase and Iancu had known of Onvyr's presence deep in the bowels of the castle dungeon, away from everything and everyone living in his territory. So who had broken him out? Not Iancu, because the general would have devoured the dusk elf, not let him escape. And the devil knew Iancu had enough brains to not report a disappearance he himself had caused.

The only person who would have a reason to free that particular prisoner was Faraine. But she should have been far away, working to find that last stone for him. The master stone for a master vampire. From what she'd described, this one should be twenty times the size of the other ones. The most powerful for the strongest vampire in existence.

After killing his father all those years ago, Atanase had been lower than only one vampire in terms of power, a reaper in the Sudan, one of the mighty Sons of Osiris. But a battle with Ra had ended in a blight on one of the clans, and in an attempt to save his kin, the master had unknowingly fallen into a trap set by several gods and a collection of magir powerful enough to topple even Atanase.

Atanase knew better than to sacrifice himself for anyone. And look at him now. Master of the strigoi, stronger and older than any other master alive today. Even the gods worried about the mighty Atanase of the Crimson Veil.

His heart thundered. *Everyone bows to me. They fear me, obey me, and know their place.*

He stared at the empty cell, the vague echo of pain and the scent of faded fae blood all that remained of his prisoner. His toy. "*My fucking pet,*" he screamed, incensed and so furious he hammered a fist at the ground.

And blew a hole in the dungeon with his rage, his Bloode Stones thoughtful enough to focus his anger into power. Fortunately, the hole blew through rock and earth and didn't disrupt the many strigoi above. Not out of any conscience or affection for his people, but because they would be costly to replace.

Yet replace them he would if necessary. Atanase's patience had come to an end.

Still in a cold rage, he returned to his receiving office and called for Mihai. But as he moved, he realized something else in him had changed. He clutched the locket, feeling with his bloode, and nodded. He'd gained the ability to teleport and to send a telekinetic wave through solid earth.

Perhaps losing Onvyr had been preordained, that sudden rage

unlocking the energy inside him, all thanks to the Bloode Stones resting against his chest.

Enthused and once again in a good mood, he sat behind his desk, contemplating the riches of his library, the ancient mahogany and burnished gold accents of his furniture. The many paintings and sculptures of himself and his kind, replaying the strigoi's many victories. As he waited for Mihai, he pressed a button to connect to his secretary once more.

"Yes, Master?" Pavel entered and bowed his head in deference.

"Pavel, send for Iancu."

Pavel obeyed and returned right away. "Anything else, Master? Can I get you something to drink, perhaps?"

"Ah, Pavel, you are so good to me." Atanase stroked the arms of his chair, the handcrafted wooden ends shaped like ravens with inset rubies for eyes. "How long have you served me?"

Pavel kept his gaze trained on the floor. "For one thousand and forty-seven years, Master. It is my honor to serve you."

"Yes, it is." Atanase chuckled. "Good strigoi. You've earned my thanks. You deserve a break from service. But first, bring Codrin to me."

Pavel gaped. "O-of course, Master. Anything you wish."

"Yes, yes. Then you can go and have a bite of one of the fresh new students we picked up today. A few of them have yet to stop screaming."

Pavel's eyes brightened. "You are too good to me, Master."

Atanase watched his man leave with a spring in his step and waited for his patriarch, his witch, and a weakened general to arrive.

Pavel returned with Codrin at the same time Iancu joined them.

His general looked almost gray, the loss of blood and limb,

and that eye and half his face, taking its toll. Iancu, though battered, appeared annoyed and obviously alive.

"Master Atanase, I am here to serve." Iancu bowed.

"Codrin is here, Master." Pavel bowed his head as he entered with a younger strigoi next to him.

Codrin bowed low. Lower than Pavel had. Hmm.

Atanase teleported to Pavel and ripped out his heart. He waited until the others understood what had happened, giving them a moment to adjust to his greatness, then sank his fangs into the pulsating organ and drank as his faithful servant died a true-death.

Codrin and Iancu froze.

Atanase finished a mouthful of rich bloode and said, "Such a good servant for so long. It was time he had a vacation." He laughed, delighted he'd managed to once again surprise his general.

Codrin continued to stare at Pavel in horror. A fledgling then, too young to hide his emotions. Atanase would have to change that.

"You, boy, are my new head servant. Dispose of the body." He took a last sip from the heart then tossed it to the floor. "That too." He turned to Iancu. "Now, it's time to get some plans in place." And fix what Atanase's inattention had broken.

He sighed, knowing he had only himself to blame. In his arrogance, he'd thought he could contain a powerful warrior fae in a cell made to contain strong magir.

But Onvyr of the Folde was no mere dusk elf. The son of two rival warriors, he'd been born to fight, the spitting image of his father with the conviction of his mother. Drinking him down had been just one joy in a pleasure of perversions.

Ah, the things he and Onvyr had shared. To his surprise, he found he missed the crazed dusk elf. Thinking he could talk to animals. That the spirit of Gaia existed, and that it existed outside of fae lands?

He chuckled and decided to kill Faraine in front of her brother. That death would cause Onvyr pain from which he'd never recover.

Even better, Atanase would take his time with the beauty. Her torture all those years ago had been too brief, her agony a symphony he had often replayed in his mind, a lovely interlude which never failed to soothe him.

Back then, he'd been loath to break her, eager to get his hands on a legendary Bloode Stone, three of which she'd already provided. And now look, she'd found five of them, with the sixth on the way.

Supposedly.

His ire dissipated as he realized the full import of what she'd done, for Onvyr's escape could be the responsibility of no one else.

Faraine had bested *him.* The greatest of vampire masters. An impossible occurrence.

Yet so was teleportation and his new ability to cut through earth and rock with a thought.

He wondered if he might just be able to break a few rules once he had the master stone, to do what no other vampire had done before. Might he not be able to breed more progeny? Someone more suitable than Varujan to uphold Atanase's legacy? To follow in the footsteps of mighty Ambrogio? To equal, no, to *surpass* his forefathers?

Thinking of all that power and fame aroused him, and Atanase decided to put his cock to good use when he had the little dusk elf under his roof once more.

Mihai knocked before entering, noticed the blood staining Atanase's face, and nodded. "It's good that you fed, Master." His expression didn't change as he noticed Codrin cleaning up the mess of dead strigoi.

"Yes, it is." Atanase smiled, and his mirth increased when he heard Iancu growl at Mihai. "Ah, general, I think I can see a milky white eye replacing the one you lost. Bet it pains you though."

"More than I would have thought, Master."

"Good. I gathered you all here because I have a plan to retrieve my property." He told them what he had in mind.

Mihai nodded. "I'll get our best hunters together. Should I go with them?" He stared at Atanase's fist wrapped around his locket.

That's right. I'm an even greater power than I was before. You understand. "No. I want you here. I have some things I must attend to. General, speed up that healing. I don't care what you have to do. We don't have time for weakness. Gather the Five." What he'd been calling the five clan patriarchs to whom he'd previously leant the stones' power. "We're going to war with the lycans."

And once I've roasted and blooded the wolves, I'll have more than enough power to feast on your soul, young Faraine. For a very, very long time.

CHAPTER SEVENTEEN

T wo nights later, in the early evening, Fara sat next to Varu in an airy workspace and studied the Bloode Stone. He'd been absent last night, doing something else for Mormo. Fara and Onvyr had spent their time moving around the house, looking for a way to escape, but found nothing.

She glanced at the strigoi, annoyed with all the silence. He'd been with her since before sunset, apparently not having to sleep during the day like the others. As soon as he'd sat down, he'd informed her they needed to figure out how to control the stone. Yeah, like that was news to her. She'd been spending her time alone studying the sentient gem and going through several texts from Mormo's library to help her figure it out but had hit nothing yet.

Onvyr hadn't been allowed to stay with her, as he had the previous days. Instead, he'd been escorted downstairs by Rolf with an excuse that the dark elf needed "better training."

No matter how many times she'd asked Varu what that meant, he ignored her.

The big oaf.

It disturbed her that she continued to dream about him and his kisses. She felt feverish to hold him again while he seemed content to ignore her. The Bloode Stone, on the other hand, hummed to her, seeming overjoyed to be near her and Varu at the same time.

It kept wanting to seep deeper inside her, but worried Varu might use it to control her, she kept herself guarded against it. And after three hours of silence and shielding, she'd had enough.

"What do you expect to get out of this?"

He blinked and looked away from the stone. "What?"

"This. I'm just getting a headache."

"Because you won't let it in."

"Oh, and you have?" She looked at him, wishing she could stop lingering over his features.

Thick, soft, black hair brushed back off his face. His dark eyes flashed with red, and that handsome though stern expression never seemed to soften, even when he smiled.

Unfortunately, his grins turned him from darkly handsome to breathtaking. And she didn't like it.

The more she studied him, the more she thought he looked less and less like Atanase. Varu could be cruel, but that meanness didn't linger. He was a killer, yes, but he hadn't killed indiscriminately, at least, not according to Onvyr, who got his information from that snowy owl that continued to hang around the house.

Varu looked back down at the gem, which rested on the table away from the dagger. "I've bonded with the Bloode Stone. We've come to an agreement."

"Oh?"

He licked his left fang and smiled, but the expression didn't reach his eyes. "Perhaps we need a break."

Him and her? Him and the Bloode Stone? "A break?"

"Yes. Come with me." He stared into her eyes, his turning a bright, burning red.

She had never seen a man so attractive in all her life. Fara smiled and rose, taking a step toward him. And stopped herself from taking another with a huge burst of willpower. *You, be nice,* she mentally roared at the stone. *I saved you from going back to a cruel master, remember.* It sighed, gave her an emotional hug, and retreated, allowing her to inure herself to Varu's power.

He blinked, swore under his breath, and forced another smile.

"Nice try." She shook her head, disappointed. "I'm not going anywhere with you."

He glared at the Bloode Stone and stood. "Let me try it this way. I'm bored out of my skull and irritated enough with you that I'm considering biting my way into your good graces."

She took a step back.

"Instead, I suggest we head into the city for a bit. Is there a place you might wish to see?"

She stared. "Really? Leave the house? Can we do that?"

He chuckled. "I can do whatever I want. I don't have to obey Mormo."

"I though he was your patriarch. Your boss."

"He likes to think so. None of us volunteered to work with Mormo and Hecate." He said the goddess's name as if it were an insult.

"You don't like witches?"

"I don't like deities. They're all a little too full of themselves."

She had to laugh. "This coming from a species who calls anyone not a vampire a 'lesser being.'"

"Truth is truth."

"You're making my point." She shook her head. "But I'm happy to leave. Onvyr—"

"Can stay here with others. Where it's *safe,*" he emphasized. "Because you and I will be out in town, and he'll be here, surrounded by protection. So you don't need to worry about him. You can see him again as soon as we're home."

The obvious implication that if she tried to escape, she'd

never see her brother again. "Fine." Despite the danger, she walked into his personal space and poked his rock-hard chest. "Anything happens to him, you'll answer to me."

"Promise?" He licked his lips, and she wanted to trace his tongue with her own.

No, nope. What the heck is happening to me?

She took a hasty step back, ignored his smirk, and left the room.

Bella met her at the door to the garage with a wad of cash. "Hey. Mr. Mormo said you guys are leaving on a break. Said to give you some money for dinner or shopping. You know, to get anything you might need for a lengthier stay."

Fara groaned, not even caring how Mormo might know what she and Varu had just decided to do. "Thanks."

"Have fun." Bella grinned at Varu, who ignored her.

After entering the garage, he grabbed a set of keys and shocked her when he held open the passenger door to a shiny black car. "After you."

Not trusting him in the slightest, she gave herself as much space as possible to get in the car without brushing against him. He closed the door behind her, got behind the wheel, then drove them away from the house.

She powered down the window and breathed in the scent of wind and rain, alarmed at how liberated she felt. "It's an illusion of freedom, I know, but I'm glad to be away from the house."

"As am I." He sighed and drove with care toward Lake Washington. He fiddled with the radio and music came on, an entrancing electronic meld of beats and sounds that made her want to move.

They drove without speaking, raindrops spattering the car, the music filling the silence between them, though she frequently felt his gaze upon her. The hour passed nine, and they continued into the crowded city filled with life. He drove north, finally stopping outside of the Washington Park Arboretum, a place she'd wanted to explore but hadn't been able to yet.

It was closed due to the lateness of the hour, but Varu didn't care. Once out of the vehicle, he took her by the hand and walked with her toward a section with signs toward the Japanese Garden.

They came across a wall of trees, and he gathered her in his arms.

"What are you—"

Before she could protest, he jumped and raced over grass and past more shrubs toward a tall wooden fence. He vaulted that and finally landed on pavers. Then he slowly set her down, as if disinclined to do so.

Not sure how they'd moved over the distance so fast, she found herself needing to catch her breath, shocked and alarmed at his contrary actions. Holding her protectively. Being solicitous now, when earlier he'd threatened to bite her. She pulled away and put space between them.

He didn't seem to notice. "I thought you might like this."

"I love it." She frowned at him. "What's your game now?"

"Excuse me?" Even dressed in jeans and a long-sleeved, black, button-down shirt, he looked elegant. Too handsome for his own good. She thought it a terrible thing that vampires had been created to be good-looking on top of being super fit, super strong, and deadly.

"You can't force me to do what you want. Mormo forbade you from hurting me, and the stone protects me from your mental games. Ah, so that's it. You're doing to try to be so nice that I'll forget you're a killer and do whatever you want. Am I right?"

He smiled wide, his teeth brilliant under the moon that decided to come out from behind the clouds. The rain continued to mist over them, and it only made Varu look that much more perfect, like a marble statue come to life as rain drops slid over his smooth, pale skin.

"That is my plan, fae. And you'll fall for it, see if you don't."

"Please. I'm more stubborn than anyone you've ever met. I've never fallen for a pretty face. I won't start now."

He stared at her. "You think I'm pretty?"

She could hear the smirk he didn't let show. "Stop talking. You're ruining the atmosphere."

She turned and left him standing there, *laughing*, while she explored the gorgeous garden. The stone underfoot hummed with happiness, well-loved and cared for in this place bursting with life despite the falling leaves.

The autumn weather was apparent in the gorgeous yellow and orange leaves on the trees around several water features, the season accentuating the lush green grass and blue-ash colored stone of the walkways. She felt Varu trailing behind her, but she didn't let him distract her from the rock singing to her of life and the many creatures living in its environs. Eager to feel more, she removed her shoes and sighed at the feeling of bare feet against the ground.

Time had no meaning as she walked around. Despite looking human, she took power from the earth in many of its forms— rock, grass, earth—and enjoyed being outside where she felt at her most powerful. The glamour didn't even bother her as she got back in touch with her true self.

Sitting cross-legged on a narrow bridge overlooking moss-green waters, she opened her eyes to see the moon large overhead. Waning since its blinding presence just a few nights ago, it shone down over her.

Over them.

She was startled to realize Varu sat next to her in a similar pose, staring at her while she'd been centering herself.

"What?" she asked, breathless and not sure why.

"Just watching you." He didn't seem to see anything odd about staring at her while she communed with nature.

She should have felt awkward, but he aroused in her a passion she didn't trust.

Fara didn't say anything more, and Varu looked content to keep staring.

"You're like a snake that never blinks," she blurted, unnerved and wishing she could do a better job of focusing on his deadly intent and not his handsome face.

"Thank you." He smiled. "A snake is the ultimate predator. Its keen focus and ability to swallow prey whole is something to be admired."

She blew out a breath. "Right, well, I'm ready to go. I'm hungry." She tensed, realizing she shouldn't have mentioned hunger to a vampire staring at her like his next meal.

"Fine. I know of a restaurant you might like."

"With humans?" She hadn't blended much with mortals in the past decade. Most of her time had been spent in out of the way places or around magir who knew how to help in her search. She found humans interesting but a little scary. They had no respect for the natural world around them and continued to encroach into Gaia's depths.

Yet they made such marvels out of stone, their buildings fascinating structures, if she could overlook some of the toxic supplies they used when constructing their marvels.

"Yes, with humans. Come." He stood and held out a hand to help her to her feet.

A trick perhaps? She glanced up at him but could read nothing in his face. Wary, she placed her hand in his, felt his immense strength as well as a vast well of power he could have used on her but hadn't, and tugged her hand back as soon as she'd regained her feet.

He quirked his lips but made no comment. They left the same way they'd arrived, with no one the wiser, and for those spare moments, heart to heart as he held her in his arms to clear the fence.

Varu hadn't realized he might like the part he'd decided to play. Being a gentleman had its perks. Fara kept watching him as if he might jump her at any moment. She seemed more suspicious about his manners than his actual threats to bite her.

They sat at a private table in an upscale restaurant on the water that had late hours for those who could afford the steep prices. He'd ordered an expensive bottle of wine while Fara stared at the menu, effectively hiding behind it while a server delivered ice cold waters and a basket of steaming bread.

He grinned to himself, astounded at how much better he felt being out from that oppressive house, once again a strigoi under his own steam.

"Wow. A lot to choose from," she said and lowered the menu.

He studied her, wishing she didn't have to wear a disguise. He would have loved to have seen her skin glow under the moonlight out in the middle of the Japanese Garden. But even looking like a human, her beauty shone through.

They had started out in simple enough clothing, nothing that would have allowed them to walk into this place. So she'd glamoured herself into a dress that molded a little too well to her curves and gave him a jacket and nice shoes and trousers to accent his passable shirt. All in black, of course.

In a lower voice, she added, "Do you eat food? Not people," she said before he could tease her. "I mean, this kind of food."

"I haven't for many years. I can, but I normally don't." Though he would order something to blend in.

"You ordered wine."

"I like alcohol."

"I don't." She frowned.

"I thought your kind preferred sweets."

She nodded. "Yeah. Elves drink, of course. But when we want to kick back and relax, we indulge in something sugary." She glanced at the menu, and he swore her eyes glazed over. "They have a lot of desserts on this menu."

He waited while she ordered a salad and entre of salmon, and he ordered a rare filet he actually thought about eating. When left in silence once more, he sipped his wine, appreciating the fine taste. And the potentially fine company. He stared at her throat, watching her rising pulse.

"Cut it out." She nibbled on bread. "I'm not on the menu."

He grinned, careful to keep his fangs hidden. "Of course not."

She fumed and muttered, "You don't have to hide your smile. I glamoured that too. You look human enough. I guess."

He did continue to get a good bit of attention, he noticed with a subtle glance around them, and none of it seemed to be tinged with horror. Fara too had her fair share of admirers. "Thank you."

"Gratitude? Be still my heart."

He chuckled. "You're a funny little fae, aren't you?"

"So patronizing."

"Well, I *have* condescended to escort a lesser being around the city. I'd think you'd be more appreciative."

She rolled her eyes.

"Huh. Now you remind me of Orion."

She grinned. "What's the deal with all you guys, anyway? I don't really understand the tribes and clans stuff. Yes, Mormo gave us a long history lesson. But it was a lot to take in. I just know vamp—um, your kind—tend not to get along."

"A lesson in politics, hmm? I'm game." He had nothing better to do than watch her eat with those tiny teeth, though he took great joy in watching her lips hugging anything at all. Varu cleared his throat. "We have ten tribes."

"I know that."

"Each tribe is made of clans. You'd think that at least clans in a particular tribe would get along. And they do if a master is in residence, or close by. Sometimes he can ensure that his patriarchs—clan leaders—have enough power to keep the peace. Unless he's strigoi," he added with a sigh. "Then everyone's at everyone's throats."

She swallowed. "Um, so, you're strigoi. But you don't seem like the others I've heard about."

"I'm not. I'm very much my own person. But at home, back in Romania, I'd have reacted to other tribes with a lot less kindness, I guess you could say."

She choked. "Kindness? You guys aren't kind."

He frowned. "We're not the monsters you think we are." He lowered his voice when a passing server looked at their table. "Well, maybe. But we do find pleasure in more than killing."

"Oh, killing it in the stock market, sure," she said to cover, and the server looked away.

"You know human customs."

"I know how human dialogue works, and I've been around enough magir to know what to say and what not to say."

He shrugged. "I'm normally hunting when out from under Mormo's thumb. I like to study my food." He glanced around. "Though I find nothing here appetizing." He glanced back at her and winked, loving her blush. "Almost nothing."

"Stop it." She glared at him but smiled up at the server who returned with their meals. After he left, she started eating. And didn't stop.

"I guess you really were hungry." He continued to sip his wine, an outstanding Bordeaux blend from a special reserve.

"Famished." She sighed. "Glamours take energy, and being around you people is stressful enough. This curse has been hell on my life."

Curious, he sipped more wine and asked, "What do you do when you're not cursed and finding lost stones?"

She started to answer but stopped when he started cutting his steak. His mouth watered, the meat's juices rare enough to entice a low-level bloodlust. Nothing he couldn't control, but he wondered about eating cow flesh after so long going without ingesting actual food. Sensing Fara's hunger, he cut a slice and held it up to her.

She blinked. "Huh?"

"Want a bite?"

She frowned. "Is this the punchline to a bad joke?"

He allowed himself a chuckle. "It should be, but no. You look like you're still hungry."

"I am." She flushed. "I eat a lot."

"You don't look it." She was small but, he recalled all too well, fit perfectly in his arms. He could almost hear the Bloode Stone humming, reverberating throughout his body.

And when Fara leaned forward and took the meat between her teeth, he sighed with pleasure, wishing to feel her fangs on him.

Yes, the stone whispered. *Soon.*

F ara chewed a slice of meat that melted like soft butter in her mouth. But as she chewed, she felt Varu's intense gaze. It felt different. Not threatening, but not kind or safe. Dangerously seductive, actually. Though she sensed he hadn't used his power of seduction on her.

She swallowed, wondering if it would be impolite to ask for another bite.

He exchanged his plate with hers. "Please. By all means."

She dug in, savoring the food and not speaking, glad he seemed content to let her eat without making conversation. When she came to the last bite, she figured it would only be right to offer him a taste of his own plate.

"It's delicious." She held the forked steak out to him, expecting him to grab the utensil and feed himself.

But Varu opened his mouth, waiting. She felt funny, the exchange a lot more intimate than she might have expected. He took the food between his lips and chewed, his expression thoughtful.

She leaned forward and whispered, "When's the last time you ate something?"

After he'd finished the bite, savoring it by the look on his face, he answered, "Early 1700s, I think. I'd had venison then, if I'm not mistaken." He sat back and dabbed his mouth with a napkin. "Wow. That was good. I'm going to have to remember to get that again."

"You do realize this meal cost quite a bit." She lowered her voice to add, "Even for humans."

He shrugged. "Money means nothing to Mormo, who's bankrolling all this. The wine was over a thousand dollars. I don't care much about the cost for the rest. Besides, we're not done. We haven't ordered dessert yet."

Fara didn't know if she should. He likely didn't realize it, but too much sugar could have the same effect on her kind as too much alcohol did on humans. She didn't think vampires ever got drunk, though she'd heard they could get fuzzy if they drank too much blood. But then, much of what she knew of vampires had been wrong, as she'd come to learn after listening to Mormo and meeting Varu and his new kin.

After interacting with Atanase, she would have thought all the stories of monstrous blood-drinkers to be true. That they reveled in death and torture, feeding off pain and fear and not to be trusted. While she didn't trust Varu, she couldn't say he regularly immersed himself in death and others' agony.

Then again, this entire night had been pretend, designed to get her to lower her guard and trust him. And damn, but he was good.

"Why are you looking at me like that?" he asked.

"I'm wondering how nice you're going to continue to be tonight. To trick me into trusting you."

His grin told her all she needed to know.

"Fine." She gave him a flat stare. "Then you'll answer some of my questions, hmm?"

"Fara, you wound me."

"I wish."

He bit back another grin. "I'm trying to be a gentleman. You've been working hard, and I have as well. We've earned a night without animosity, haven't we?"

"So that's a yes? You'll answer my questions?"

"Perhaps." He drank more wine.

She said to hell with it and ordered the fancy caramel date cake. "Okay, Varujan. Why don't you tell me how old you are?"

He rubbed his chin, and she recalled it had been smooth before the glamour as well. Did vampires grow facial hair? She was interested in him. Really interested, and that bothered her.

"I'm one thousand and twenty-four years old."

"Wow. An old man."

"Young by Master standards."

She cringed. "Yeah."

He watched her, no doubt filing away everything she did and said. "How old are you?"

An innocent enough question, she supposed. "I'm three hundred and six."

"Young, then. Your kind live well into thousands of years."

"Unless you're hunted. Then you figure you get a few centuries and be happy you had them." Before he could ask her about that, she added, "So your dad killed your mom. You never knew her?"

He didn't look sad at the mention. "No. Strigoi mothers don't exist. We are a paternal society. Mates are only around to breed. Once they produce, they go on their way." He frowned before she could ask her next question. "We don't kill them. Usually. My sire is an extraordinary creature." He snorted. "A fucking brute. But that's another discussion entirely."

"So your father didn't love your mother?" Weren't mates about more than breeding? Lycans typically felt affection, even love, for their mates. And her parents had loved each other before remembering they shouldn't.

Varu scoffed. "Our kind don't love. We take, we possess. But we don't debase ourselves with such emotional nonsense."

"That's dumb. Love isn't a weakness. It's a powerful force."

"A force that incites murder, war, and strife. A weakness," he repeated.

Though he had a point, he'd missed the mark entirely. Without love, Fara and her brother wouldn't exist. Such a powerful force had brought enemy warriors together to create life. She didn't think Varu would appreciate the sentiment, though.

"What was it like growing up where you did? Where did you grow up, anyway? Transylvania?"

He laughed. "Stereotypes. Yes, I did grow up in northern Romania. But much of my time was spent in large cities across Europe, close enough to humans to learn how they think and act. I was used as a scout and information specialist on humans and other magir. I spent the last hundred or so years in Cluj-Napoca, a larger city in Romania." He paused. "And if you didn't already know, humans are a violent race much more barbaric than mine."

"Seriously?"

He nodded. "We have rules. You break them, you die. But we don't... *I* don't kill for the sake of killing. There's no fun without a challenge. No joy in hunting weak prey." He smiled at her. She should have been chilled. Instead she was turned on. He added, "You're not weak, are you?"

I'm not right in the head, lusting after you. She coughed. "Right. Well, so, another question. How did you end up with Rolf and the others? They seem kind of an odd group. You're all so different." She'd seen enough of them together to know that.

He snorted. "You're telling me. I came to Mormo to settle a bloode debt. Apparently, the others did too. I have the feeling Mormo engineered events to get us here. But I can't prove it. All six of us are extremely powerful, and all from different tribes, bringing different strengths to the table. Mine is leadership. I'm immune to most dangers." He cautioned her, "Even the sun cannot kill me outright."

Crap. Just what she'd always feared, that she'd end up near a vampire with insane powers.

"Can it kill your dad? He'd be more powerful than you, right? His eyes narrowed on her. "I don't know. I would think so."

"Oh?"

"It would kill the others in my new clan. Orion is partial to water though most of us aren't. I don't swim; I sink. But as I don't actually need oxygen to breathe, it won't kill me. Kraft loves wolves and has a rage state that's unbeatable. And he can't drive worth a damn though he's always begging for the keys. Khent reanimates the dead and has an ego to rival the gods. He's very smart and very annoying. Rolf has magic near equal to Mormo's and a terrible sense of humor. He's constantly pranking the others, and none of us like it much. Duncan is incredibly fast and so affable he at times seems like a real friend. He's dangerous to me, because I like him and might hesitate to kill him should he move to harm me."

He stared into her eyes. "And even with all that information, you will never be able to win against us. Not when the stone sings in my heart and whispers promises of power, of making my every desire come true."

She stared into fathomless eyes that beckoned her to come closer.

She thought about leaving her seat and joining him for a kiss sure to melt that glamour right off him. In another second, she'd make that move.

He leaned back, dropped all that intensity, and smiled at her as the waiter arrived. "Ah, look, dessert."

. . .

Saved by date cake so good she had ordered another to go, along with an extra steak she planned on giving Onvyr. Varu paid the bill without missing a beat, and as they left, he kept a hand on the small of her back, as if being mannerly and possessive, like a man on a date might act. She let herself enjoy the fiction of being cared for. Just a little.

Fara settled into the car and wondered if all mortals felt so, well, normal. As they drove back to the house, she went over her evening in detail. She'd had dinner with a human-looking male at a restaurant where humans ate, after visiting a place humans toured for fun.

"Remove the glamours," Varu ordered, then added a soft, "Please."

She did, and he eyed her with approval before giving his attention back to the road.

As much as she'd enjoyed her night, she admittedly preferred him as a strigoi. At least she knew how to handle him that way.

They drove in silence, the windows down, until she grew chilled. Fae could tolerate extreme temperatures better than humans, but not like vampires, who didn't seem affected by snow or scorching heat.

He rolled up the windows, and she felt almost closed in, too close to him.

She watched him drive, competent behind the wheel, sure of himself.

"What?" he asked, his voice low, tempting.

Not good.

"I didn't say anything."

"I can feel you burning to ask me more questions."

She tried to pull on the Bloode Stone, asking it to help her see if Varu could be trusted. The stone warmed her, and she asked the most important question she could think of. "Now that you have the Bloode Stone, what will you do with it?"

He shrugged. "I think the question should go to Mormo. As in, what does *he* want done with it? I can tell you he doesn't want vampires getting any stronger than they already are."

"Doesn't that bother you? That he's trying to limit your kind?"

"Have you met many vampires?" he asked drily. "I barely like the ones I'm bonded to."

"You're a strange race."

"You should talk. Your brother is both light and dark elf, and you're gray. A beautiful color, don't get me wrong, but how are you two so different? Do you have different parents? I thought dusk elves, though rare, took after one parent or the other."

"We have the same parents. I don't know. Onvyr and I just turned out this way." She shrugged. "But I'll let you in on a little secret." That wasn't so secret or she never would have told him.

"What?"

"We're never safe in fae lands. Dusk elves are an anathema. To be killed on sight."

He frowned. "Why?"

"Because like you, we're considered too powerful to live." She snorted. "What a joke."

He glanced at her before returning to the road. "I don't know. Your brother is more powerful than any fae I've ever run across. Well, except one annoying male, but he's in a class all by himself. A real asshole, actually." He paused. "You're pretty strong too. You stopped me and your brother from killing each other. You made my ears bleed and threw me across that empty building when you escaped that first time. That's not something just anyone can do."

She flushed. "It's not me. I ask Gaia to borrow power, and she listens. Sometimes."

"Yeah, well, that 'sometimes' is something I respect. I won't underestimate you, fae."

"Back at you." She glared, trying not to feel so pleased to have earned his admiration. She shouldn't care how he felt. It had to be the stone softening her toward him. And that would get her killed before she could fix what she'd done.

Fara was losing control of the power gem. "You didn't answer me about the Bloode Stone."

"Worried I'll be able to rule the world with it?"

"Yes."

"Well, relax. I don't need a sentient gem to make me powerful. I'm already more than you and all your kind put together can handle."

"You're so arrogant."

"And honest. But that Bloode Stone?" He shook his head. "That's not something anyone should have to worry about. It needs to get lost again. I can only imagine if a master got his hands on it. We'd have an apocalypse that would destroy worlds. Hell on earth would become a reality if that happened."

And Atanase had five of them. She swallowed. "I know."

They glanced at each other, their shared worry enough to quiet them both, lost to thoughts of what should never be.

Fara should have been happier about that, but she wasn't. Varu wanted the stone gone. But he'd need it to destroy Atanase. Without it, he'd never be able to defeat the master vampire and all the vampires he could now call kin. Not just the strigoi, but any of the clans from other tribes he might gift with a Bloode Stone.

The question became, how did she get Varu on her side and listening? Especially when he still considered her a lesser being?

She sighed. A worry for another day. She'd focus instead on her date cake. Though she'd thought about giving it to Onvyr, he could make do with the steak. She needed it more.

With extra caramel sauce.

CHAPTER
NINETEEN

Three days later

Mormo turned the corner of the basement corridor and nearly ran into a snowy white owl. "Watch it," he snarled, missing the bird's obnoxious rejoinder.

When had the house become a way stop for divine animals, anyway?

He needed to have a word with his mistress.

That was if he could find her.

Instead, he ran into Duncan in a version of Hecate's speakeasy passage, just a small square of the basement outfitted with a bar and sexy bartender. Fortunately, Mormo didn't see any doors or other-realm creatures around.

Duncan flirted with a dead lamia who had an aversion to clothing. He shouldn't have been able to access Hecate's crossroads. Even Mormo couldn't without her present. But Hecate had a soft spot for the charming revenant. She said she loved his accent. Personally, Mormo thought it more likely she had a thing for the way he filled out his jeans.

Duncan did wear them a little too tight, to Mormo's way of thinking.

"So then I told her, oy, lovey, snuggle up and we'll share the heat you're making." Duncan wiggled his brows and leaned over the bar countertop toward the bartender, his accent thicker than it normally sounded.

The lamia purred and leaned toward him as well, her naked breasts plastered against the bar top. Her skin had a greenish-gray cast, her long white hair slithering over her shoulders in the same way her lower half slithered over the ground. Having a body half human and half reptilian had never been a problem for the bloodsucking creature, ensnaring humans with ease with those bountiful breasts and beautiful face.

Personally, Mormo found her a bit too much to take, but Hecate liked the lamia working the sunset hour.

The lamia saw him and smiled. "Magician." She flicked him a kiss, and he caught the wisp of a forked tongue tasting his scent on the air.

Duncan sighed with pleasure. "Ah, that's one wicked tongue you have. Does it dance like the rest of you?"

Mormo cringed. "Can we at least keep the dead clothed around you?"

Duncan flashed Mormo a smile. "I sure hope not."

The lamia giggled.

"Duncan." Mormo reminded himself that Duncan hadn't done anything wrong, exactly. He couldn't help being charming or attracting Hecate's admiration.

Duncan left the bar with an apology and joined Mormo, who stalked down the hall, past a group of angry Amazons threatening to gut each other, toward a ghoul arguing with Mars about the right way to filet a liver. So much for Hecate keeping the crossroads from the vampires.

"A lot of dark talk down here," Duncan muttered and moved closer to Mormo. "You see why I prefer the naked lovelies."

"Yes. Hold on." He turned to separate the Amazons, directing several toward the fae plane and the others toward Niflheim, the Norse underworld. After making sure Mars had no intention of gutting the ghoul king, he rejoined Duncan. "Have you seen Bella, by chance?"

"Last I saw, she was getting cozy with the dark elf." He frowned. "Something barmy about that one."

"Bella or Onvyr?"

"Yes."

Mormo chuckled, his mood settling. "You're better off not down here when the mistress isn't."

"Can't say as I've ever seen her. Is she as lovely as I've heard?"

"More so. If you'd seen her, you'd know." But would he? Hecate and her damned games. Mormo loved her to bits, would do anything for her, but she definitely made his life a challenge.

Duncan walked in silence with him back up the stairs, continuing toward the room in which Mormo stored the Bloode Stone, a place where Varu and Fara were to spend time working with it. Though Mormo had wanted to use a spell to force Fara to tell them all she knew, Hecate had warned him to have patience, to let the strigoi ferret the answers they needed.

He heard voices and cautioned Duncan to keep quiet. He and Duncan stopped outside the doorway, watching the strigoi and the dusk elf talk. When they'd started working with the stone, the pair had sniped at each other, only Mormo's command to leave the dusk elf in one piece keeping Varu from killing her. Or so Mormo had thought.

A few days ago, the pair had gone out to take some respite from training. When they'd returned, Varu had seemed pleased, while Fara acted hunted.

Now, whenever Mormo saw Fara, Varu stood in her shadow. He held the door for her, held her chair for her when she sat. Fetched her things to eat and drink and had already mentioned he planned to take her out for another outing among humans this evening. Each time, Fara looked suspicious and uneasy. She'd tried to keep away from him, but Mormo needed them to work together and told her so. The others found it hilarious, but Mormo had forbidden them—especially Rolf—from interfering, so they'd been keeping their distance from the pair.

And keeping her brother under watch.

"How's Onvyr doing?" he asked Duncan in a low voice.

In an equally quiet tone, Duncan said, "He's all over the place. One minute he's all smiles and gobby with the racoon that's been living in one of the new rooms upstairs, the next he's attacking Orion for looking at him sideways. The lad's 'round the bend, you asked me."

"Don't kill him, at least, not yet," Mormo said.

They both paused as Varu stood and moved to Fara's chair.

"Stop it. I can get myself out. You act polite one more time and I'll suck you through the floor." She scooted herself out and away from him. "And stop looking at me that way!"

She stormed past Mormo and Duncan. Varu stared after her, a sly smile on his face that had even Mormo feeling cautious.

"What are you up to?" he asked as he entered the room. The Bloode Stone, no longer on the table, sat in Varu's palm. From a small distance away, Mormo could feel the heat generated by the connection.

"Damn, Varu. Looks like you've seriously bonded with that thing." Duncan approached, more laidback than usual. "Can I touch it?"

"Sure." Varu started to reach out to Duncan, and the stone glowed brighter in his palm.

Then vanished.

"What happened?" Mormo had been against letting Varu tinker with the stone from the beginning, but Hecate said it had to be done. That the Bloode Stone sought its true master. She would rather it be Varujan than his father, but frankly, Mormo was having second thoughts about Varu holding onto it.

Since meeting Fara, the strigoi had been changing. Even the others had noticed it, or so Mormo's spies had mentioned to him just last night. Not even a week past his first encounter with Faraine and the Bloode Stone and Varu was already acting like his father. Mellow yet treacherous, smiling while ready to pounce at any moment. Thoughts of Atanase getting his claws on the Bloode Stone was bad enough. But this stone *wanted* to bond with Varu, which would make it—and Varujan—even more powerful.

Varu stared at his palm in awe. "I... It's in me."

"*What?*"

"It's hiding, I think. Playing a game with Duncan." Varu looked shocked. "I can't get it to come out yet. It wants to leave with Fara."

"Are you sure it wants to leave, and Fara's not somehow manipulating you?" Duncan asked.

Varu shrugged. "I don't think so, but I could be wrong. I guess we'll see." He should have sounded more worried.

Mormo shook his head. "You can't leave with her tonight."

Varu faced Mormo, and Mormo felt a hum of danger.

Especially with both Varu and Duncan, the one nice, sane vampire, now glaring at him in warning.

Exactly what he'd warned Hecate would happen—Varu was taking over the position of patriarch.

Good. Then you can get back here and take this meeting with Atanase, she roared in his mind.

He winced and rubbed his forehead, and the strength holding Duncan to Varu disappeared. "You okay, Mormo?" Duncan asked. "You don't look so good."

Varu frowned. "I feel someone powerful. I feel... Is my father close by?"

"Yes and no. Don't worry. I'll handle this. You take Fara wherever you think she needs to go. But be careful. We have enemies near."

"Don't we always?" Duncan snorted. "I'll back up the strigoi."

They watched Varu follow after Fara.

"Take Orion," Mormo ordered Duncan.

Duncan frowned. "Why?"

Mormo wanted to say he worried Duncan wouldn't be strong enough to fight against a horde of strigoi, should Atanase's hunters search out and attack Varu. But that might not be true. Duncan hid his power behind smiles and an easygoing attitude. But Mormo had seen what the revenant could really do.

"Fine. Take Rolf, if only to give me and Onvyr a break. The draugr won't leave the dark elf alone. And we all know it doesn't take much to get Onvyr to snap."

"Fine." Duncan sighed. "But at least let Seraphina know I'll be back later."

"Who?"

"The half-naked lamia."

"For fuck's sake. Go." Mormo pointed to the door. "And send Orion to me. He and Kraft can guard Onvyr."

Duncan chuckled and left, but not before firing a parting shot. "For a lesser being, you're pretty funny."

Lesser being my ass.

Mormo went in search of Hecate and ran into Bella instead. "You."

She wiggled her fingernails at him. "What do you think, Mr. Mormo? Hecate likes purple now, so I'm going with that. She called it dark elf-lavender." Bella smiled wide. "Because Onvyr's soooo dreamy."

Mormo groaned. "I need to talk to you, but first, I have to see to an uninvited guest." One who'd been transported to Mormo's receiving room in a pocket dimension the moment he stepped on the welcome mat to the front door.

Atanase's intent to walk in, as boldly as he pleased, had triggered the defensive spell.

Mormo teleported and found Atanase seated and waiting, the small sitting area one Mormo liked to use for discussions with important magir, isolated away from danger. Just Mormo and his guest or guests.

"Ah, Mormo. There you are." Atanase nodded. "Please. Have a seat." He waved to a nearby chair, as if inviting Mormo to join *him*.

Arrogant bastard. Mormo studied the master vampire, seeing the features and physical presence his son had inherited. But it was there in the eyes, a subtle distinction that made all the difference. Atanase cared for nothing but his own power.

Varu had always given his loyalty first to this clan. And lately, he'd been showing a softening, a willingness to forgive mistakes and faults for which he'd normally punish the others. That Onvyr still lived was a surprise in itself. Despite the fact Mormo had ordered them to leave the dusk elf alone, Onvyr didn't make that request an easy one, constantly challenging the others to fight.

Though the vampires appreciated the dusk elf's love of battle, his spurts of weird power made him too dangerous to leave on his own.

But Varu hadn't eliminated a threat to the clan, doing what he could to keep in Fara's good favor.

Did she control him through the Blood Stone? Or was something else happening? Something Hecate had been hoping for?

"Master Atanase, an honor, as usual." Mormo bowed his head, an easy enough thing to give the master his lead.

Atanase subtly relaxed. "I come to you because I think you

might have something of mine. Rumor has it the dagger you once crafted for me has made its way back to its creator."

Mormo smiled. "You are mistaken. The dagger has ever been yours. I am not a strigoi or vampire, with no link to the gem it can carry. Were I to do so, I'd suffer the same fate your earlier subjects did." He knew how awfully those few magir had died. Handling the Bloode Stones could only be done by one Of the Bloode.

Which still made him wonder how the hell Faraine had touched one. Even holding it by way of the dagger.

Atanase steepled his fingers beneath his chin. "A dark elf was spotted in the city. He killed one of the Seattle upir, and supposedly the Night Bloode clan took care of him."

Mormo said nothing.

"There is also word of a female who accompanied him, also presumed a fae."

"I have heard the same. But none of my vampires have seen either."

"Then you won't mind if I search your home."

"I very much mind." Mormo smiled to take the sting out of his words. "My mistress is at work with some inter-demesne politicking. The Norse are at odds with the Tuatha Dé Danann."

Atanase's smile was forced. "Ah, those pesky fae gods."

"Yes." Mormo sighed. "I want to help you, but my hands are tied."

Atanase vanished and reappeared behind Mormo, choking him with a lengthening nail digging into his throat, drawing blood. The master whispered, "Be glad you still have hands to be tied. If I find you lied to me, I'll feed you to my clan for an eternity." He nipped Mormo's ear and licked the blood away. "Damn me if I don't."

Then, before Mormo could expel him from his private safe room, Atanase disappeared.

Mormo sagged, not having expected such power. What had Atanase been up to have grown so strong?

With a burst of will, he teleported back into the house and reinforced the spells keeping it safe. He didn't sense Atanase inside, but he hadn't expected the master vampire to be able to leave his safe haven either.

Mormo could only imagine what an evil beast like Atanase would do with the might of the Bloode Empire behind him.

That could never, ever, be allowed to happen.

Bella walked out of the kitchen with Onvyr and saw Mormo standing in the middle of the living area, still bleeding. Mormo touched his throat, the pain excruciating. *That bastard. What had he coated his nails in?*

"Mr. Mormo?" Bella sounded scared.

Onvyr put himself between the human and Mormo. "Where's the danger?"

Khent exited the corridor, arguing with Kraft. He saw Mormo and froze. "Mormo? You're bleeding excessively."

"Thanks, Captain Obvious," he snapped. "Help me." He gestured for Kraft to come closer. "Heal me."

"I don't.... Oh." Kraft leaned close and licked the blood from Mormo's neck, sealing the wound with his saliva. "That's *wunder* —" He passed out cold on the floor.

"Thank you for not sharing," Khent drawled.

Mormo felt the toxin beneath the wound begin to dissipate, finally. He waved his hand over his robes and the floor, and the blood disappeared. "Good. Khent, I need you to reach Rolf and Duncan. Master Vampire Atanase is looking for the Bloode Stone and two dusk elves. Make sure you guard Varu and Fara, with your lives if necessary. He's brought hunters with him, I'm sure." He looked Khent in the eye. "He's become a Power. Do *not* attempt to challenge him."

Khent nodded and left.

"Mr. Mormo, what happened?" Bella was on the verge of tears, and Onvyr pulled her in for a comforting hug, his big body its own form of protection.

"Will you stop that?" he hissed, remembered who he was talking to, and swore under his breath. "Apologies, but Mistress, I need your help."

Onvyr frowned. "What—?"

Bella scowled, put Onvyr in a freeze, and stepped out of his arms. "Really? I was enjoying him. He likes to cuddle."

"The master vampire is a threat. He's grown in power. I think the stones have given him a second awakening." Mormo didn't like that he hadn't heard or sensed the power, but what else could have made Atanase so incredibly strong?

She frowned. "That's not good."

He explained what had just happened, and she cooed over him, looking him over to make sure he had fully healed, something she could have done earlier but had been too busy canoodling with the elf.

"Mormo, you know better than to play with strange vampires in our home."

He lowered his head. "Apologies, Mistress."

"But all is well. You fortified the house, and I added a few of my own incantations. But I can't do too much. I'm busy elsewhere."

"I know." Mormo's three-faced goddess could split herself to take care of multiple problems at once. He hadn't been lying when he'd told Atanase she was trying to prevent a war between the Norse and the Tuatha Dé Danann. A real mess that kept taking place on the border between realms.

She only kept a presence here because she liked "her" vampires.

Bella waved at him and showed off her new purple nails then

moved back into Onvyr's arms. She wiggled, and he grew animated once more.

Onvyr frowned. "Bella? Are you okay?"

She sniffed. "Could you carry me to my room? I'm scared."

"It's okay. I'll protect you." Big, strong, strapping Onvyr carried Bella away.

Mormo rolled his eyes and waited for Orion to arrive.

The big vryko stared down at Kraft and growled, "Why do you continue to pair me with this imbecile?" He showed sharp teeth.

"I'm so not in the mood," Mormo growled back.

Kraft shook himself awake and swore in German. "Don't know how Varu sucked him down, because Mormo put me on my ass."

Orion blinked. "You tasted him?"

"Sweet, like candy." Kraft winked. "Not like chicken."

Orion started laughing. Kraft did too.

And Mormo had to do his level best not to blast them into the underworld while instructing them on what to do when—not *if*—the strigoi invaded.

O*h, that blasted vampire is on my last nerves,* Fara thought as she stomped her way into the library down the hall. She hated how much she wanted to be with Varu. Since that evening spent visiting the Seattle Japanese Garden three days ago, the connection between them had changed. Deepened.

She wanted to keep her distance and figure out how to manipulate him with the Bloode Stone, but Mormo kept throwing them together, and she refused to act intimidated around him anymore. Varu liked when she catered to his moods, so she'd been trying to do the opposite and pretend he didn't bother her.

Except she had a feeling he could see right through her.

Damn it. I'm not a fighter. I'm a dusk elf who just wants to play with her rocks and enjoy the outdoors. And to go human shopping, if I'm honest.

That night at a real restaurant surrounded by humans had been eye-opening. Mundane activities carried out by mortals had been so stress free and calming. She wanted to try more of that.

"Faraine, hold."

Shoot. Varu had caught up to her. She should know better than to try to hide from him in the library. The vampire loved to read.

Yet another reason she liked him more than she should. He didn't tease her for studying, the way Atanase's minions had. He just sat with her and poured through volumes of text as well. Not speaking, just there.

She would have thought the other vampires would give her grief, but they kept their distance. Because Mormo had told them to? Or because Varu had not so subtly staked his claim?

"What?" she said more loudly than she'd intended. "Varu, did you need something?"

He smiled. Trying to get on her last nerve, no doubt. He'd taken to being extra nice because he knew how off-putting she found it. "I wanted to take you out for some shopping and then a dessert shop. It's early enough. The sun just set, so we have a good hour and a half before store closings."

Just what she wanted. Hmm. *Are you telling him things about me?* she asked the stone, which had started talking back to her, no longer communicating only in images. She didn't know if she should find that more or less alarming.

No. Should I? The stone sounded eager.

Please don't.

Varu waited. When she didn't speak, he shrugged. "That's fine. I just thought you could use the break. I know I can. The stone has been frustratingly quiet lately."

Ha. Not with me. She really wanted to go out. "I guess it would be okay to leave for a little bit. Might give us a new perspective when we come back."

He rubbed his palm, distracted.

"Varu?"

"Yes, let's go."

He didn't give her time to reconsider and hustled her out to the same car they'd taken a few days ago. While driving, he glanced at her and smiled. Ack. All the smiling. He'd been doing that a lot lately.

"You look very nice in that."

"Thanks," she murmured, hoping he hadn't seen her stroking the sleeve of the soft cashmere sweater he'd purchased for her a few days go.

The strigoi kept giving her small gifts and pieces of clothing. Hell, she kept waiting for him to drop a dead body at her door in some retro vampire courting ritual. She kept her hysterical laughter to herself, wondering when he would get the hint and realize his trickery wasn't working. She wasn't going to obey him because he kept being nice and treating her well.

She totally wasn't.

Not at all.

Except she did love the sweater. So soft and warm. He'd told her he'd bought it because it matched the color of her eyes.

"Can you take off the glamour?" he asked. "No one can see us in here."

The tinted windows took care of that. The car sped silently over the road, energetic music that had a soft beat and mellow vibe spilling between them.

She lifted the glamour, freeing herself from the constraint of looking human, trying not to love that he preferred her natural appearance. His eyes flashed to red before turning black once more, his gaze on the road.

"Why the shopping trip?"

"It would make you happy," he said, as if that answered everything.

"Why do you care? I'm not part of your clan. I'm a prisoner."

"I like when you smile."

She had no comeback for that, especially because he frowned when he said it and added, "I like your scent when you're happy."

"I have a scent?"

He shifted in his seat and gripped the wheel, not looking at her. "It's always gentle, like flowers and earth. And it soaks into me, so that I'm carried by it when I go about my daily routine. You've seeped into my senses, probably because of the Bloode Stone." He let out a breath. "I should be angry about that, but I'm not. When you're happy, that scent intensifies, and I feel something of the same."

"You feel my feelings?" She'd gotten a few sensations she'd swear were his, but they hadn't lasted, and she'd wondered at her imagination.

"No. I can't feel your feelings or read your thoughts. I just feel a measure of peace, and that's something extremely hard to come by when you're strigoi."

"Oh. That's a good thing, then."

"So long as we're safe, yes. But I need all my wits when we're unprotected. Like now."

"Wait, you feel relaxed now?" She liked that. A lot. Maybe she could start using the stone to make him do what she wanted. Should she try? And why did she feel a pang of guilt for wanting to use him when he'd just been opening up to her?

She frowned. This was about survival, for her, Onvyr, and a lot of innocent beings. She needed Varu's cooperation. For all that he'd said he would never want his father to have the Bloode Stone, he was strigoi first and foremost. She couldn't trust him to do the right thing.

And surprise surprise, she really wanted to.

"Fara?"

She realized he'd been speaking. "Sorry. What did you say?"

"It's not important." He paused. "Shall we do the shopping first? Or would you rather grab dessert?" They pulled into the entrance to a parking garage in Bellevue, a city just north of Mercer Island, where a man in a uniform stood waiting.

Many stores remained open, and she didn't want to wait any longer. "Shopping. I want to look at shoes and purses. Many women shop for these." She thought about it. "Not so much the shoes, since I like going without those. But bags are nice. And this sweater is very comfortable. I might want more like them."

He nodded, waited for her to glamour them both, then left the vehicle to give the man in uniform his keys.

Once away from the parking garage and in the outdoor center, facing the stores, he said, "Mormo has been fetching you clothes from somewhere, but I don't like to ask him to explain his magic. He drones on about it. A lot like Khent does if you ask him something he thinks he knows about."

She had to laugh at that. "You like your new kin. Admit it."

"They aren't as likely to die by my hand as they were when we first met. I guess that's something."

They walked toward a store called Neiman Marcus. Many other humans walked around, talking and laughing despite the darkening sky.

The clear evening and lovely stores obviously attracted a crowd, though it didn't feel overly bustling.

She looked at a small fountain surrounded by shrubs and flowers. "Duncan seems nice. You seem to talk to him a lot."

"Ah yes, Duncan. He's as happy to sink his fangs into a female as he is his cock."

She stopped and stared, wide-eyed, at him spouting a crudity she hadn't expected. "Wh-what?"

"He's happy to bed any female that strikes his fancy." Varu shrugged. "Just warning you, because I believe fae like to bed and wed in short order."

"I— You— *What?*" she sputtered. "First of all, I don't think of Duncan in that way."

"All females do."

"Sure, he's handsome. But so are you." At his look of interest, she flushed and hurried to say, "It's a predator thing, I know. Your kind were built to attract prey. Secondly, not all fae like to couple up with bed partners. A lot of us are happy with just sex."

"Oh?" he practically purred.

"Not me. I mean, sex is okay." *Stop talking, Fara.* "I like sex a lot. But only with someone I trust. And like. He'd have to be attractive to me, sure. Nice and smart too." *I'm babbling. Stop babbling.* "Sex involves trust."

"On that we agree."

She was bursting with curiosity. "Is that why you don't go out with women?"

"Who says I don't?"

A flare of jealousy took her by surprise. "Oh, so you do?"

"No, but one should never assume"

She saw him smirk. He was *laughing* at her. "Well, you certainly seemed happy enough to kiss me the other day."

"I was and am." He let her see his human-looking teeth as he grinned. "I'd be more than happy to show you again right now."

She followed his nod toward his front and glanced at the length jutting between his legs. "*Varu.*"

"Yes, little fae," he said, his voice thick. "Anytime you want to ease me, just let me know."

Fara swallowed. Loudly.

He groaned. "That would work too. I need ease, and I can remember too easily how soft and sweet that mouth is."

"Stop talking. Right now." Because the dragon-tongued male had aroused her with nothing but words. "Let's concentrate on our shopping trip."

"If that's what you want."

She saw a cupcake store and headed for it, needing something to calm her nerves. Several cupcakes and macaroons later, she felt happy and excited and worry-free. Taking Varu's hand in hers, she clasped it tight, loving his surprised expression. He grinned and squeezed her hand, holding for a second before he let her slip away.

"Too handsome for your own good," she murmured and turned to explore the stores, ready to shop to her heart's content.

VARU HAD a difficult time not pulling the female into some dark corner to sink into her. And not with his fangs.

He knew the devious little stone in his hand had to be responsible for his softening feelings for the elf, but he didn't care. And that worried him even more.

He wanted her. The feeling had been building since that first kiss. And it had grown more and more impossible not to just possess her. What a strigoi wanted, he took. Though he'd never had an unwilling donor or lover, he'd never wanted one with such passion.

Still semi-erect, he moved with Fara through several stores, purchasing whatever she wanted. Oddly, the little fae didn't want much. She had a lot of fun trying on clothing and looking at jewelry though.

Though she tried to spend the money Bella had been giving her, he wouldn't allow it, needing to provide for her himself. He bought her several purses, a few necklaces, and a sweater for Onvyr because he could feel how much she wanted the items. The stone seemed content to sit inside him, though he couldn't feel it through his flesh. It was a part of him though, and he wondered how he'd absorbed it into his skin. Strigoi couldn't ingest inorganic material. And he hadn't swallowed it so much as it had dissolved into his hand.

Fara laughed at something an attendant said, and he realized she was agreeing with the woman. "I know. He's so handsome. And mine."

Varu gave a low chuckle, entertained in the knowledge that the sweets had made Fara a little bit... drunk.

Perfect.

He escorted her to several stores, urging her to try on a few things. In one particular store, he found a sheer garment that would cling to her curves and show off her lovely breasts, so of course he secretly added that to her purchase with the help of a circumspect sales clerk.

When Fara had finished, he demanded they buy a few more cupcakes to make up for all the energy she'd expended. She agreed, seeming sober once more but still relaxed, not so on edge with him.

He'd been having the best time, watching her smile, seeing her joy. His heart thumped in time with hers, and he didn't understand why it had taken him so long to see what she clearly was meant to be—a gift from his forefather, delivered by the Bloode Stone itself.

A mate.

He'd never thought to have one. Never thought he deserved one since Atanase had—

Damn it. He shook his head, aware the gem had once again messed with his mind. It wanted him with Fara very badly. He would have gotten rid of the sentient gem if one, he could get it out of his body, and two, he didn't need it to keep Fara close. He had to find a way to start using *it* instead of being the one manipulated.

But.... She smiled at him as they left the shop with all her bags and headed toward the car. He nodded to the valet, who ran to get it for them, and started to say something but stopped, sensing his kin nearby. Vampires could sense their own kind, and kin especially.

Ah, there, Rolf and Khent approached, strutting toward them as if unaware of the many looks being shot their way.

Khent with his long dark hair and arrogance branded on a face mistaken for a god's, and Rolf with his own flowing locks of gold, a smirk on his face as he admitted to one passerby that yes, he and his friend were actors and on a film shoot, as a matter of fact.

Fara eyed them with misgiving. "Huh. What are they doing here?"

Khent joined them first, his eyes darting all over the place. Looking for danger, Varu just knew.

He also sensed Duncan nearby. "Is Duncan here?"

Khent nodded. "You can't see him, but he's watching from a distance, looking for danger."

Rolf joined them. "Atanase's in town. Mormo wanted us to warn you."

"You could have called," Fara said, but she moved closer to Varu, her fear impossible to miss.

"Would have if Romeo had remembered to bring his phone," Rolf said with a smirk. He tossed Varu's phone at him. "Idiot."

Varu ignored him. Having been a part of Fara's happiness for too brief a time, he refused to let anyone ruin things. Including his father. "I have an idea. With me." He held onto Fara by the arm and moved into the darkness of the garage, stopping in front of the human behind the wheel of his car.

"Thank you." Varu sensed the valet's attraction and worked his seduction on the male. "You never saw us."

The human beamed. "Never saw you, sweetie. Good night." He took the cash Varu handed him and walked away, his mind fogged.

Varu made a decision. He unlocked the vehicle and placed all the bags into the trunk. Then he said to Fara, "I need you to cast a new glamour. Make us look like wealthy humans, and make Khent and Rolf look like you and me." To the vampires, he said, "Distraction. I'll bring her back later. For now, get the strigoi after you." He mentally searched for those of his kind, his reach extended thanks to the Bloode Stone. "They're south of us, closer to the house. Make them think we returned but be prepared for a battle. Feel free to thin the strigoi."

Kill as many as you can.

Rolf and Khent shared a smile that shifted into an eerie mirror-like display, Khent looking like Varu and Rolf looking like Fara. Varu looked down at himself and saw his own changes. In the reflection of the vehicle, he saw that Fara had turned him into a handsome human male with dark skin and smiling eyes.

"Nice. You're looking good for a human," Rolf said with a laugh.

A glance at Fara showed a tall blond man. "What?" she said in a man's voice. "I always wanted to try this."

"Kinky," Rolf said, earning a glare from her.

"We'll grab Duncan and go." Khent nodded at them and pushed Rolf toward the car. Moments later, the car turned around to drive deeper into the garage.

"Act human, not frightened of things you should be frightened of," Varu told Fara.

"Sure, Jack," she—he—answered.

"What?"

He found it odd to look at her in man's body, knowing what she really looked and sounded like.

"Your name is Jack. I'm Tom. We'll be humans together."

"Right." He walked with "Tom" back up toward the shopping area, keeping his hands in his pockets, his stride easy.

Tom walked alongside him.

A quick glance at his phone showed a few hotels nearby. Wanting a bit of space from where he and Fara had last been seen, Varu walked with her several blocks away and entered W. Bellevue.

After seducing his way to their best suite, he left the woman at the counter panting after him and walked with Fara into the elevator.

"Hold our images until we get in the room," he murmured, to which Tom nodded.

Once inside, he felt the glamour slide off him, relieved to see Fara as herself once more, pale gray and gorgeous.

Need surged, riding him hard.

"Are you all right?" He looked her over for signs of any injury or strain, though he knew she might only be tired from expending energy on their glamours. Still, he needed to hear her tell him she was okay.

Odd, because he rarely cared about others outside his clan. But he was almost frantic to see to Fara's comfort.

He held onto her forearms, staring into her lovely lavender eyes, and sensed a sudden shift deep inside himself. Where they touched, he felt an instant connection, her essence sliding into his and tangling with the carnal need building for his fae.

Awed, he realized the little conniver was controlling his emotions, stoking the fires of his lust to create an opening for herself. His respect for her swelled to new heights.

What she didn't realize was that he was tired of fighting that driving need for her. Tired of trying to dig past her thick walls to the heart of her. Perhaps, if he let her, he could later backtrack to find a way inside *her* mind. Because his way hadn't been working, and he was honest enough with himself to realize he wanted her more than he wanted the stone. More than he wanted to get away from Mormo, his father, the growing danger, all of it.

He just wanted Faraine. So he smiled and let her bring his head down for a kiss sure to doom them both.

CHAPTER TWENTY-ONE

F ara was exhausted. Between holding glamours at a distance
for four individuals, trying to think through the sugar rush
that had been blurring her thoughts, and denying how much she
wanted Varu, she felt for the one thing that had been constant
since finding the Bloode Stone.

Her need to control it.

"I need it," she whispered as she dragged Varu down to her,
bemused by how much she should have said, *I need you.*

"Then take it," he replied before their lips touched.

Heat stole through her, desire racing through her blood,
spiking her adrenaline with a swell of lust so intense she could do
nothing but feel.

Never had she felt such need for another, and she could do
nothing but give in to the rising tide of a fever that would not be
denied.

She kissed him, taking back the power from the stone that
throbbed... in his hand? The touch of his palm on her arm sang of
belonging, and she wrapped it around herself, entwining the
power of the Bloode Stone through Varujan, so that she wouldn't
burn from the intense bloode heat, safely embraced in his hold.

Varu kissed her back, just as hungry for her. Ever since their first kiss, she'd been holding back, trying to deal with her desire and the danger all around her. Responsibility had never been so trying, making sure to protect her brother, herself, and still manage to hold onto the one weapon that might destroy a creature bent on breaking worlds.

But none of that mattered as she joined herself to Varu, sinking into his kiss.

She didn't feel him lift her in his arms. Only as he lowered her to the bed did she realize he'd taken charge.

And she let him, lost in the burning red gaze that looked her over from head to toe.

"I need to be inside you."

She watched him undress, saw the evidence of his arousal, and knew this could only be stopped with bloodshed. Varu looked beyond control. As it should be. The bloodlust built, and she wanted to bite him. To make him lose himself in her, where *she* held the power.

He didn't give her time to think, and she didn't want to. She helped him take off her clothes, and then his mouth was over her breast, sucking her nipple to a stiff peak.

Sensation cascaded through her body and mind, echoed need, his and hers magnifying, playing off each other.

He sucked hard at her other breast, and she felt him thick and hard between her legs, seeking, probing.

"Yes, Varu. In me."

"Not yet," he managed, his words gritty. "Need you so much." He was kissing her, rubbing that cock over her sensitive center, pushing her past one orgasm straight into another. The kiss went on and on, his tongue winding with hers, stroking then retreating. He pulled back to whisper into her ear, "You're mine. Forever. In my bloode. In your blood." He licked her ear, nibbling at the sensitive point and driving her mindless.

She shifted, so slick and needy. "Look at me." She heard their voices together, one, coming from her mouth. "*Mine.*"

He nodded, waited as she spread her legs wide and arched into him, notching him at the entrance to her drenched sex.

She swore a fire blazed in those red eyes as she ordered, "Now. Come now."

He watched her without blinking as he thrust deep and jerked, moaning as he came in that first deep push.

She felt the stone throbbing, and the echo of ecstasy rippled throughout her body, her orgasm crashing over her once more.

Varu wasn't nearly close to being done, because he started moving, watching her as he claimed her in a dance shared by the very first of his kind.

"Yes," he hissed. "Mine. My mate," he pledged before kissing her once more.

She gripped him tightly inside her and felt him pulse again, filling her with seed.

But Varu wouldn't stop, and neither could she. Not yet. Not while the stone remained unfulfilled.

Varu kept moving, his hips pumping, while both of them struggled with the new wave of pleasure cresting close. "Bite me," he said, panting. "Take my bloode inside you."

She let her fangs sink into his chest and seized in a rapture she could never have fathomed as his bloode trickled down her throat.

Then she felt a sharp pain at her neck while Varu did the same, sucking then licking the wound shut. He slammed into her with desperation and cried out when he came, their communal bliss a sign to the stone that the act had finally been completed.

Varu continued to release inside her, braced on his hands as he stared down at her in a daze.

She stared right back, not sure what had happened but loving it regardless. The stone now lay completely open to her, Varu's power hers to command.

But none of that mattered as much as the feel of her mate finally claimed, finally inside her, where he belonged.

"Yes," he said, his voice deep, sexy. So very sexy. He jerked inside her once more, getting as deep as possible before slowly withdrawing.

Together, they'd made a huge mess, and she wanted to care. But not yet. "Do you think we could worry about what all this means later and take a bath now?"

He opened his mouth, showing her those sexy—no, *sharp*—fangs, then closed it. "Yes. Worry later. Much later."

Varu scooped her off the bed as if she weighed nothing. "Come, female, time to bathe. We've got a lot more claiming to do before we rejoin the others."

She felt the satisfaction inside him clear to her toes.

"And so many places I have yet to taste." His smile was nothing short of wicked.

She shivered, met his gaze, and smiled back.

VARU FELT no such urge to sleep, but his new—*female, not mate*—needed rest. Considering how much energy she'd expended on her earlier magic and the stress of all she'd been through, he figured she deserved to relax.

Plus, the moonlight streaming through the glass windows by the bed painted her gray skin in a vision of loveliness. He stroked her, gently caressing, and enjoyed her sigh of pleasure. The touch wasn't sexual but soothing, and that need to see to Fara's comfort felt right. As it should be.

Varu should be more upset about losing control to the fae, but in truth, he had never felt such incredible harmony with another. As if he'd been missing a part of himself for so long and had never known until he'd found her.

His mate.

Mate?

He ran his fingers over her shoulder, through her hair. Such soft, dark hair streaked with white, like the softest feline's fur. He fingered the tips of her ears, and she sighed and shifted her hips.

He smiled. A pleasure touch he had yet to thoroughly investigate. He'd make sure to pay strict attention to those sweet ears later.

A glance between his legs showed him hard once more. Not a surprise given how aroused he'd been since getting a taste of her essence. Her spirit, wrapped in a kiss, had ensnared him. And all he could think was, *thank fate*—a concept he didn't even believe in.

He sighed and snuggled behind her, drawing her into his strength.

The stone now followed Fara. And he followed the stone.

Whatever she wanted he'd give her. He chuckled to himself, knowing Mormo would be apoplectic once he learned what the crafty dusk elf had done. Taken both Varu and the Bloode Stone as her own.

But he didn't care, because he now lived inside her. He felt her true heart, knew her past hurts, her need to do right and protect those she considered her own. Surprisingly, Fara was a lot like him, except she'd never known safety, never known acceptance.

He planned on changing all that.

He had to.

Oddly, he considered what he'd once told her about his kind. Even after such an intense bonding, he still maintained a vital truth. Vampires did not love. He felt possessive. He coveted her. And now that he knew what it felt like to join with Fara in the most intimate of ways, he wanted no other.

Perhaps time would cure his insatiable need. That or the experience of having sex after such a long time had fried his senses, along with fucking with a Bloode Stone inside him.

Yes, that actually made sense. He couldn't identify his feelings—emotionally—for Faraine. But he wanted her with everything inside him. And yes, pleasing her pleased him. But that had nothing to do with affection and everything to do with sexual gratification.

Didn't it?

Yes, that had to be it. In making Fara happy, he'd smoothed the way toward his own happiness. Of course he had a rational explanation for his irrational feelings.

Pleased to have come to a reasonable conclusion about the new sensations concerning—not his mate, no, he'd been mistaken in that—his new *lover,* he relaxed and listened to her heartbeat, soothed by her nearness.

Finally finding a moment of peace, he let himself enjoy the scent of flowers and earth on his pillow and hugged her tighter, lost in the feel of her hair against his cheek.

HE HAD no idea how long he'd drifted, for he never napped at night. But it couldn't have been long, for the moon remained in her spot high in the sky. He rolled onto his back to find Fara climbing over him.

"Little elf, what are you doing?" he asked, his voice hoarse, as he watcher her crawl on her hands and knees between his legs, stopping above his stiffening shaft.

"I'm hungry and need something sweet." She leaned down to lick him from root to tip, and a jolt of seed spurted from him.

"It's pink," she said with a grin. "I like pink."

He flushed, feeling ridiculous for his embarrassment. "I'm vampire. Everything about me revolves around bloode."

"But you're actually sweet." She licked him again, and her eyes widened. "Literally."

He groaned, incredibly aroused at the sight of her mouth on him, those full breasts swaying as she engulfed him, bobbing up and down.

"Fara." He gripped the sheets and tore through the fabric. "You'll make me come too soon." And he had plans for her fine body.

She slowly sucked until he popped free from her mouth, leaving him incredibly aroused, his cockhead slick. "But you recover fast, don't you?"

"I do, but—"

"Then let me have some more. Is this part of your kind's ability to seduce? Sweet seed to addict the fae?"

He was speechless to answer as she took him to the back of her throat and moved faster, sucking harder.

He couldn't believe what he was seeing, a fantasy come to life, and he cupped her cheek as he watched. "I'm coming. So hard, Fara." His balls were like knots, steel tight as he readied to climax.

Instead of pulling away, as he'd expected her to, she bore down.

And swallowed a mouthful as he jerked, the orgasm stealing all sense as he released with a roar.

She pulled away, and still he came, even harder when she milked him with those small, strong hands.

They watched as he spilled onto her hands and his belly, and he did his best to catch his breath once more.

"Wow. That's a lot."

It always is with mates. He swallowed his first response and answered, "It's because of you."

Not a lie. And a fact that pleased the Bloode Stone to no end.

"Oh. I like that." She mounted him, absorbing more of him as she seated herself until she had taken all of him inside her. She closed her eyes and sighed. "I feel you. So much of your essence is in your seed."

"Yes." He sighed, feeling drunk and vulnerable with another and not caring. He'd never had an orgasm leave him so open, never been so helpless and deliberate about it.

"I have to move. Will you stay hard?" she asked and planted her hands on his flat stomach as she rode him. "Oh, wow. You're really big."

"For you." *And only you.* He felt an urge to breed with her. To plant life inside her sexy belly. And more. To be there, to protect, to provide. She needed pleasure. He'd give it to her.

He sat up, shocking her, and drove deeper, sucking her breasts while she rocked over him, up and down, pushing him to more pleasure than he'd ever had. And still he came while she milked him dry, grinding against the fingers he'd shoved between them as he teased the hard knub between her folds.

"Varu, yes, please. All in me," she moaned and seized, ripping another burst of seed from his balls, the pleasure almost painful.

He hugged her tight, teething her nipple with his fangs, since she seemed to like that, tightening around him each time he did.

She ran her hands through his hair and finally stopped moving, basking in their shared pleasure.

They were both breathing hard, exhausted, and he felt the onset of sunrise begin.

Fara looked at the wide glassy windows, looked back at him, and moved faster than he'd ever seen her move before.

She pulled the shades and curtains closed, encasing the room in darkness.

A sliver of light came through a different side of the room, so she hurried to close that as well.

Varu, who rarely slept during the day anymore, and never when not in a secure location, starting to drift into a doze.

Alarmed yet too dazed to do anything about it, his lids started to close.

"It's okay," Fara whispered from right next to him. "I won't let anyone come near or let the sun in. I swear."

He felt her hands over his face, felt her press a kiss to his lips, and sighed.

"I promise. I'll take care of you, Varu."

"That's my job, mate," he murmured and lost himself to the fog of the Bloode Stone and Fara singing him to sleep.

CHAPTER TWENTY-TWO

D uncan glared at Onvyr, wondering when Mormo would
realize the dusk elf needed to die.

This was the fourth time in as many hours when Onvyr turned
bat-shit crazy. It took Duncan, Orion, *and* Kraft to keep the
bastard down before tossing him into the holding cell under
the gym.

"Can't faff around all day taking care of this arse," he growled
to Kraft as Rolf joined them, studying their angry "guest."

"What?"

"We're wasting time with him when we should be going after
Varu." Duncan rubbed his chest. Something had changed. He
could feel it.

Though he played the charmer who tried to get along with
everyone, he had a different agenda than playing nice. His old
patriarch had been a decent chap, as were his father and uncle.
Duncan owed his loyalty to the clan who'd raised him.

Chosen to pay back the bloode debt incurred by his patriarch,
he'd done his duty thus far and had even come to like the others.
Mostly. Kraft, frankly, scared him. Funny, but way too powerful
when in a wolf-rage. He could easily overpower Orion, though

Kraft thought he was keeping his abilities a secret from the others.

Right.

Duncan knew information on all his kin, including the fact Varu had the hots for Faraine but kept trying to hide it. Onvyr, though annoying, had also seen through Varujan's failed attempts to seduce the dusk elf.

"Bet he's balls-deep in her right now," Rolf was saying, about as low class as one could expect from one of his kind.

Onvyr looked on him with rage but didn't try to break through the dragon's breath bars again. Perhaps because he couldn't. Which reminded Duncan to give a more careful study to the dusk elf's unique weapon, which Duncan had hidden in his room for further study.

"Shut it, Rolf," Duncan said offhandedly, not really caring about Onvyr's feelings but pretending he did.

Rolf flipped him the finger and left, complaining to Orion about the all strigoi he'd been forced to ignore on their way back from Bellevue.

Apparently, Mormo had a plan. Making sure the strigoi focused on Fara and Onvyr here in the house, under Mormo's protection, was more important than the needful killing of strigoi.

Fucking magician.

Onvyr stared at Duncan, who stared back, wondering what to make of this creature who could blend light and dark elf traits. They called him a dusk elf, but come on, the guy was currently pitch black with white hair. Nothing dusky about him.

"Duncan," Bella's voice came over the intercom, breaking his concentration.

Duncan turned from Onvyr, not surprised when the bloody fool tried to come at him through the bars and almost knocked himself silly.

Idiot. Duncan pressed the intercom. "Yes, Bella? It's Duncan."

"Hey, handsome. Would you mind telling Onvyr to relax? Mr. Mormo told me he might not make it up here in the next few hours. And Onvyr's supposed to play cards with me when the sun comes up. But he won't be able to if he keeps getting in trouble. "

Duncan turned to Onvyr, who looked at him sheepishly. "Sorry. I can't help it sometimes."

Duncan felt for him, but that didn't make it any easier to handle the elf. "Whatever." He pressed the intercom. "He heard you. I'm coming up."

"Thanks!" Bella's perky answer amused him. For a human female with no power, she did surprisingly well among creatures of the night. Varu, that brooding bastard, always felt like a powder keg about to explode. Then there were Orion and Kraft, two hulking brutes who didn't know how to spell the word charm, let alone use it. Khent had his nose stuck so high in the air it was a wonder he could walk.

And Rolf.... Duncan avoided running into a sheet of plastic wrap stretched across the end of the hallway and turned toward another set of stairs buried in the east wing of the basement.

"Shit," he heard Rolf swear. "I thought for sure I'd get him the way I got you two yesterday."

"I hate you," Orion growled.

"I hate Rolf more," Kraft said before cursing the blond bastard in German.

Duncan shook his head and continued past Hecate's odd half realm, where he saw all manner of creatures, divine and not, though he hadn't seen Seraphina or her magnificent breasts in a while. Such a shame.

He joined Bella upstairs and drank a pint of blood, hungry because Varu was hungry.

Duncan had made sure to bond to the most powerful of them upon first arriving at the home. He kept tabs on the strigoi, though

Varu didn't know it. Or if he did, he hadn't cared to sever the connection.

But with the Bloode Stone now in play, they were all majorly fucked.

He sat stewing, simultaneously annoyed to be having to deal with Varu's issues and pleased he'd been chosen from his tribe to fix a goddess's problem.

Mormo soon entered, and the others joined them around the kitchen island while Bella made herself scarce. He doubted she'd be able to find Onvyr in that maze of a basement, especially since the underground cell had a secret entrance.

But then, Bella ran the place and worked for Mormo. Who the hell knew what she could do?

"Say, Mormo, do you own a pair of jeans?" Orion asked, the burly vampire leaning against the counter with his arms crossed over that massive chest.

Kraft murmured something under his breath that made Orion laugh.

Mormo grinned. "I do." He said nothing else.

Khent huffed. "Congratulations for having jeans. Now, can we please talk about the strange shit happening with the Bloode Stone? Power has shifted, and I don't like it."

"Yeah, what he said," Rolf agreed, still smiling.

Always smiling, even when trying to bury a dagger in your back because it might be funny. Duncan scowled at him.

Rolf pointed to himself, made a heart shape with his hands, then pointed at Duncan, who did his best not to laugh. No point encouraging the dickhead.

Mormo nodded. "Good point, Khent. Glad someone is keeping us on track."

Khent now appeased, that stick up his ass still in place, waited for Mormo to continue.

"Right. Here's what we know: Master Vampire Atanase is in

town with strigoi hunters intent on reclaiming our elves and the stone. He knows we have them, and he's already proven a lot stronger than he was the last time I saw him, which was just a few months ago. This is not good."

Duncan agreed. Everyone was intently listening to Mormo, so he figured they'd also realized the problems they faced. Maybe enough to stop putting plastic wrap in hallways or putting banana peels on already slippery floors.

"I have a bad feeling the Bloode Stone we have isn't the only one out there." Mormo paused. "I think Atanase has the others."

Rolf stopped smiling. "That's a death sentence for the rest of us—draugr, revenant, you name it. You know Atanase will move to kill all his rivals. The Bloode Stones are powerful weapons, but they don't work on everyone."

Orion frowned. "They don't? Then why is the one here affecting all of us?"

"Because Varu is its rightful master," Khent said, his eyes shrewd. "You thought we didn't know about him," he said to Mormo. "But you were wrong."

"Wait. What do we know?" Kraft asked, his accent thick, meaning he was worried.

Mormo turned to Duncan, surprising him. "Would you like to tell them, or should I?"

Duncan hadn't realized Mormo had known about his information collecting. And he didn't like it, but he'd deal with Mormo later. "Varujan is the son of Master Vampire Atanase of the Crimson Veil. The Bloode Stone calls to Varu because he's powerful. Even without it, he can connect our kind."

"I thought that was the Bloode Stone," Orion said with a frown. "Or just that he's older than most of us."

"He's not that much older than I am," Rolf cut in, "but he commands naturally. He's likely already a master, correct?" he asked Mormo, who nodded.

Duncan sighed. "A master with a sense of decency his sire lacks. Atanase will do whatever it takes to destroy his son, which means as his clan, we're all in danger."

"As is Faraine," Mormo said. "She broke her brother out of Atanase's prison, and the vampire was rather fond of him."

Duncan had been missing that piece of information. "So that's why Onvyr is so troubled."

Mormo nodded. "Years spent with Atanase damage the soul." He shook his head. "There is no way we can let the strigoi have the Bloode Stone or the dusk elves."

"You mean the stone that's now inside Varu." Duncan had been waiting for Mormo to divulge that, surprised he hadn't.

The others looked concerned.

Khent swore. "The stone is *inside* Varu? Then why do I feel a stark fae presence at all times?" He shared a look with Rolf, and his eyes took on a surprising twinkle when he said, "Is is because our Varu has been, how shall I say, inside a fae of his own?"

The others laughed, though Duncan had a bad feeling about this new tie between fae and strigoi. "Hold on. Fara brought the Bloode Stone to Varu. He's the rightful master of the thing, and it helps connect all of our kind. Making us an unstoppable army, right?"

Mormo frowned. "It does more than that. It also elevates the Bloode, stimulating an awakening in the more powerful."

"Meaning the magic in a vampire. It grows," Khent explained.

Mormo paused. "I think that's why Atanase has become more powerful, because he somehow found the other Bloode Stones."

"There are six according to myth," Khent said.

Rolf rubbed the back of his head. "And we're thinking Atanase has a few? Where did he get them? And why is he waiting to attack, if that's the case?"

Duncan wondered if maybe Atanase was waiting for Varu's Bloode Stone to be brought to him. By his own son or someone closely involved with him. Someone like a frail, sexy little dusk elf who might have used the lot of them in her bid to save her brother.

He met Khent's gaze but said nothing. He'd need to talk to the others later, away from Mormo's ever-listening presence. Something about all this didn't make sense, and he trusted no one but himself and his fellow kin to make it right.

If only he could include Varu in that group. But he had a feeling the strigoi was lost to them, at least, for now.

WHEN VARU WOKE, he woke all at once. Not with a slow yawn and stretch or blinking awake.

One moment he was asleep, the next he sat up and stared around him, conscious and ready to kill. His eyes were wide open and red, his claws out, his fangs wicked sharp and illuminated by the dim light by the side of the bed.

Fara had been awake all day, needing to be alert to protect him. That he'd slept next to her had told her exactly how much he trusted her, something she never would have believed if she hadn't seen it herself.

The myth about vampires sleeping like the dead was true. His chest never rose or fell, and he didn't breathe while asleep.

Awake and deadly, he should have scared her to death.

Instead, she wanted him all over again.

By the sight of his erection tenting the blanket over him, he wanted it as well.

He turned, blinked at her, and relaxed with a small smile. "Ah, little fae. You're ready for me."

"I, what?"

He pounced, tossing her gown aside before mounting and sliding inside her with a sigh. "I smelled your need."

"Oh, well, yes." She couldn't argue the point, especially as slick as she was. She had no idea what yesterday had turned into, and it had fogged in her mind when she tried to understand it. Perhaps because the Bloode Stone wouldn't let her remember in greater detail.

She only knew she had power over Varu in some fashion, and that she wanted him as much as he wanted her.

"Gods, yes," she moaned as he continued to graze that sensitive place between her legs, his girth and length hitting the pleasure spots deep inside her. Being with him was like riding a wild earth demon, dangerous and satisfying all at once.

"Bite me," he moaned and sucked her nipple, making her susceptive to every lick and nibble.

She bit his shoulder, her fangs tiny in comparison to his, but her bite made him shiver.

"Fuck, yes. Fara, please. By the Bloode," he swore as he moved faster, thrusting harder with each push and pull. "Need to get deeper."

She scratched at his shoulders and linked her ankles behind his back, enthralled with his strength. "Yes, deeper. All the way inside me," she moaned, lost to his scent and taste.

He kissed her, his fang scratching her lip. And when he tasted her, he shoved hard one final time and had her coming seconds before he joined her.

The release echoed through them both, the pleasure overwhelming. Powerful. And doing something to the Bloode Stone that worried her.

Later, after Varu left her to use the shower and give them both some space, she realized she wasn't as in control as she should have been. Yet, she knew for a fact she'd tied them both to the stone, and of course, to each other.

Varu would never hurt her. She felt that deep in her bones. He wanted her like no other, a fact she couldn't deny, a truth in her blood. Not Bloode. *Blood.*

She somehow knew he didn't see the difference between them anymore.

She joined him by the glass wall of the shower, not even pretending not to look at his magnificent body. Corded with muscle, pale from the sun, shadows of his strength grew as he turned and washed his hair, slicking it back from a face filled with secrets.

He raised a brow. "You coming in to join me? Or are you just happy to watch?"

To her shock, he held his cock in hand, and she saw it stiffen as he rubbed it. "I want you again," he growled. "All the time. I... don't understand it. But we are connected."

My mate, he'd called her.

Had they mated? What did that mean? She remembered what he'd said about mates, how vampires felt possessive and didn't love anyone. How strigoi sent their mates away.

In the end, it didn't appear to matter.

She only knew she kept wanting him, and it wasn't natural.

This is your doing, she sent to the stone. The little jerk ignored her before understanding her unspoken insult.

Not nice. It sulked.

She hastily replaced "jerk" with "gem" in her thoughts before shielding herself from the overly dramatic stone.

Varu continued to watch her with a broody stare. "Come to me," he said, his gaze mesmerizing, and that had nothing to do with his power of seduction. Everything in him called to her, and she could no more deny him than she could deny anyone she cared for.

She entered the shower with him and stood idly while he washed her, taking care of his *possession.* She didn't like the thought, needing more from him. Then, as if she'd coached him, he changed the tone of his ministrations, his strokes now caressing, his touch careful.

He kissed her neck, her cheek, and whispered, "Turn around to face the wall. That's it." He continued to kiss her neck, scraping his fangs over her throat but not piercing her skin. Then he nudged her ankles wider and pulled her hips back.

Before she could ask him what he thought about them together, he entered her from behind, the taking slow, deliberate, and full of care. He continued to whisper sweet words, his hands everywhere, especially between her legs as he pushed her to know even deeper levels of pleasure. And all the while he took her, owning her as he thrust deeper and harder.

Until he came with her, filling her once more. But this time he left a part of himself behind, a sense of affection she could all but feel echoing in the stone. As if Varu had come to realize he did in fact care for her.

But he didn't speak of it, and neither did she.

They finished the shower without talking, but Varu's kisses didn't lie.

The strigoi felt something for her, even if he couldn't say the words. And she wished his affection didn't mirror what she felt for him as well.

After Fara had glamoured them both again, Varu convinced a pretty female cab driver to take them back to the house then forget about them. Because Fara watched him carefully, he gave the driver an extra tip before she left.

Not that he wouldn't have provided for the human for doing a service, but he might not have been so generous with his cash.

Baffled at what this new connection with the fae meant, he nevertheless craved more of it.

Coming inside Fara was like finding a slice of the afterlife. He could linger inside her and feel nothing but goodness, pleasure, and peace.

With her, Varu knew belonging and the need to be more. She made him want to be... good?

It confused him and filled him with purpose at the same time.

But he didn't get two feet in the door before the others swarmed him.

"Where the hell were you?" Duncan.

"Answer your phone, dipshit." Orion.

Kraft nodded. "*Ja.*"

"What is this bonding between you and the female?" Khent gasped. "She possesses both you *and* the stone?"

Everyone grew quiet until Mormo clapped. "Hurray, Varu's back." His fake enthusiasm had everyone amused, even Khent. "Now, boy, let's talk about you two and what you've been up to."

At that, Rolf appeared and nodded like a toy bobble head. "Oh yes, let's."

Varu growled, needing some violence to sate his constant hunger.

Fara placed a hand on his arm, and he stilled. "Can I see my brother?"

Bella arrived behind the others with a yawn. "I'm beat. Oh, hey, Fara. Where have you been?"

"Um, out with Varu."

It amused him to see her flush, especially because she'd unraveled her glamour the moment they'd entered the house. And now he could see pretty purple highlights dancing over her cheeks.

"Out, huh?" Bella chuckled, and the others turned to see her blushing as well, a pale pink over her human cheeks. "Oh, well, I was *out* with your brother earlier. He'll be coming along shortly." She smiled at Mormo. "Mr. Mormo, sir, I'm going to go clean the basement if that's okay. You guys are pretty messy."

Mormo frowned, saw the others looking at him, and cleared his expression. "Yes, thank you, Bella. I apologize for our household."

"I'm not messy," Rolf tried.

"You keep leaving evidence of your pranks behind," Khent said with a sniff. "The whipped cream in the face was not amusing."

"Getting his ass handed to him was. You did a good job, Khent." Orion grinned and took a step toward Fara.

Varu moved so swiftly everyone stared in awe, and he couldn't blame them, shocked at himself.

"Um, did he just teleport?" Kraft asked. "Because that's new, right? Or can he do that because he powered up with all the fucking?"

"Kraft," Mormo admonished.

Fara slapped a hand over her eyes. "I can't even."

Varu growled at Kraft. "Really? You want to keep that big mouth, maybe close it."

"Right. Yes. Okay." Kraft stepped behind Orion and chuckled, but not quietly enough because Varu still heard it.

"You are such an ass," Orion muttered.

"He just moved like Atanase," Mormo said thoughtfully.

"My father was here, wasn't he?" Varu made sure to keep Fara behind him. Safe.

"In a manner of speaking." Mormo waved the matter away. "Don't worry. He was in another dimension. The house is protected. But we need to talk. All of us." He looked at Fara, who glanced away, her cheeks still flushed. "The Bloode Stone is now active, and it needs to come out of Varu before it takes him over."

Fara darted a glanced at Mormo. "What do you mean takes him over?

"Before it kills him."

"*What?*" Fara yanked Varu's hand up, staring down at it as if she could see the stone. Hell, maybe she could.

Varu didn't know what Mormo was talking about, but he didn't think the magician was telling the truth. The stone fit inside Varu, a part of him. If he wanted it to leave, he felt sure it would. He only kept it close because with it, he could protect Fara. And it had become vitally important that he keep her safe at all times.

She dropped his hand, and he missed the contact. But he didn't let anything show on his face, unnerved at the attention he seemed to be getting.

"Onvyr," Fara cried and raced to the big lug who appeared and lumbered toward her, yawning.

"Hey, Fara. You'll never guess who's back." He smiled and hugged his sister, the black pitch of his skin wrong. His presence wrong. His closeness to the female an affront. The dark one was not kin.

"Fara, come back. Now," Mormo said quietly.

The vampires around Varu were tense, all of them ready to attack her brother, Varu noticed with surprise. Then he realized he felt a lot of anger... from the stone.

My mate, it conveyed. *Mine.* Because Varu and the stone were one.

Yes, but he's only her brother. Added protection from our enemies, he told it, and it relaxed its hold on the others.

Fara slowly stepped away from her brother but kept her hand in his. "Wh-who's back, Onvyr?"

Her idiot brother didn't realize his danger, because he grinned at the others. "She Who Walks Between Worlds."

"What?" Mormo frowned as a familiar giant battle cat snarled and stalked down Fara's hallway toward Onvyr. "Why will you not stay gone?"

The feline paused to rub her face against Onvyr before sneering at the others. To Varu, she gave a respectful nod before disappearing down a stairwell that emerged before her in the middle of the marble floor.

"Whoa. That's a new one." Onvyr followed her with a wave to Fara. "See you later, Sister."

Everyone gaped at the weird steps going down before they gradually vanished.

Duncan broke the silence. "Bugger it all. This house is fuckin' weird." He walked into the kitchen and grabbed a beer from the refrigerator.

"Good idea," Orion seconded and joined him, soon followed by the others.

Varu took Fara's hand, relieved she didn't try to pull away after she'd felt the cloud of violence toward her brother. "Come on. I could use a beer myself."

"You drink beer too?" She gave him a shy smile when he looked at her, and his heart raced for no reason he could think of. "I have all kinds of questions about you."

His lips curled. "Me too."

"Ahem." Mormo, that annoying weirdo, cleared his throat. "If you two love birds could contain the flirting for now? We have questions."

"And we'd like answers." Rolf wiggled his brows. "Preferably with videos and pictures. So who was on top?"

Varu wanted to gut the male, but Fara's laughter was contagious, and he found himself laughing with her. He laughed even harder at the stunned amusement from the others. Until they all joined in.

For the first time in forever, he felt a part of something greater than the strigoi, than his tribe, or even his kind.

He felt surrounded by real family and a female he'd claimed. *All mine,* he thought with satisfaction, unaware his eyes glowed a bright, bloode-red.

MORMO COULDN'T BELIEVE the change in Varu as he stood with the others in the kitchen, drinking a beer and conversing, as if they were all *friends.* Fara smiled with them, a part of their clan now. He could sense it, the Bloode Stone forging a new path of connection for the seven creatures who should never have bonded.

Even more interesting, Varu had clearly become their patriarch. Mormo's magic couldn't hold onto them through the layer of bloode-magic wrought by the Bloode Stone. Yet Varu didn't seem conscious of his power.

Mormo cleared his throat, and everyone looked at him. "I'm sure by now you can feel that the structure in our clan has shifted. Varu is your new patriarch."

All but Duncan nodded. The revenant seemed perturbed by the change. Interesting.

"I'm still kin, so to speak, thanks to Hecate's power. But you're now truly a new clan under a powerful leader."

Khent glared. "Not my leader, though I'll claim him as kin."

"What he said," Orion growled, and Kraft nodded.

Rolf shook his head. "Boys will be boys. I guess I'll go with the popular vote."

"Mormo's talking a lot of bullshit," Varu said, glaring at Mormo with a familiar annoyance that felt normal. The magic in the strigoi's bloode felt stable, so at least Mormo didn't have to worry about that.

Mormo ignored Varu, deliberately needling him. "The patriarchy is not significant at the moment. What's important is that Atanase is a clear danger. We'll need to be on our guard. Fara and Varu, continue to practice channeling the power of the Bloode Stone. We can all feel the energy inside it affecting us. Even me, and I'm only a peripheral part of your clan."

Duncan watched Fara with wariness. "Yes, and she's not a part of us either, though she feels like kin. It's unnatural." He looked at Varu. "But we'll deal with it. If Atanase comes for the stone, he'll bring others—*a lot* of others. Remember, he's a master." He gave the others a grim smile. "But so is Varu."

"I'm no master." Varu frowned. "It's the stone amping our connection."

"If you say so." Duncan shrugged. "But you need to figure out just what it, you, and the rest of us can do against a master or we're going to have serious problems."

Fara spoke up, watching Mormo. "Why can't Hecate interfere? She's the one who brought everyone here, correct?"

A good question. Hecate's answer each time he asked her about the vampires? *Love will find a way.*

What in the all the realms did that mean?

Since they waited for an answer, Mormo gave them one. "It doesn't work that way."

Varu pinched the bridge of his nose. "Here we go again."

"My mistress oversees the crossover boundaries between all worlds. As important as this one is to all of you, there are many, many more crossovers where wars threaten to break out at any time."

Duncan sighed. "Yeah. I saw a bunch of Amazons fighting with each other not too long ago. There's some dodgy shit going on in the basement."

Orion turned to him with a frown. "What?"

"I want to see Amazons," Rolf said, his fangs visible when he grinned. "The stronger the woman, the better. And they taste spectacular."

Kraft perked up. "Oh, really?"

"I could eat," Khent said offhandedly, and the five of them left for the basement while Varu, Fara, and Mormo stared after them.

"They just left." Fara shook her head. "We were talking about serious danger from a master vampire. Duncan mentioned Amazons in the basement. And they left."

"Always thinking with their fangs," Varu said with a sigh. "But I have to admit I'm curious. I'll be back." He gave her a kiss on the lips and left.

Mormo saw the elf's surprise. He felt it as well, astounded over that incredible showing of affection from Varujan, and needed badly to talk to Hecate about the matter.

Fortunately, she rang in his mind.

"Apologies, Fara, but my mistress calls."

"You know, I'm tired. I think I'll take a nap." Fara paused. "The house is spelled against Atanase though, right?"

Because you know how it feels to be in his clutches, don't you? "Yes, it's safe. For now."

"I'll take what I can get." Fara smiled at him, and Mormo knew what Varu saw in her.

A pure heart and a giving spirit. Someone who could accept a blood-drinker and give him what he needed.

That was if a certain someone's father didn't kill her first.

Mormo sighed, heard his mistress demanding he hurry the hell up, and disappeared in a flash of light.

CHAPTER TWENTY-FOUR

Two days had passed, and Varu spent time with Fara, getting to use the stone through her, and with her. Together, they were controlling a small group of upir out near Tacoma, convincing the dozen vampires to leave a gathering of university students partying in the woods alone.

Fara was adamant about that, though Varu thought the vampires should have at least been allowed to kill a few of the humans, to thin the herd.

One of the women, wearing a short shirt that emphasized her large breasts and trim belly and an even shorter skirt, sneered at Fara. "Nice hair, bitch. What is it Halloween?" She tittered, her gaze clinging to Varu and centering on his crotch. "Oh wow. Yum. Come on, pretty man. You can do better than her."

Varu stood near Fara, so the female assumed they were together. That pleased him. Though he didn't like her comments.

The upir pretending to be fellow students stood around, annoyed because their fun had been interrupted.

"We were only going to snack," one of them said sulkily. He seemed young because he should have known better than to talk out of turn.

Had he been one of the Crimson Veil clan, he'd have been either whipped or had his tongue ripped out. In front of Atanase, he'd have been killed after being skinned.

Varu waited to see what the upir in charge of their gathering would do, because it couldn't possibly be the young one.

Another upir shook his head and said, "Calm down, Leo."

"But I'm hungry." Leo stood behind the mouthy woman and pulled her closer to him, rubbing his hand over her belly and up to her breast. "This one's so fine."

"I really am." The woman laughed, and a few of her friends returned to partying, turning the music back on.

"I could kill them all." Leo turned a covetous eye on Fara. "That one too. Bitch looks tasty."

"Do you see?" another of the upir said as he drifted closer to Varu. "We don't mean offense, but they are ripe with life. Delicate, so easy to rend."

Varu nodded, noticed Fara's irritation, and raised a brow. He felt her jealousy through the stone and wanted to laugh. But he did his best not to reflect his pleasure over her jealousy, by expression or by emoting, used to keeping himself shielded.

The Bloode Stone had bonded with him, but it also allowed him to keep some thoughts separate. So far, his plan to ensnare his little dusk elf was working. Yes, she pretty much owned him, but he found her so enticing that he he didn't mind.

In or out of bed, she entranced him. He liked watching her expressions, so clearly displayed on her face. Though he disliked her glamour, he knew out here, around the humans and other magir, that she needed it. Tonight though, in the dark, he'd asked her not to put a human-seeming on him.

It was best the upir acknowledge him by sight before they felt him take over. They needed to know he was not to be trifled with, and that the Night Bloode had power. With any luck, they'd chalk up their need to obey him to his status as clan patriarch and not due to any a hint of the Bloode Stone still inside him.

"I'm not hungry, Fara." He caressed her arm. "I ate earlier." He winked at her, pleased to see her blush. "But the upir are on a hunt, and it would be cruel to leave them hurting."

"Since when do you care about being cruel?" she muttered.

He didn't allow himself to grin, though he wanted to. Since being mated—bonded—to the female, he had started to find humor and delight in many things, feelings he'd never experienced while in the Crimson Veil.

"Well, I *do* care about my kind. If we supervise their feeding now, you won't feel guilty later, because they won't have killed someone."

One of the humans must have overheard, because she darted away.

Varu sighed. "The drive to hunt isn't going to help matters stay calm."

He watched the bloodlust grow. One of the upir hunted down the running female and dragged her back, kicking and screaming, so loud she could be heard over the music.

Someone had the sense to turn it off, finally.

The mouthy woman from before pulled away from kissing Leo and stared at her screaming friend. "Okay, we're leaving."

Leo didn't listen, because he sank his fangs into her neck and drank, holding her still.

Fara glared.

Varu sighed, but he wanted to make her happy. "All of you will stop what you're doing and listen." The power behind his command punched through everyone at the party, to human and upir alike.

Fara patted him on the arm. "Thanks."

"I am at your service." He gave her a slight bow.

"Can you tell the women to leave and forget all this?"

He did as she asked as she asked it, reading her intent through the Bloode Stone. The humans departed, then he drew the upir closer. They'd been useful for his and Fara's experiment with the stone. Time to let them go. "Go home. Tell your patriarch there's a new master in town."

The others stared at him in concern.

"But I have no interest in upir territory. Just the Night Bloode."

They as one bowed their heads and vanished—all but Leo, whom Varu held back with the force of his will.

Fara stared at the young upir. "Varu?"

"Can you show me what you did to the upir who recorporated, you know, that night when I first captured you?"

She flushed. "You heard about that, huh?"

"You've shown to have power over the earth. But what I learned from the upir we first questioned was still startling. I'd like to see."

"It will be uncomfortable for him."

Varu snorted. "I don't care."

The upir under his thrall didn't move though he clearly wanted to.

"Okay." Fara knelt and put a hand on the ground. She closed her eyes and whispered a plea to Gaia. Varu heard it through the stone and felt a vast power answer her call.

To Leo, he said, "Next time, maybe you'll remain silent in the presence of your superior." Varu narrowed his eyes in warning. "And you never, ever, threaten *this* female." He nodded to Fara. "Or I'll rip out your heart and crush it while you stand watching." He mentally reached out with the stone, closing a fist of energy around the upir's heart.

Leo gasped and clutched his chest, locked in agony until Varu let him go.

"Learn well. You won't get a second chance."

Leo nodded violently then shrieked in pain.

Varu watched as he started to, well, melt. Flesh and sinew, blood then bone, all dissolved, licked up by the earth beneath his feet.

Varu stepped back, thoroughly impressed.

"That's it, but it takes a lot out of me." Fara stood, shaky, and accepted his arm to balance. "The upir's okay. He's just a little gooey at the moment." She glared at the mass on the ground seeping up from the dirt. "I don't appreciate being thought of as prey."

To Varu's surprise, his dusk elf felt a little bit like him. Much more predatory than she'd seemed before. He wondered if the stone was changing her, or if bonding to him had brought out the predator in her. For all that Fara didn't seem to consider herself a fighter, she had plenty of backbone.

He suddenly had to know all about her.

"I think we're done here." He guided her away from the reforming upir.

They walked back through Bresemann Forest, and he sensed her delight at being outside.

"I like it here."

"It is nice," he agreed, annoyed the clouds covered the moon. His enhanced vision allowed him to see well enough, but he was disappointed not to see Fara's skin shining under the moonlight. "You have an affinity for power gems and the earth. Yet your brother talks to animals and fights like a vampire. What are your parents like?"

She started when he reached for her hand and smiled at him shyly, gripping him as they walked. "My parents.... Well, my mom was a light elf. My dad a dark elf. They were sworn enemies who happened upon each other in the woods one day. Though my mother could have killed him, *should have* killed him, she let my father go.

"He returned, day after day, until he found her bathing by a pool under the moonlight." She smiled, and he felt his heart catch. *Ridiculous. Must be the stone's doing.* He shrugged off soft sentiment and listened, needing to learn more.

Varu cleared his throat. "Trapped by his own lusts. That I can understand."

She squeezed his hand. "Shush. It was more than lust. Well, probably an attraction at the beginning, sure. But my father talked to my mother, got to know her. They realized they only hated each other because rival clan leaders a thousand years ago had fallen out with each other. My parents fell in love and mated. Onvyr came first, then me. But one day not long after I was born, my mother had a change of heart and went back to her people. Years later, while I was still young, she came back with a group of them, and they found me all by myself, studying my rocks." She paused and bit her lip then looked up at him, her eyes shining. "She died protecting me. My father had been off with my brother, hunting. They came back and found a squad of light elves dead around us, with me protected in her arms."

"A warrior, your mother."

She smiled through tears. "Yes."

He didn't like her sadness. "Stop it." He carefully wiped her eyes, her tears like magic, burning into his flesh, making him grieve with her.

"I loved my mother, just as I love my father and brother."

"Where is your father now?"

She sighed. "He kept us hidden for hundreds of years, but a village elder found him out. Father hid us with a small caste of dusk elves deep in Stone Fell, a magical place of beauty and peace." *And boredom*, he swore she thought but didn't say. "Unfortunately, to make restitution for harboring dusk elves, despite us being his own family, Father was forced to life-swap with some of Danu's children."

"The Tuatha Dé Danann ?" He had always wondered about the elves. "You elves worship different gods and goddesses, yes? In different pantheons."

"Yes. And lately the gods have been arguing about our kind. So to make peace, Father has been serving on The Wild Hunt. He likes it but says Danu's children are really full of themselves."

"You should meet Gwyn ap Nudd. He's a legendary hero and has an ego the size of Orion's feet."

She chuckled. "Funny. Anyway, with Father gone, it's been just me and Onvyr." She quieted.

"Fara?"

She walked a few more paces before lifting her wounded gaze to meet his. "It's my fault. All of this. Atanase, my brother being tortured. I'm responsible."

"What?" Finally. He sensed she meant to spill the truth. And he would listen.

FARA'S GUILT had been building for years, especially the past few months, since rescuing her brother. "If I hadn't left Stone Fell, I never would have been caught by Atanase."

"But you were cursed." Varu waited, his gaze patient, his curiosity aroused.

She could feel bits of him through the Bloode Stone. Always present, his power hers to command, but his feelings came and went though his desire was never in question.

"I lied." When he didn't blink, she continued, "Your father found me when I appeared through a gate that put me near the strigoi stronghold. I have no idea how I got there. I was bored at home, and I asked a druid to send me somewhere different, where I could wander and see a new world.

"It was only supposed to be for a short while. I wouldn't be gone long enough to be noticed. Onvyr spent so much time training with our warriors, and no one paid me much mind. I told him I'd be traveling for a bit and not to look for me.

"Then I stepped through a gate. Right into a clan of strigoi." She shuddered, remembering what a nightmare that had been. "The only thing that saved me from being drained was that they saw my true form, knew me as a dusk elf right away. They took me straight to their patriarch. Unfortunately, he was in a meeting with Atanase at the time, and I overheard them mention a search for power gems."

Varu's gaze narrowed. "Who mentioned the gems?"

"The group of strigoi where I first landed had been hunting for Bloode Stones for Atanase. I knew if I didn't make myself important to him somehow, he'd kill me. So I told your father I had an affinity for power gems. He demanded proof, and I found him a gem to amplify his senses, buried near where that clan had been searching. We had a discussion, and in return for letting me live, I would find Bloode Stones for him." At his hard look, she swallowed and said, "So it was kind of a curse."

"How many stones does he have?"

"Five." She blew out a breath. "But they're all really small. The one you have is huge compared to them." She paused. "And so much more powerful. At first, I didn't think it was a big deal. I'd never heard much about the Bloode Stones, but I was curious. And the more I learned, the more they fascinated me. But Varu, I didn't know what they could do." She swallowed. "I watched Atanase test out that first one with a draugr. He let the vamp hold a Bloode Stone. And with it, the draugr commanded two dozen strigoi with ease. Atanase took it back of course, had the draugr killed, and ordered me to find the rest.

"I was scared. And weak." She felt so ashamed and looked away from Varu. "I found him two more, but then I couldn't continue. I knew what he wanted with them by then. To rule the

Bloode Empire, and to turn the worlds into a feeding ground with him at the helm. So I stopped."

"And he took your brother," Varu said.

She glanced at him through tears, not expecting to see compassion on his face. "Yes."

He gathered her in his arms.

Fara cried, for the first time letting herself feel all that anguish and guilt for what she'd done. She didn't know how long they remained embraced but finally pulled back and wiped her eyes. "Sorry."

"How long did he have Onvyr?"

"Four years." She had to catch her breath. "He tortured me for just a few days and I wanted to die. But he had Onvyr for so much longer. I did my best to slow the search, to look for any way around obeying him. But I had to save Onvyr. I managed to find help and broke my brother out of Atanase's prison. By then, though, I'd already given him five stones. Then I learned about you."

Varu cocked his head. "What about me?"

"A contact mentioned you just might be the answer to ridding the world of Atanase."

"Being his son doesn't make me strong enough to battle and defeat a master. And trust me, he has no love for me. He won't hesitate to kill me."

"I know that now. But you're powerful. Even without the stone, you had a lot more power than I'd figured. With it, you can fight him."

"No."

"Yes," she said, willing him to believe it. "Varu, don't you get it? I brought you the Bloode Stone so you could fight your father and stop him. It's not just a matter of stopping a master who's determined to conquer the world. It's stopping a monster who's planning on conquering everyone and everything, bringing nothing but destruction." Even among masters, Atanase was considered a cruel leader.

He groaned. "I'm not disputing the fact he needs to be stopped. Hell, *I* want to end him. I have for a very long time. But I serve this bloode-debt to Mormo at my father's behest. I'm still, though it pains me to say it, under his command. I can't beat him, Fara. Not with this Bloode Stone. And not with Hecate or Mormo or anyone's help. He's my sire, and that means I can never, ever kill him. Not while our bloode is tied."

No matter how many times Fara argued with him on the ride home, Varu told her the same thing. A truth she didn't want to acknowledge.

Varu was pledged to his father until Mormo released him from the bloode debt. Yet without the bloode debt keeping him allied to Mormo's cause—and keeping Fara safe from all harm—Varu would be his father's pawn. An awful case of Varu being helpless against Atanase. He hated it, but then, he'd always been at the mercy of his sadistic sire.

"You act like I don't want to end him. I do." Varu growled as he put his foot on the gas. "He killed my mother a few years after my birth. He's killed or injured anyone I ever cared about, until I learned not to care, that strigoi have no feelings and no desires other than what their master decrees. I've seen him behead servants for breathing too loudly. For taking females for some fucked up perversion. He's a monster who's only grown worse—and more powerful—with age. But he's smart, and he's tied me to him. We share bloode, a magical bond from sire to progeny. Patricide, in vampire culture, is only a forgivable sin if the progeny wins. But if I try to raise a hand against him, he'll simply tell me to stop and I'll be forced to obey."

"So you won't fight him?" Fara looked ready to cry again.

"Sweet, I *can't* fight him. You're not hearing me. The moment I step foot in our territory, my loyalty will snap back to him automatically. His orders are mine to carry out, no matter how much I might hate him."

"The Bloode Stone can counter it. You have a new clan now."

"A clan built on magic from a goddess and a magician. Magic that's already been weakened by the Bloode Stone. And while we're a newborn clan made of members from different tribes, we're still small and fragile compared to the strigoi. My father has shaped them, remember. He's got more than a few hundred strigoi surrounding him at any given time. They would massacre us before we could make a stand." He felt her frustration. "Maybe with Mormo's help, we can figure a way around my bond."

"Maybe." She slumped in her seat, and he felt her pain. If they could transfer the stone to Rolf, or maybe to Khent, they might be able to sharpen Varu's focus, enough for him to work around his bond to his sire. Once Mormo absolved him of his bloode debt, Varu could try to keep connected to his new clan, with any luck severing his bond to the Crimson Veil, and thus giving him more distance from Atanase. The stone muddied his thoughts too much, yet Varu needed its power. But if Mormo were to be believed, the stone belonged to Varu due to his parentage. A conundrum he needed to figure out, because he couldn't let Fara down.

He frowned, caught between two masters now, apparently.

"What's wrong?"

"Why do you ask?"

"You look like you're about to break the steering wheel."

He released his grip on the wheel and glanced at her, listening to what the Bloode Stone had to tell him. A shocking addition to add to his troubles. "*You* think to take my loyalty from my sire."

"Yes."

He liked that she didn't lie to him. "But I've told you my kind don't feel much beside basic hungers. Lust, not love. Pleasure, not affection."

She watched him, her lavender eyes bright. "You feel nothing for me but desire?"

"Yes." He scowled. "It's just sexual."

"Uh-huh." She no longer seemed to be upset.

"Are you smiling, female?"

"No."

"You are," he growled. "I'm not lying to you."

"I know."

Still, she seemed a lot happier about their circumstances that hadn't changed.

Contrary elf.

THE NEXT EVENING, Varu watched as Duncan tried to tackle Fara on those hated gymnasium mats.

"Come on, Fara," the revenant complained. "Act like you care about saving your own life."

"I do, but I'm not a warrior. I study rocks," she huffed and glared at him. "Try again."

Duncan knocked her on her ass and would have punched her right in the face if Varu hadn't teleported to stop him. He caught Duncan's fist an inch from Fara's lovely nose and snarled, "Back off."

Duncan danced back with a smile. "I would have stopped. Nice power you have there."

Varu felt a rage beyond words. Once he could speak, he warned, "Touch her and I'll kill you."

"You can try."

Before he could launch himself at the stupid vampire, Fara caught his arm. "We were just training. And he's right. I need to get better at this. We're all in danger now."

"We always have been." Duncan shook his head at her. "You're his weakness. And you make this all so much harder than it has to be."

Varu shrugged her off and would have hit Duncan if Onvyr hadn't gotten in the way, taking the knock to the stomach Duncan should have had.

"Oof." Her brother bent over, moaning. "That hurt."

"You should better pay attention to where you walk," Duncan offered then added, "We're surrounded by idiot fae."

"Onvyr." Fara darted to his side an shot a glare at Duncan. Then at Varu, as if it were *his* fault her brother's head was too often in the clouds.

"Don't blame me, I was aiming for that fang-head."

Duncan flipped up his middle finger and laughed as he sauntered out of the room, only Kraft and Orion keeping Varu from tearing after Duncan and ripping his head off.

"I hate vampires," Onvyr muttered and let his sister lead him to the corner of the room.

Rolf jumped into the middle of the gym and nodded. "Me too, Onvyr. They're so testy." He shook his head at Varu. "You need to save all that rage for your sire. Because without it, you're nothing."

"I know." Varu had been telling Fara and Mormo that since Fara had explained her plan to use him to kill his father. "I want to end him. But he's my sire."

"And he holds your leash and your loyalty," Orion said. "Bummer. My old man is a decent guy. He drinks a lot, but we have too much sun at home. What else is there to do?" Orion grinned. "Then again, we have a lot of mermaids with a thing for vryko. Not all of us need a mate for an excuse to fuck."

Onvyr cleared his throat and looked down at his sister.

Orion shrugged. "Sorry."

"No, you're not," Kraft muttered. "Big mouth."

"Jealous?"

"Hell, yeah." Kraft snorted. "You think I don't want to see a naked mermaid? Of course I do."

"Isn't that redundant? Aren't all mermaids naked?" Rolf asked.

"Yes," Onvyr said. "The ones I've seen are. In fae lands, at least."

"Oh, interesting." Rolf sat cross-legged on the mat and propped his chin in his hand. "So Onvyr, you were tortured by Atanase for years, right? You and Varu have something in common."

Onvyr stood and gently nudged Fara aside. He looked at Varu, then back at his sister, and smiled. "Oh, well. Okay then."

Rolf and Varu exchanged a confused glance.

Before Varu could ask what exactly was okay, the intercom buzzed and Bella's voice sounded. "I'm sorry, but could Fara come up here? Mr. Mormo wants to talk to her."

Fara stood. Orion pressed the buzzer for her, and she smiled her thanks and said, "I'll be up, Bella."

"Great. Head up to the second floor. I made cookies."

Once Fara had gone, Varu studied her brother. "We need to talk."

Onvyr nodded.

The others watched, but Varu didn't intend to put on a show. He nodded to the back and started walking down a corridor.

Onvyr followed, as did a snow-white owl.

"Don't mind her," Onvyr said. "She likes me."

"Whatever." Varu continued. Using the stone, he mentally shoved back the two vampires who followed.

Orion and Kraft chuckled and Kraft yelled, "We felt that," before they turned back to the gym.

Varu rounded the corner and walked up a set of stairs that led to a small sitting room on a floor not associated with any in the home. He had no idea where it actually existed, but it had been a safe, quiet place for him to decompress while living in this house of mystery.

He sat down in his favorite seat, ignoring the television mounted to the wall in favor of the tall, black dusk elf staring at him, a snowy owl with huge talons perched on his shoulder. Varu waved at the empty chairs and watched as Onvyr sat and the owl hopped to seat itself on the arm next to him.

"So." Onvyr nodded. "You want to wed my sister."

"*What?* No." He coughed and cleared his throat. "I wanted to talk to you about Atanase."

Onvyr's shuttered expression told him the elf wouldn't be talking about his time spent in captivity.

"What I mean is, how did you escape?"

"Faraine came to free me."

"But how? How could she know about my sire's special cell?" All strigoi knew the master had secret places for the truly unfortunate prisoners. But no one had ever seen them and lived to tell the tale.

"A strigoi helped her. That's all I know."

"You don't know who? Did you ever see anyone but Atanase during your time there?"

"Two other vampires. Both male."

"We're all male."

"Hmm."

What did that mean? He needed to know about the others there, curious as to who might have helped Fara. And why.

"They had dark hair and dark eyes. And they weren't nice to

be around." Onvyr shrugged. "Why don't you want to marry my sister?"

Varu should have known better than to try to get answers from Onvyr. "Never mind."

Onvyr remained seated, his focus on Varu palpable. "Why not?"

"Vampires don't marry."

"They mate." Onvyr nodded. "Ambrogio and Selene mated for life."

"True. But they were the first."

"You're a first."

"No, you're mistaken. I'm not a master." Then again, Mormo and Duncan seemed to think he might be. But Varu thought that was because of the stone.

"You are. And a Primus." Primus—a pureblood ruler of vampires, able to lead any of the tribes. The stuff of legend.

"How do you know about the Primus? Has Mormo been talking to you?"

"No. Atanase said some things. He liked to talk." Onvyr's gaze darkened.

Varu sat up straighter. "Like what?"

"Like that stones aren't stones. And the power is in the combination of talent and touch. Thought and feel. Bloode and bloode."

"What?"

"I know he waits for you. To kill you and mate my sister." Onvyr frowned. "But can he? He already mated and had you. And killed her, because she was more than him. Stronger. The bloode of Selene in her light."

Confused, Varu just listened, feeling an odd pang of sympathy for Onvyr's twisted mind.

"But you mated my sister." Onvyr smiled. "Congratulations."

"I didn't. Not really." Though the stone seemed to think so.

Varu's passion for her had not yet abated. They'd been spending her sleep periods in her room, enjoying each other.

Onvyr exchanged a glance with the owl and stood, waiting for her to land on his shoulder once more. "She said you don't need it anymore. Open your hand and it'll come. Then put it back in the dagger until you're back with your sire. But I wouldn't go back if I were you. No matter what, unless you believe in love."

"What the hell are you talking about, Onvyr?" Varu was getting a headache.

Onvyr turned with owl and said, "I know. I tried, but he's like a rock. Ha. Just like the Bloode Stone. Get it?" He chuckled as he left.

Varu didn't understand anything Onvyr had said. He wished it were as easy as opening his hand, calling for the Bloode Stone, then poof, confronting his father and stabbing him through the heart, setting him on fire, then dousing the ash with the Waters of Nu. True-death for any vampire in any realm.

He opened his palm and concentrated.

The stone rose out of his skin to sit atop it, glittering prettily.

Stunned, Varu closed his eyes and wished for a magical gate to transport him to Atanase.

But nothing happened.

He sighed. "Figures. You're good for nothing, Hecate." Yeah, he'd recognized her in that snowy owl. "And I mean that."

He swore he heard feminine laughter. Then nothing.

But at least he was free of the Bloode Stone.

So why didn't he feel any different?

Time to find Fara and see if she had any answers.

CHAPTER TWENTY-SIX

T hree nights later, lying in her bed at midnight wide awake, Fara didn't know what to think about all she'd learned.

After Varu had somehow removed the Bloode Stone from his palm, she'd expected to feel cut off from the stone's power. But her connection to the gem and to Varu felt the same.

Mormo continued to talk in circles about her getting stronger and learning how to work with Varu to stop a growing threat. He talked a lot about the coming chaos, but she sensed there was much he hadn't told her. Things she needed to understand and didn't.

She sighed, wondering if tonight Varu might join her.

He'd avoided her last night and the night before, and it bothered her that she had yet to see the inside of his room. A silly thing, but she felt distanced from him because he kept a wall between them. A physical wall at that.

She believed him that most vampires didn't care about love or affection. Unfortunately for him, the Bloode Stone kept showing her visions of him as someone who'd once loved. Varu as a little boy so in love with his mother. As a younger man with soft feelings for friends and crushes on females. Periods he'd forgotten having lived a long life, but they'd once existed. Before Atanase had wiped away much of Varu's emotions, Varu had loved and laughed openly.

In his many years serving the Crimson Veil, he'd made bonds of, not friendship, but loyalty. He always kept himself closed off, but she could feel that small part of him that would do anything for his strigoi patriarch, Mihai, whom he still respected very much. And for an old servant who had done his best to make sure Atanase never looked too hard at his son's rare indiscretions.

Saving a wild hellhound from dying. Giving blood to an aging strigoi from a rival clan, because that strigoi had once been a great war hero. Killing a pack of lycans who'd preyed on a young girl in the wilds of his homeland. A human girl he'd rescued and returned home to her mother, unblooded.

She'd seen Varu's memories through dreams and visions from the Bloode Stone. Incidents that turned her respect and affection into something more.

But she had to wonder what he'd seen of her. Something that made him avoid her, obviously, because he was keeping his distance.

And it bothered her.

The more she knew of him, the more she admired. How had he grown up with a conscience with Atanase for a father? How had he remained his own person, a strong warrior with definite ideas about right and wrong, no matter how others in his old clan had behaved? Varu kept to his own path, not influenced by what others did. He didn't consider weakness a challenge, had never slaughtered the innocent, and considered sexual congress with the unwilling to be beneath contempt.

It was as if some part of his mother remained inside him, protecting him from Atanase's corruption. A fanciful idea, but the stone liked it and continued to tease her with glimpses of Varu smiling and loving. And loving *her*.

He strode through her door without knocking, and she barely held back a scream as he shut and locked the door behind him.

"Oh, it's you." She sat up and put her hand over her chest, wearing the see-through garment she'd found tucked away in the armoire last night.

He appeared enraged, his eyes red, his fangs shining and his nails long and sharp. "This is all *your* doing."

She should have been afraid. But Varu had stopped being someone to fear since he'd first become a part of her.

Carefully, she asked, "What's my doing?"

"I tried to stay away. The Bloode Stone is no longer a part of me, so you should no longer be a part of me."

That hurt.

"But I think of nothing but you," he continued, looking as upset as she'd ever seen him. "The stone tells me nothing. Do you really think that by keeping me away I might start to care?"

She had no idea what he was talking about. "Look, you—"

"I *crave* you," he admitted on a guttural moan as he stripped naked, his glorious chest heaving and his erection impossible to miss. "I miss your laugh, your smile," he snarled and stalked her, staring at her as if starving. "Your beautiful body, that lovely, pale gray skin. I have to plan a defense against a pending attack, and I worry about protecting *you.*"

"I worry about you too," she said softly, conscious of his anxiety.

Poor Varu, he was feeling, and he had no idea what to do with his emotions.

The stone throbbed inside her, pouring love, fear, hate, and acceptance—all of it for her and him and the mess that had become of their lives.

Fara knew so much about Varu, though she still knew little. She knew his heart, what made him tick. But she didn't know the simple things. What did he like doing when not trying to save the world from his father? Did he have hobbies? A favorite type of prey/food? Did he want to have a mate and young? How much sex did strigoi like to have, because he'd been insatiable before doing his best to avoid her?

He yanked the covers off her body, and his eyes brightened as he looked her over.

With a groan, he joined her on the bed. "I knew you'd look this beautiful. And now you're in my brain, and you won't go away."

She gave a low laugh, ignoring his growl. "You want me to go away?"

"No, damn you. I don't." He yanked the thin garment off her body and latched his mouth to her breast. He sucked, and she quivered under him, her legs automatically spreading to cradle him close.

He continued to suck her nipples, alternating from one breast to the other. Then his hands trailed down her belly, grazing her sensitive ribs and easing a sigh out of her.

"Yes, mine," he whispered against her, licking and teething and making her wet.

His thumb found that sensitive spot between her legs, then his finger was inside her, in and out, stoking her desire.

Varu hurried from her breast to her mouth, kissing her with a passion that stunned her. Desperation mixed with desire, and suddenly he was thrusting that thick cock inside her while licking past her lips to stroke into her mouth.

With each push, he continued to build her pleasure. Varu always saw to her needs first. He seemed to grow more aroused with her, their bodies in tune, their energies in perfect accord.

She felt like, at the moment right before orgasm, she could see into him, his wants and dreams, and they matched hers. To love and be loved, to feel safe, and to cherish that which gave such pleasure.

"Yes, that's it," he said, and she didn't know if he meant her thoughts or he'd just gotten that much closer to coming. But then he added, "That's what I want. You, Faraine. All of you." He ground harder against her, throwing her into a rapture that stole her breath.

She tightened around him and kissed him once more, causing him to jerk and pump inside her, pulling his mouth away to latch onto her neck and bite.

As he sucked her blood, she climaxed harder, the ecstasy growing, especially when she felt him pouring into her. Trust and affection, a seething build of something close to what she'd call love.

She held him tightly while he moaned her name, always so tender when he finished, acting as if he treasured her.

After finishing, he remained inside her and rose on up on his elbows above her. "Vampires possess." He kissed her, lingering over her mouth. "We covet." He moved his kiss to her throat, licking across the already healing bite marks he'd left. "We take what we want."

"What do *you* want?" She played with the hair at his nape.

He closed his eyes, as if lost in bliss. When he opened them, he stared down at her and said his truth. "You my little elf. I want you."

Then he started moving again, her strigoi never satisfied just once.

WHEN FARA FINISHED CLEANING UP, she dressed in a pair of jeans and a new sweater, just as soft as the one Varu had gotten her, but in red, the color of his eyes. She didn't tell him that, because it was bad enough he knew how much she desired him. The arrogant vampire probably still considered her a lesser being, for all that he couldn't seem to do without her.

But she did like that he kept trying to convince her that she belonged to him.

For all that the "higher" being acted like he was her boss, Varu constantly tried to take care of her. Like now.

"You should eat," he said again.

She rolled her eyes behind his back.

"I saw that."

She grinned as he turned around, frowning.

"It's not funny. You're getting too thin."

"Stop." How sweet. "I need to talk to Mormo again. I had a thought about the Bloode Stone."

"I'll come with you."

"Okay."

He vanished from her room naked and returned moments later carrying clothing.

"That teleportation thing you've got going is pretty neat." She paused then blurted, "Why haven't you ever let me see your room?"

He finished putting on his clothes, a tee-shirt that showed off his muscular biceps and chest and a pair of jeans. "Come."

Well, I guess we're not talking about him keeping his distance.

She put her hand in his, and he winked them away.

She blinked and found herself standing in his room. "Whoa."

He steadied her. "It takes some getting used to."

"Your room or the zipping around?"

He shrugged. "Probably both." He walked around, and if she hadn't known better, she'd think him nervous. "This is my room. It's a place I can come to sleep or store my things. Just clothes. A few necessities."

She noticed beige walls and a large, made bed. The dressers had nothing but a light and a succulent plant on one. No photographs—vampires *did* show up on film—no knickknacks, or hints to his personality anywhere. Just that plant and an orderly room with a large bathroom attached.

In there, she noticed the towels hung perfectly, the soap dispenser and sink spotless, and the same with the shower. She stared at the toilet and bit her lip.

He saw and sighed. "What now?"

"Do you really need that?" She glanced at the toilet. "And is your face turning red?"

"Yes, I use that, and no, I'm not red."

Yet she thought she saw a faint flush on his cheeks.

She snickered.

"Damnable fae."

She laughed. "Sorry. But you don't eat."

"I do drink. The liquid has to go somewhere. We don't recycle waste, you know." He glared. "We're not ghouls."

She blinked. "Wait. Ghouls recycle waste? They never have to go, you know?"

"No. So are we finished? Any other intimate details you need to know?"

"Do you floss?"

"I— What?"

"Your teeth. Your fangs are kind of spaced apart, but your teeth that aren't fangy look normal. I see a toothbrush. Do you floss too?" She paused. "Oh, wow. Do you use condoms? I know magir can't get diseases and some can regulate pregnancy, like us elves, but can you impregnate anyone you want?" She blinked. "We probably should have talked about that before."

Varu didn't know how to answer her. Except this was why he had started to have so many pesky feelings about his dusk elf. Those intrusive questions would be ridiculous from anyone else.

But Fara asking made her that much more adorable. Did he use the toilet? Did he floss? Did he use condoms?

Had he ever been asked such mundane questions before? More, had anyone cared about his answers? She looked interested, and she continued to smile at him, even after he'd been rude enough to ignore her for a few days, trying to get her out of his mind.

By the fucking gods, he had a feeling he really had mated her. Which would put her in real danger, even more so than what she already faced.

Atanase didn't countenance his people having anything he didn't approve of, and since his sire already wanted Fara and her brother as prisoners, he would move the seven hells to take her from Varu.

Which was unacceptable. The Bloode Stone flared hot inside him, and he let it, needing it to protect this precious female. His feelings for her did make him weak, so on that level, he understood why his father might have wanted to kill his mother. But how could Atanase have harmed someone so special to him, knowing he could only ever have one mate?

How could any strigoi send a mate away, keeping behind the male child only for others to raise as unfeeling warriors?

Varu stared at Fara, enamored by her questioning eyes, so deep and purple as she watched him. Her skin, a lovely stone-gray and filled with a richness under the moonlight. He couldn't think past having her safe and close, away from anything that caused her pain.

The need to take her again pressed him, and if he'd had time, he might have. She welcomed his physical affection, her eyes hot, her body flooding for him. He wanted to taste her again, there, between her legs, to feel her feminine essence all over.

Mate. Mine. The stone kept hammering home how much they

fit, and Varu couldn't argue. Not with a truth he felt to his soul. The one person he knew would never betray him. A female, for the first time in his life, that he felt something more than need for. Something akin to that softer, weaker emotion, that odd love she spoke of—

"Varu! Open," Orion barked as he hammered at the door.

Varu put himself between the door and Fara and opened it, ready for anything.

"Strigoi have entered the house. They're in the basement and fighting with Kraft and Khent."

"Fara, take that stairway up," he ordered after pointing to a doorway next to the armoire. "It's private and safe. No one can get you there." He kissed her and left, feeling a rush of fury, that anyone would interfere with his kin. Fuck with *his* clan in his own *territory?*

He teleported himself to the threat, the need to kill and protect uppermost in his mind. The world turned red, and he let the bloodlust fill him as he stepped into a war zone.

CHAPTER TWENTY-SEVEN

F ara had no idea what was going on. Before she could manage to ask questions, Varu and Orion vanished. She rushed to the door, her thoughts on finding her brother, and ran into Bella.

"*Oof.* Sorry." Bella helped her steady herself. "Mr. Mormo wants you and me upstairs. Come on."

They ran down the corridor toward the living area and saw Onvyr—at least, she thought the elf under the glamour was her brother—and Rolf battling a dozen strigoi.

"There she is," one yelled and pointed at her. "He wants her and the other one. Find him."

Her brother had taken on a vampire-seeming. He fought with a vampire's strength and had short, dark hair, fangs, and a pale complexion. He saw her and winked before yanking off a strigoi's ear.

"Go up," he yelled to her as he punched another vampire in the face then laughed.

Next to him, Rolf drew runes in the air and wiped out four of the strigoi approaching, turning them to ash.

Good night, but that was scary. Rolf saw her and gave a short bow, barely managing to avoid being gutted with a blade. "Ladies."

Bella dragged her by the hand around the corner of their hallway then through a doorway that suddenly appeared. "In here. Go." Bella shoved her ahead, and they ran up the stairs.

Once at the top, Fara recognized Mormo's office. But there was no Mormo to be found.

"Okay, sweetie, time to talk."

Fara turned around and saw a svelte woman with sun-kissed skin walking toward her. She had large, expressive eyes in a bright, inhuman-blue color that fluctuated with black, and long, dark hair that swirled to an invisible current. The woman's face morphed several times, finally settling on Bella's features, but with a more serious expression than the happy human liked to wear.

"You like it?" The woman wiggled her fingernails to show off a shiny black polish. "I call it vampire-night, for my Night Bloode. Appropriate, eh?"

"Um, yes." Fara thought hard and let herself feel with all her senses. "Are you... Hecate?"

"In the flesh." Hecate smiled, those teeth blindingly white and surprisingly sharp before the image blurred and she appeared witchy but human once more. "Now we need to talk, Faraine de Cloche Jherag."

"Sure, um. Right." Fara didn't know what to call her. Ma'am? Your worship? Not Mistress. Fara didn't worship Hecate. At best, she paid tribute to Gaia with respect and love. But gods and goddesses of other races didn't make much sense to her. An elf was a creature bound to the very essence of all the worlds, a spirit of growth and rebirth.

"Sit here, little sister. And call me Hecate."

"Okay." Fara joined Hecate on the couch in front of Mormo's library.

"I like it here. He has a wonderful collection of books."
Hecate sat with her arm over the back of the sofa and tapped her
nails against it. "Fara, the shit has hit the fan. As we speak, we're
being overrun by Atanase's strigoi."

"But how did they get in? Why now?"

"How and why indeed?" She whistled, and Mormo appeared.

"Seriously? I was trying to keep the vermin out," he said, his
tone waspish and his face healing from a myriad cuts. "Oh, hello,
Fara."

"Are you okay?"

"No." He didn't exactly glare at Hecate, but he didn't seem
pleased with her.

"You're hurting my feelings," she murmured.

He gave an exasperated breath. "You're hurting my house!
There are dozens of strigoi invading, and they don't seem keen to
leave. Why did you let them in?"

Let them in?

Hecate turned back to Fara. "You need to get Varu to give his
father the Bloode Stone."

"I'm sorry. *What?*"

Even Mormo looked at Hecate as if she were loopy.
"Mistress?"

Hecate sighed. "Time is short. The battle wanes. We've
blooded the dusk elf. She's gathered Ambrogio's tears, and I've
handled the bones of the abomination." Her sly grin told Fara she
was missing something. "But we're missing a true sacrifice."
Hecate stared into her eyes. "Varujan of the Night Bloode must
face his sire in the place of his birth. He alone must deliver the
Bloode Stone."

"But then Atanase will become all powerful," Mormo said.

Hecate nodded. "With the stone in his possession, yes, he
will."

"He'll kill Varu."

"He'll try. Varujan might die, but does he ever stay truly dead?"

Fara had hope. Hadn't Varu said that even sunlight didn't kill him? "I'll try to convince him."

"Varu *has* to face off with Atanase. And you and your brother will fulfill the prophecy."

"Prophecy?"

"There's always a stupid prophecy." Hecate sighed. "I hate them, but the Fates and Furies demand them. Personally, I blame Apollo. He's always been such an ass. Him and his oracles. Just an excuse to keep them virginal until he 'blesses' him with his cock, really."

Mormo nudged, "Hecate?"

The goddess cleared her throat. "Right. Sorry. Anyway, you're running out of time. Get in there, rescue your brother, and get out. Let Varu battle his father. One way or another, he has to win."

"But what if he can't?"

"He has to."

So not an answer.

Hecate's expression softened. "Fara, hear me. If Varu doesn't face Atanase, chaos comes, and the worlds will end. If he fights, we still have a chance to beat back the darkness."

But at what cost? "How can I help him?"

"You will make a choice."

"What?"

Mormo stared at Hecate, a frown on his face. "Mistress, that's not—"

She snapped her fingers, and he disappeared.

Hecate watched her. "You must sacrifice a love to save a love. The answer will become obvious to you, but it won't be easy. To save us all, you must accept your fate—to truly wield the Bloode Stone." Hecate paused. "But to hold the stone is to die."

"I don't understand."

"Poor child." Hecate looked on her with pity. "You will. One can only hope the other has more hope and hate than despair."

"Hecate?"

"Go. Your brother and another are gone. Time is ticking away, Faraine. Be true to your heart and all will work out as it's meant to be. Find Mormo when you've decided."

"But that's not an answer, is it? What's meant to be?" Fara asked, scared out of her mind, fearing she'd lost the two people she loved most in the world: Onvyr and Varu. And yes, she did love the stubborn strigoi. So how could she sacrifice one of them to save the other? That made no sense. Wait. She'd have to wield the stone? She'd have to *die?*

Still confused, she rushed down the stairs and ran into a bloodied group of vampires.

Rolf, Khent, Orion, Kraft, and—*Varu*, she saw with relief. But not her brother or Duncan.

"Where are they? What happened?" She hugged Varu, beyond relieved to find him okay, aware he held her with strong arms wrapped tightly around her.

Varu answered, his voice cold, "Atanase teleported in, grabbed your brother, and teleported out. Before he did, Duncan managed to latch on to try to slow him down. He disappeared as well. The strigoi left as soon as their master left. He laughed at me before he vanished. Ordered me to bring you and the Bloode Stone to him or Onvyr and Duncan will die."

"Let's go."

Varu grabbed her when she would have raced to grab the stone. "We can't give him the Bloode Stone. He'll destroy us all if he has it."

"No, he won't. Hecate said we can save him."

"How?" His eyes narrowed.

Sacrifice a love to save a love. But to hold the stone is to die.

Fara had been prepared to die before, to make up for giving

Atanase those stones. And then he'd grabbed her brother. Now he had Onvyr again, and Hecate wanted her to take Varu with her to face his sire? Wouldn't that be putting Varu majorly in harm's way? She couldn't sacrifice him to save her brother. No. There had to be another way.

She had to put her faith somewhere, and Hecate seemed to want to help her.

"I think if we give him the Bloode Stone, we can save everyone," she tried, and the others drowned her in noes and rejection.

"Stop," she shouted, pleased when they quieted. "Listen to me. Hecate said Varu has to willingly bring the Bloode Stone to his father at the place of his birth."

"No." Varu growled, "I don't follow the gods and their bedamned prophecies. I never have and never will."

"But Varu, we—"

"He's right," Khent said, looking fierce. "We make our own way. We'll all go. The four of us will distract the strigoi while you two use the Bloode Stone to defeat Atanase and save Duncan and your brother. You need to believe in us, Fara. Not a goddess with an agenda we don't understand."

"But Hecate said—"

"Fuck Hecate," Varu snapped. "We're leaving. Someone get Mormo. He can make us a gate." Varu left to fetch the dagger holding the Bloode Stone. "This is mine. It sings to me still. It won't willingly go to my sire. Work with me, Fara. Together we can save them." His eyes turned flat. "I will no longer let that bastard take the lives I can save. He gets nothing from me but a hard death."

Apparently, Varu no longer had a bloode tie to his father.

The others grunted and cheered their agreement.

Rolf said, "I'm getting my magic bag and a spell for the Waters of Nu. You four grab your weapons. It's time to make war on the strigoi. This is going to be so epic."

Kraft grinned. "*Ja.* We finally get to kick some strigoi ass."

Surrounded by battle-hungry vampires, Fara realized she couldn't win this argument. And it hurt, because she knew in her bones she would have to make a choice. She could only hope she'd make the right one.

MORMO JOINED them soon enough and made a gate on the back porch, a black portal through which they'd arrive near the marshlands inhabited by the ghouls in strigoi territory. Far enough away they could regroup to handle the vampires in the main keep, they hoped.

"Be careful, you nutty vamps." Mormo grinned. "I gave Rolf some healing potions in case you get swamped. Get it? Swamped?" He chuckled and kissed Fara on the forehead, ignoring Varu's growl. Then they were gone.

They arrived in a swampy dark land filled with the scent of death.

"My kind of place," Khent said in a low voice and started reanimating dead strigoi lying nearby. Oddly, they hadn't decomposed. They rose, a tangle of limbs and sagging flesh, and walked away, presumably toward the main keep.

Rolf strapped a bag around Fara's back, under her sweater, holding a spell for the Waters of Nu in addition to a few healing potions. Then he divvied out more potions to the others.

Varu quickly showed them the basic layout of the stronghold. "We are vastly outnumbered. The only way to survive is to pick them off one by one and keep to the shadows. A small fire will distract them easily enough. I suggest near the livestock."

"Livestock?" she asked.

He blinked. "Er, the humans they keep for feeding."

"Oh, sure. Right." Livestock. She felt squeamish.

'They're well taken care of, actually," Rolf said, sounding

chipper. "Most of the humans sign up to live a carefree life where they donate a lot of blood but live in a mansion with gourmet foods, a top notch gym, and to-die-for entertainment. No pun intended."

"Rolf." Varu sighed. "Good luck. It's been interesting knowing all of you."

Kraft held a hand over his heart. "Touching, Varujan. I think a tear just trickled down my cheek."

Orion snickered.

Even Khent smiled.

They parted ways, and Varu kept Fara close. "We have to work together to defeat him. I know you're scared, but we can do this."

She stopped him and looked deeply into his eyes, feeling that her end was near. "I think I love you, Varujan."

He stared with intensity and kissed her, putting his feelings into that connection, even if he didn't know it. "Vampires don't love."

"I know." Her eyes misted. She sniffed and squared her shoulders before toeing off her shoes and socks. "Let's do this."

She followed him on nimble feet toward the keep, over a miracle of rock that begged her for communion.

As if he heard her thoughts, he murmured, "When we're done, we'll come back here and you can do that thing you do with stone. This is an ancient place, and I bet it will talk to you."

"Yes." Too bad she probably wouldn't be around to appreciate it.

Once they reached the point he'd decided to teleport from, hoping he had the ability to reach his destination over such a distance, he paused.

They heard an explosion, then shouting.

He took her into his arms. "Remember, together."

She nodded.

They arrived in a crowded courtyard where Atanase stood over two kneeling prisoners, held in place by strong guards. Oddly, both prisoners, Onvyr and Duncan, were laughing in his snarling face.

Atanase wheeled around to see them arrive.

"Wait," Varu ordered.

And every strigoi in the courtyard froze.

Atanase's face turned paler than it usually was. He glared from his son to her. "The little fae bitch returns." He started laughing. "He doesn't know, does he?"

She had no idea what Atanase was talking about, but with Varu using the stone, she felt free to focus on everything else around them.

Though Varu held the largest of the Bloode Stones, Atanase possessed *all* the other five.

Not good.

Duncan was slowly bleeding to death—she could feel that through the Bloode Stone Varu held, embedded in the dagger, the same tool he planned on wielding to cut off his father's head. He would have tried to hide the stone in his palm, but it refused to leave the hilt of the dagger.

Are you going to help? she asked it.

The stone sighed. *You're doing it wrong. And you're going to lose.*

CHAPTER TWENTY-EIGHT

F ara's heart raced.

"He has no idea you belong to me," Atanase said.

Varu hissed, his eyes narrowed, looking more like his father than he ever had. "Your end is near, you bastard."

"Is that any way to speak to your father?" Atanase tsked. "Ah, I sense our bond has been severed. You're a master, are you?" He laughed hard before sobering to say, "Faraine, darling, thank you for bringing him to me. I hereby release your brother safely to you." He nodded, and his men released Onvyr. "Feel free to keep the revenant too. He'll be dead soon." The other vampires released Duncan.

Varu shot her a sharp look.

Fara understood Atanase's plan. *Ah, trying to divide and conquer. It won't work.*

Onvyr crossed to her, looking crazed. He spoke in mrykálfar, muttering death threats and curses she'd heard long ago from a distant past.

"It's okay," she told him in the same language. "We'll get out of here."

Duncan glared as he made his way to Varu. "Varu, she's been playing you this whole time. She's in it with Atanase."

Still speaking dusk elf, her brother said, "The master has been talking about you in front of us, planting seeds of doubt in Duncan's mind. He won't believe you're innocent, and he's going to tear you and Varu apart. The stone needs you to be together to defeat him."

"How do you know?"

"The owl told me. She's Hecate's pet, an animal guide." He studied Varu. "You're his weakness, Faraine. Varu feels for you."

"Vampires don't love."

"Maybe they do."

They both watched Varu battle his doubts while holding those in the courtyard in check.

Duncan moved between her and Varu, guarding him from *her*.

"If he continues to cleave to the notion he can win on his own, he'll lose. Everything." Onvyr sounded surprisingly clear-headed.

On impulse, Fara reached out to the Bloode Stone and found it having a difficult time battling the other five stones, which were bound to Atanase's control while he tried to get Varu's stone to join the others. And it wanted to. Badly.

She found that odd but didn't have time to dwell on it.

With Varu's will splintered, trying to hold everyone else at bay while keeping his mind centered on the stone, he took a step in Atanase's direction. So intent on keeping everyone safe, he refused to let her in to help.

The beginning of the end, the stone said with a sad hum.

Fara had to protect Varu, her brother, and all the others. Atanase only had the power he did because she'd given it to him, after all. *My fault, my responsibility.*

A thought came to her, of taking charge and doing what needed to be done. She sent the idea to the Bloode Stone and knew it was a chance to work a happy ending for most everyone. Well, everyone who mattered.

"Brother, follow my lead," she murmured in their language.

In a louder voice, she said to Atanase, "I've done what you ordered, my lord. Varujan was so easy to manipulate. You were right." She forced herself to look him over, as if she found him distasteful.

Atanase chuckled. "Ah, I underestimated you. You're delightful."

She could feel Varu's pain, sensed the crack in his hold over the Bloode Stone.

"Fara, no," Varu said, his voice thick with stress.

"I pledge your brother's safety," Atanase said, sounding surprisingly truthful. "I give you my word. *Onvyr* can go."

But not me. She heard what he hadn't said well enough.

Atanase smiled. "Onvyr, I'm sure I'll be seeing you again soon. But Duncan and Varu, I'm sorry. Your time is at an end."

"You bitch." Duncan would have knocked her over, but Onvyr shoved him back. As weak as Duncan was, he fell to his knees.

Varu frowned at her. "I don't know what your game is, but it won't work. Stay with the plan, Fara."

"I'm sticking with the plan. *My* plan. Varu, you say vampires don't love. Well, neither to dusk elves. Everyone hates us. And when you grow up being hated, you learn to hate as well. I could never mate you." It broke her heart to say it, because she could see the pain he tried to hide under a stoic front. *Sacrifice a love to save a love.* She'd rather Varu hated her and live than love her and die, even if he didn't believe in the soft emotion.

"Mate?" Atanase barked a laugh. "Don't tell me he's still trying to make friends after all this time. Such weakness, fledgling. You know better."

Varu scowled. "She lies."

"Why would I?" She mentally gripped the Bloode Stone,

doing her best to let it mask her movement through Varu, controlling it. His fingers around the dagger didn't help. She'd need to take hold of the physical connection this time. Those stones Atanase had were hurting her connection, and she a bad feeling she knew why. "I had to get you here to earn my brother's and my freedom. Atanase was playing you the whole time, Varu. And you fell for it." She laughed.

That sent him over the edge. He snarled and lost that last bit of concentration he needed to hold command over the stone.

She pushed all her energy into the gem. *Come with me and let's do this,* she told it.

The power jumped into her, an ability to direct Varu's energy.

Varu felt betrayed, she could see it in his eyes. He pushed thoughts through the stone at her, desperate to believe. *You're setting him up, aren't you? You have to be. Why?*

She'd never worked so hard to force herself to look unmoved. *Gaia, help me have the strength to do what's right.* She felt a surge from underfoot and used it, steady like a rock.

"Take Varu and Duncan if you want," she said to Atanase. "Hell, take the others too. They're around here, somewhere. But let my brother go."

Atanase nodded. "Go, and be free."

"Onvyr, I'll see you soon." In dusk elf, she added, "Yank that dagger from Varu and give it to me. *Now.*"

He nodded and hugged her, saying his goodbye. Then he shot to Varu and grabbed the dagger from him.

Varu fought to hold onto it, confused and enraged and so badly hurt.

Onvyr landed a punch while the vampires all around surged to attention, no longer held back by Varu. Once again under Atanase's power.

"No, wait. I want to watch," Atanase told them, his eyes bright. "This is the best thing I've seen in ages."

Onvyr tossed the dagger near Fara.

She and Atanase saw it at the same time. She'd never be able to beat him to it if he teleported.

"May I deliver your stone, my lord?" she asked quickly.

"Why not? And kneel while you deliver it."

She nodded, bowed her head to him, and gathered the dagger. The moment she touched it, she burned with a power not meant to be hers.

"It hurts, doesn't it?" he asked with a smirk.

"Yes." *Stones, come,* she called, using the Bloode Stone's power to urge its pieces back home, to make it whole.

The more she'd thought about it, the more it made little sense that one Bloode Stone should be so much larger than the others. And then she'd remembered its odd grooves, knew its similar facets to the ones she'd already found—mere chips off the main stone. The same stone in the dagger.

She held onto the dagger and dropped to her knees, staggered by the power thrumming into the Bloode Stone from all its pieces.

Atanase hadn't realized what was happening. But he'd know soon enough.

That was if she could stay conscious long enough to do what had to be done.

VARU'S HEART, if he'd had a heart to begin with, had broken. The female he'd trusted had betrayed him, a pawn of his father's all this time.

And now they had the dagger. Duncan looked near death, and Varu had just had his ass handed to him by a fucking dusk elf.

"Wait," Onvyr hissed, not hurting him as much as he was delaying him.

Varu wanted to trust that he'd misread everything, but the pain of losing Fara to his father overwhelmed sense.

He struggled to get free and watched in astonishment as she held out the dagger to his father on bended knee. No. He couldn't believe it. Didn't *want* to believe it.

"Splendid," Atanase said, sounding like a proud father. "I do believe we're going to mate after all," he told her.

Varu literally felt ill.

But something wasn't right. He still couldn't believe she'd turn on him like that. Or that the stone would let her give it to a vampire not its master.

No, it couldn't possibly.

He reached out and felt with his power, with what made him strigoi, and sensed something happening on another plane.

A reaching, from the Bloode Stone to its... fragments. *Fucking hell.*

She was gathering the rest of the power blocked from the original Bloode Stone—their Bloode Stone. But as she drew the power, his father would start to realize what he'd lost.

"You bastard," Varu yelled to get his father's attention. "She's mine! I'll kill you. Then I'll kill her. *Fuck you both.*"

Atanase turned to face him with a wicked smile, ignoring Fara for the moment.

Behind him, Mihai strode into the courtyard with Iancu not far behind, though the general had looked better. He appeared to be missing a hand.

"Look, general, patriarch." Atanase sounded drunk on his own power and amusement. "My progeny has returned. And such a wonder. He's brought my missing dusk elves and the last Bloode Stone. Now I have all six."

Mihai's expression flickered with disbelief, but only for a moment. Iancu didn't react. The rest of the strigoi remained frozen, not sure what to do.

"You're dead," Varu threatened. "And I won't just kill you. I'm going to parade your worthless head in front of the other tribes, so they'll know what a loser you really are."

Atanase's expression turned ugly, and he went on the attack.

Varu met him blow for blow, master to master, though he was at a clear disadvantage. Younger and not as strong, he did his best, but his father had both power and a crazed anger he utilized to the fullest.

They teleported all over the courtyard, and Atanase nearly blasted him into a pile of smashed flesh and bone several times, an insane amount of telekinetic power at his beck and call. He crushed several of his clan and didn't seem to care, lost in the battle and addicted to the pain he readily caused. Knowing how his father's mind worked, Varu used that to his advantage, keeping clear of Fara, Duncan, and Onvyr.

Duncan and Onvyr stood close, neither talking as they watched the battle, but Fara remained on her knees, fighting on another level. Varu tried to help, not knowing if she'd get the power and still turn on him or not. But he couldn't let Atanase have the stone in its entirety.

His father suddenly wavered and looked at Fara "What are you—"

Varu struck. His hand plunged into his father's chest but missed his heart. *Fuck.* He'd only managed to break a few of Atanase's ribs in the process.

But he'd drawn a master's blood.

A *huge* deal.

The courtyard went silent, only Varu's and Atanase's voices to be heard. They swore at each other and fought. Varu nearly lost an eye. Atanase gouged into his belly then broke Varu's left arm. But Varu fought back, doing serious damage to his sire as he healed. Unfortunately, his father healed just as fast.

Atanase shoved Varu aside and froze in place. He turned to

Fara. "You fae whore," he shrieked and tore at the pendant at his throat. He opened the locket, but nothing was there. *"Give them back."*

Varu looked at Fara to see her skin turning a darker gray, closer to black, her eyes deep wounds. "Take it," she whispered to him. "Take it and fight." *Win, Varu. For me.*

She threw the dagger at him, and he teleported to intercept it before his father could.

He caught it and crouched over Fara, alarmed to see her breath faltering, her eyes deep flames as she burned from the inside out, her skin completely black, the red flame within a magical burn, a punishment for playing with a Bloode Stone never meant for one not Worthy, one not Of the Bloode.

"Good. She's dead." Atanase spit on the ground; his wounds finished healing as he spoke.

Varu healed as well, but the wound in his heart gaped wide open.

"She's dead," Duncan said, amazed. "No, no. She was one of us after all."

Onvyr had tears pouring down his cheeks. "A sacrifice to save those she loved."

Varu's pain lit up the stone, rage, hurt, and an emotional storm brewing to take him from strigoi to Master of the Night Bloode, a worthy Primus.

"Die," he yelled to his sire, the one responsible for so much death for such a long time.

The strigoi around them woke up, attuned to the dagger and the one who wielded it. As a group, they drew nearer, prepared to obey their master.

Atanase laughed. "You can kill me all you want, but Faraine is gone. And nothing you do will ever bring her back. Oh, the pain of that bitter truth. Or maybe I won't die at all. Because what can a weakling like you ever do—" He gasped as Mihai drove a fist through him from behind.

"Take it." Mihai yanked back the heart then threw it at Varu. "You know what, Atanase? You talk too much, you sick fuck."

Iancu snarled, "You're mine, traitor."

"Yeah, you're next," Mihai sneered and attacked.

Strigoi started fighting amongst themselves, a love for battle and favored leadership underway. Those loyal to Mihai battled those loyal to Iancu, Atanase forgotten in favor of fresh bloode.

But Atanase was already regenerating, and Varu didn't have time to waste.

He struck at his father and missed. So he struck again, only to find Atanase fleeing to safety.

But Varu wasn't alone. He spotted Khent climbing a wall and Orion not far behind, on another tower. Kraft, bloodied but in good spirits, appeared next to Duncan and handed him a healing potion.

"No you don't," Onvyr yelled and moved like lightning toward Atanase, who disappeared into the castle.

Varu faltered, torn between leaving Fara and going after his sire.

"Go. I'll watch her," Duncan rasped.

Varu teleported into a chamber he knew his father might visit, full of healing herbs and sorcerer-made concoctions.

He made it in just as his father appeared, Onvyr wrapped around him like a constrictor as the dusk elf tried to gouge out Atanase's newly grown heart.

"Onvyr, get back," Varu ordered and rushed to drive the dagger through his father's chest seconds after Onvyr leaped away.

He mashed the internal organs, hoping to slow his father down while Atanase shoved claws through Varu's body, trying to dig out Varu's heart.

Another stab and his father slowed enough that Varu could reach his throat.

With a mighty yell, he plunged the dagger into his father's neck and sawed through flesh and bone, tearing off his head.

Getting closer. He needed something to burn and noticed a torch on the wall. Varu nodded to Onvyr. "The torch."

Onvyr grabbed it.

"See if you can find something to throw the ash into." Vampires were flammable. Only a small touch of fire and his father's body would *burn*. But without the Waters of Nu to neutralize regrown tissue, his father would only regenerate again, something only a true master strigoi might accomplish.

Fara held that water spell strapped to her back.

And Fara was now dead.

He couldn't handle the pain, not yet. Not until he'd done his job.

He set fire to his father's body and ignored the decapitated head laughing at him. "Fuck you." He set fire to the rest of Atanase and watched the head spark into ash.

With Onvyr's help, he gathered his father's remains into a glass bowl. Carefully teleporting out with it, he found Duncan right where he'd said he would be, over Fara's body, which had curled in on itself, as if she were hugging her knees to her chest in a gentle nap.

He carefully tried to remove her sweater to get to the bag and found it charred.

He had to crumble it away and fought the dagger of grief lodged in his heart. After finding the pouch, he dug through to remove the spell holding the Waters of Nu. Reciting it, he channeled the waters into his father's ashes, clouding the bowl.

The moment the magical water touched his father's ashes, a loud screech rent the air, and everyone froze.

The Bloode Stone in Varu's grip sang out loud, and everyone turned to him with respect. And a question.

Mihai stepped closed and knelt, and everyone followed. "What now, Master?"

Varu didn't know. He'd stopped a mad master vampire from taking command of the strigoi and lost his heart in the process.

"We should head back," he said, not sure how to get to Seattle, if he even should or wanted to go.

Onvyr knelt over his sister, weeping. And then he sang, and the dulcet sounds of grief filled Varu with an exquisite pain, a longing so fierce he felt a single tear trickle down his cheek. Followed by another.

The strigoi watched in awe, and emotion filled them as well.

Duncan put a hand on his shoulder. "Come, Varu. We'll take her back with us."

Mihai joined Onvyr and nodded at Fara. "She did what she said she would. She would not want to be buried here, I don't think." It had been Mihai who had helped Fara, apparently. Varu had wondered and now didn't much care.

Onvyr looked up, spotted Mihai, and sighed. "No, she would not." He looked to Varu. "I think she would want to go home."

"To fae lands," Varu said, feeling hollow.

"No, with you."

And that hurt even more.

CHAPTER TWENTY-NINE

F ara looked around, still sore, feeling like a rock herself. In death, she'd taken on the shape most familiar to her patron, a black ash-stone that was light but solid, a contradiction and one of Gaia's most primitive forms. *Look at me, I'm Lava Woman.*

She walked around the dark speakeasy, amused at the many creatures gathering together. Animal and fae, troll and god, lycan and medusae. And every pantheon seemed included.

And there, Hecate, with her beautiful face, this one with dark eyes and ruby-red lips. "How do you like the color?" she asked, flaunting pale blue nails.

"Nice, but not as lovely as vampire-red."

"Not vampire-black?"

"No. I like red." The color of the Bloode Stone and Varu's eyes when he looked at her.

They stood in the corner at a bar table, watching the throng of customers drinking and moving from one plane to another, through doors and fields and skies.

"This is my duty," Hecate said, "watching over the boundaries. I am a liminal goddess; I protect the between."

"The between?"

"Life and death. Oh, and ghosts, necromancy, witchcraft. Etcetera, etcetera." She wiggled her fingers. "Boo."

Fara laughed. "I don't feel dead."

"Sadly, you are." Hecate sighed. "And your mate is a mess. It's been a month. He won't eat, won't sleep, barely talks to anyone."

Fara's heart raced. "Really?" She paused. "Hold on. What happened to Atanase?"

"Oh, he's true-dead. In the deepest hell and suffering for an eternity. That bastard." Hecate frowned. "Mihai now rules the strigoi. He killed the general and grew so angry he awakened into a master. Or else Varu shoved him into the position. I can't be sure. I do know Varu didn't want to become a master of the strigoi. He wanted to come back here with you and the others." She paused. "He pines for you. Every night he sits in the back and listens to the stone sing. I think it misses you too."

"That's sweet." Was it wrong to be glad Varu missed her? "Can you tell him I miss him too? I didn't want to die when I felt like I had so much to look forward to. But it was worth it. I want him to live. Onvyr too."

"Your brother, now he's a mess." Hecate sighed. "He's taken to killing better than the vryko and nachzehrer combined."

"What?"

"You're missed, Fara. You did better than I could have hoped. A smart cookie." Hecate winked. "And speaking of cookies, Bella made some peanut butter ones that are to die for. Maybe you could bring them up to Onvyr."

"But I'm dead."

"I think I rule death's door." Hecate smiled. "But it is peaceful in the afterlife, if you're so inclined. After all, vampires don't love. Want to ask him what he thinks?" Hecate nodded to a doorway, through which Fara could see Varu sitting on a bench next to a narrow stone box the length of a body. The moon overhead was thinning, the clouds large spools of cotton trailing through the night sky.

The fresh breeze had the scent of water on it, the lake behind Varu calm, rippling ever so slightly in the wind.

She walked through the portal and glanced down at herself, back to her original pale gray. Now clad in the lavender sweater he'd once bought her and a pair of jeans. All clean, her hair soft and flowing, her feet bare, feeling the earth's welcome under her toes.

"They say vampires possess. They covet. They take what they want," she said and watched him turn and stand, staring at her in shock.

His eyes turned bright, shining red. "Fara?" He took a step toward her, and then she was in his arms, and he was hugging the breath out of her. "Fara. Mate. Mine. Oh, Fara." He stuck his head in the crook of her neck, dampening her sweater with... tears?

"Varu?" She pulled back and saw him crying.

He hurriedly wiped his eyes and frowned. "Are you here to haunt me?"

"I don't know." She blinked. "Should I?"

"Yes, for ever doubting you." He gripped her shoulders and pulled her in close again. "*By the Night,* I missed you. My heart has been hurting. Nothing is right without you." He pulled back to kiss her, the song of the Bloode Stone sweet in her mind once more, now tinged with Varu's soul, she imagined. Rich and red and full. "I think maybe vampires do love. At least, this one does."

She smiled. "I think we mated."

"Yes, we did. You're mine."

"And you belong to me." She tapped fingers over his heart. "I can feel this racing."

"For you."

Hecate joined them, appearing from out of nowhere. "Well? Was her sacrifice in vain?"

"Sacrifice?" Varu asked.

"She released her hold on you to save you, sacrificing her love for you to save you—her love. Tricky tricky."

"She gave *her life,*" Varu roared. "Everything for *you.*"

"No, strigoi. Everything for *you.* She loved well. But do you?"

"Yes, I do. She's mine. She's in my heart and bloode. I'm not letting her go. If you take her back, I'm going with her."

"Hmm."

"No, Varu. You're needed here." Fara felt that. His journey, his mission, wasn't over. "You only have one Bloode Stone. There are five more out there, and I have a feeling more will be resurfacing soon."

Hecate nodded. "She's right. The others will soon appear. And the chaos still comes."

"What?"

Hecate sighed. "Look, I'm tired and thirsty, and there's a dusk elf with my name on him."

Fara frowned. "Do you mean Onvyr or—"

"I need you working with me, Varu. There's a lot riding on this."

"Then Fara stays." He put a possessive hand around her waist.

"Fara?" Hecate asked. "Is this what you want? You've more than earned your place at Gaia's side in the afterlife."

"But I'd be lonely without Varu." She smiled up at him, her heart full. "And someone needs to keep an eye on Onvyr." She didn't know if she liked Hecate taking such an interest in her brother. "Besides, he's good with animals and tracking. He can help us find the other Bloode Stones."

"Whoa. It *is* Fara!" Duncan yelled.

She glanced over at the upstairs patio landing to see the rest of

Varu's clan staring at her. And then Onvyr joined them and started jumping for joy. Literally jumping around and pounding the others on their backs.

"Your clan is going to get weird," she warned her mate. "Because you're adopting two dusk elves."

"And a magician." Hecate pointed to Mormo, who pulled up in raft on the water, kicked back and for once not wearing a robe. Instead, he had on a Hawaiian shirt and shorts. In forty degree weather.

He waved. "Hey, Fara. You back to stay?"

"Does Mormo have to be part of the package?" Varu complained, a twinkle in his eye.

"Yes." Hecate tapped her foot. "Well?"

"Fine. But *I'm* in charge of my kin. And Fara's in charge of Onvyr." He waved at the gang on the porch before turning to Fara, smiling. In a clear, deep voice, he announced, "Faraine de Cloche Jherag, I love you."

"Whoop. Told you," Onvyr said. "Pay up, suckers."

Everyone but Rolf handed him money. The blond draugr waved at them. "I believed in you!"

Varu sighed before turning to Fara. "Vampires take what they want. And I want you. Let's go make up for lost time."

"So am I an undead then?" she turned to ask Hecate, who'd vanished.

Mormo too.

"You're perfect, is what you are." Varu paused at the stone box. The others joined them, gathering around her coffin, she guessed.

When Varu opened it, there was nothing there.

Duncan poked her. "Wow. It really is Fara."

"Hey."

He grabbed her in a big hug. "I'm so sorry I doubted you. And

I'm so glad you're back. Varu nearly willed himself to death to be with you. So you can never leave."

Varu shoved Duncan back. "Yeah, yeah. She's staying. She's my mate. And I'm keeping her."

"Our new patriarch's going to be a huge pain in the ass," Orion growled. "Now we have to deal with a mated strigoi?" Orion looked her over, his expression easing. "And his sexy mate?"

"You got that right," Kraft agreed with a wink.

Khent looked her over, gave her a half smile, and walked away.

"Well, *I* love you," Rolf said and kissed her on the cheek, dancing away when Varu took a swipe at him. "So much that I promise to only try to kill your mate once a month. Will that work?"

Fara stared. "What?"

"Enough of you guys," Varu growled. "My mate and I need a happily ever after if you don't mind."

"Good." Onvyr nodded, and his smile grew wide at something behind them. "Oh yeah. It did all work out. You were right."

The giant battle cat was back and stalking over the backyard grass toward her brother.

The others gave the feline a wide berth. But Onvyr talked happily to it as they made their way back into the house.

"This place is like mayhem incarnate," Varu murmured, lifted her into his arms, and teleported them into his room, which had been filled with her things.

"Varu?"

He kissed and hugged her tight. "Night's truth, I missed you, Fara. Don't ever leave me."

"I won't. I promise."

"Because sometimes vampires love. And this one loves you true."

He really does, the stone told her.

Then Varu made it hush and kissed her again.

And they did make up for lost time.

Over and over and over again.

EPILOGUE

Hecate lay next to Mormo in his raft on the water, her head pillowed on his shoulder, staring up at the sky as they floated in the middle of Lake Washington. The stars winked down at her, while the moon whispered words of warning, staring out at things Hecate didn't yet want to see.

"That was a nice thing you did," Mormo said.

Hecate smiled. "Yes. I did enjoy our strigoi's pain, though. Imagine thinking you're beyond love. What a crock."

Her head spun, and she watched a multitude of issues needing her attention and tried to ignore them. She needed a break. Hades and Asmodeus would have to chill out for a bit over that shared border. *Not my undead monkeys, not my satanic circus.* Just maybe, if she were lucky, Bella could manage a few more snuggles from one sexy dusk elf with the nicest ass.

She sighed. "Well, we did okay for a first step. We just need to gather the rest of those stones."

"I'll put Duncan on it tomorrow. He's got one hell of an informant network, though he's not as sneaky as he thinks he is," Mormo muttered and trailed a hand in freezing lake water.

October in Seattle was no joke.

"Oh, he's sneaky. But that's a good thing." Hecate dearly wanted to relax, but that image appeared again. "Damn it."

"What's wrong, Mistress?"

She patted his chest, safe with her protector, her beloved servant and friend. "Mormo, honey, we have a slight problem."

"When *don't* we have something to worry about?" He groaned. "I need a drink."

"Right? Me too. Paddle us back home, hmm?"

He did, and they walked down through the lawn that opened up beneath them, into a passage toward the basement. They made their way to a dead witch making cocktails.

Hecate accepted one and took a long sip. *Yum.* She drained the glass. "It's not great."

The witch frowned.

"Oh, not the drink, Catherine. This is fabulous."

The witch beamed.

Mormo nudged her. "What isn't great?"

"Our little problem."

He groaned. "Which is?"

"Remember that witch Duncan thought he was pumping for information?"

"What do you mean, *thought* he was pumping?"

"Turns out *she* was using *him.* And oddly enough, that grimoire of mine stolen seven hundred plus years ago? Yeah, it's been found by our clever witch. Except she's been casting spells that could put our vampires out of commission. For good. No more waking at sunset. No more whining about the clan name you gave them that everyone hates."

He sniffed. "I thought Night Bloode was inspired."

"No more vampires period."

"You're serious?" Mormo started. "That would mean no more protection against the Big Evil coming for all of us."

"Yeah, that," Hecate said sourly and guzzled another drink.

Huh. At this rate, she'd need to give Catherine a raise. These things were *amazing*.

Mormo nodded. "I'll have a talk with Duncan. But tomorrow, okay?"

"Sure, sure. Vampire annihilation tomorrow. Tonight, Witches & Bitches Kill Snitches." Her favorite new drink. In a louder voice, she said, "Catherine's special—on the house for everyone."

The crowd let out a cheer.

Well, all except for one demon with a grimoire to find and a goddess to kill.

THANK you for reading the first of the Night Bloode's adventures! There are five more to go…five more stubborn vampires who need someone to love and fight for. Check out Duncan's story in Between Bloode and Craft!

And to read ***special bonus chapters*** to learn just how a certain red-haired witch found a special grimoire, then how the spell she cast on Duncan *really* worked, go to my website and join my newsletter!

GLOSSARY

INTELLIGENT BEINGS CLASSIFICATION:

- **Demons**—creatures from any of the hell planes, tricksters, evil-doers, and powerful beings with a bent toward dark desires, associated with fire
- **Divinity (gods and goddesses)**—those of a divine nature and whose power is derived from creationism and worship
- **Humans**—mortal beings from the mundane world, not born with magic though some can harness its power
- **Magir**—an all-encompassing term to describe those supernatural creatures living among the human population in the mundane realm (e.g. lycans, witches, druids, mermaids, gargoyles, etc.)
- **Monsters**—animalistic creatures that aren't human or magir but do have magical properties/abilities (like fox spirits, gryphons, dragons, manticores, etc.)

Vampire Terms:

- **Ambrogio**—the first vampire ever created, born from a curse given from the god, Apollo. Father (Primus) to the vampire species, husband to Selene, the mother of the species.
- **Bloode**—that intrinsic vampiric essence within a blood-drinker that makes him a vampire, as opposed to a demon or other dark-natured creature
- **Bloode-debt**—vampiric debt incurred by a member of one's clan, passed on through familial members until fulfilled
- **Bloode Empire**—the name for the vampire nation created in 727 BCE
- **Bloode-magic**—magic in a vampire's bloode, manipulated through the Bloode Stones or a deity with power over blood and the dead (i.e. Hecate, thus Mormo)
- **Bloode Stones**—six droplets of Ambrogio's blood or tears (split mythology on origin) congealed into power gems when they made contact with the earth. It is rumored that only a Worthy vampire can handle a Bloode Stone and instill peace within their species.
- **Bloode Witch**—a witch who uses bloode to power herself, serves his or her vampire clan and is considered kin. Very rare, more common in older times.
- **Clans**—groups of vampires within a tribe that act as family, led by a patriarch, comprised of kin (brothers/fathers/sons), anywhere in number from ten to sixty members
- **(The) Ending**—the period of time before vampires came into existence

- **Guide**—also known as bloode-guide, someone not related who mentors a young vampire through adulthood
- **Kin**—family, those vampires who do not instill an urge to kill. Another word for vampire brother, father, or son
- **Kin Wars**—legendary vampire civil war, thought to have been fought several thousand years ago, brought about by a foul curse from the gods, turning vampire against vampire and forming the ten tribes
- **Master**—vampire leader of an entire vampire tribe
- **Mate**—a vampire's bonded female partner, with whom he can sire offspring
- **Of the Bloode**—another term for vampire
- **Patriarch**—vampire leader of a vampire clan
- **Primus**—the first vampire, the father of all (Ambrogio), also refers to a pureblood vampire leader
- **Sire**—a vampire's father, also sometimes used as a term of respect for the Master of a tribe
- **Tribes**—the ten large factions of vampires, bound together according to particular traits. The tribes are as follows: Strigoi, Upir, Nachzehrer, Reaper, Draugr, Revenant, Jiangshi, Sasabonsam, Vrykolakas, and Pishachas.
- **Upir Gold**—term used to denote vampire bloode and brains, a divine delicacy
- **Vampire**—a blood-drinker and descendant of Ambrogio, always male, always naturally born. "Vampire" is also a generic term in reference to describing a blood-drinker from any of the ten tribes. Other names for vampire are: Of the Bloode, blood-suckers, blood-drinkers, vamps, fangers, and death-bringers.

- **Worthy**—characteristic of a vampire who is the quintessential essence of the Bloode, who has the true heart of Ambrogio in his body, courageous and powerful, a leader who will do what's best for his people

THE REALMS:

- **Celestial**—the homes of the gods, no matter what pantheon
- **Death**—also called the afterlife, the plane that harbors the dead, looked after by Hecate and several other deities, not to be confused with the hells; also sometimes referred to as the Netherworld
- **Fae**—home of the fae, to include the lands of the elves, dwarves, and faery, as well as elemental spirits
- **Hell**—the underworld planes, of which there are many, usually inhabited by demons, devils, and dark spirits, not to be confused with the Netherworld
- **Mundane**—earth, the mortal plane where humans dwell
- **Pocket**—small planes, or "pockets" of reality, created by powerful magic-users

SPECIES:

- **Dark Elves**—Fae creatures who prefer the night, they often live in the caves and underground with dwarves in Nidavellir, which is part of the fae realm

- **Demons**—those who live in the hell plane, tricksters, evil-doers, and powerful creatures with dark desires, associated with fire
- **Druids**—humans who can do natural magic and commune with fae spirits
- **Dusk Elves**—rare (and often hunted, unwelcome among the elves) blending of light and dark elf parents, live in fae realms. Also known as mrykálfar.
- **Dwarves**—also known as dvergar, fae creatures who live in Nidavellir
- **Fae**—those who live in the fae realm, an alternate world comprised of elves, dwarves, sprites, and other creatures from a multitude of pantheons
- **Light Elves**—fae creatures who live high in the mountains in Álfheim in the fae realm
- **Lycans**—shapeshifting creatures who can assume the form of a human or large, magical direwolf
- **Mages**—magir-born, long-lived mortals who practice magic for good (also sometimes used as slang for magic users of all kinds)
- **Nymphs**—beautiful magir partial to water, generous in spirit, often sexual creatures in tune with nature
- **Necromancers**—humans who can harness death magic and command of the dead
- **Shapeshifters**—rare creatures who alternate between human and animal forms at will
- **Sorcerers**—magir-born, long-lived mortals who practice magic for evil purposes
- **Warlocks**—humans who perform magic for evil purposes, typically utilizing sacrificial magic
- **Witches**—humans who perform magic for good purposes, typically utilizing celestial or earth magic

ALSO BY MARIE

Zack & Ace

Derrick

Hale

DAWN ENDEAVOR

Fallon's Flame

Hayashi's Hero

Julian's Jeopardy

Gunnar's Game

Grayson's Gamble

CIRCE'S RECRUITS 2.0

Gideon

Alex

Elijah

Carter

SCIFI

THE INSTINCT

A Civilized Mating

A Barbarian Bonding

A Warrior's Claiming

TALSON TEMPTATIONS

Talon's Wait

Talson's Test

Talson's Net

Talson's Match

Roadside Assistance

Zero to Sixty

Collision Course

THE DONNIGANS

A Sure Thing

Just the Thing

The Only Thing

ALL I WANT FOR HALLOWEEN

THE KISSING GAME

THE WORKS

Bodywork

Working Out

Wetwork

VETERANS MOVERS

The Whole Package

Smooth Moves

Handle with Care

Delivered with a Kiss

GOOD TO GO

A Major Attraction

A Major Seduction

A Major Distraction

A Major Connection

BEST REVENGE

Served Cold

Served Hot

Served Sweet

ROMANTIC SUSPENSE

POWERUP!

The Lost Locket

RetroCog

Whispered Words

Fortune's Favor

Flight of Fancy

Silver Tongue

Entranced

Killer Thoughts

WESTLAKE ENTERPRISES

To Hunt a Sainte

Storming His Heart

Love in Electric Blue

TRIGGERMAN INC.

Contract Signed

Secrets Unsealed

Satisfaction Delivered

AND MORE (believe it or not)!

ABOUT THE AUTHOR

Caffeine addict, boy referee, and romance aficionado, *New York Times* and *USA Today* bestselling author Marie Harte has over 100 books published with more constantly on the way. She's a confessed bibliophile and devotee of action movies. Whether hiking in Central Oregon, biking around town, or hanging at the local tea shop, she's constantly plotting to give everyone a happily ever after. Visit https://marieharte.com and fall in love.

And to subscribe to Marie's Newsletter, click here.

amazon.com/author/marieharte

bookbub.com/authors/marie-harte

facebook.com/marieharteauthorpage

instagram.com/marieharteauthor

twitter.com/MHarte_Author

goodreads.com/Marie_Harte

Made in the USA
Coppell, TX
09 February 2022

73244166R00178